T. Torrest

REMEMBER WHEN

A Romantic Comedy Novel

D1502666

For Michael

T. Torrest
Remember When

Cover design: Dana Gollance
www.ateliergollance.com

Printed in the United States of America
First paperback edition

REMEMBER WHEN

Prologue
COME SEE THE PARADISE

Years before Trip Wiley could be seen on movie screens all over the world, he could be seen sitting in the desk behind me in my high school English class.

I'm sure I don't need to tell you who Trip Wiley is. But on the off chance you've been living under a rock for the past decade, just know that these days, he's the actor found at the top of every casting director's wish list. He's incredibly talented and insanely gorgeous, the combination of which has made him very rich, very famous and very desirable.

And not just to casting directors, either.

I can't confirm any of the gossip from his early years out in Tinseltown, but based on what I knew of his life before he was a celebrity, I can tell you that the idea of Girls-Throwing-Themselves-At-Trip is not a new concept.

I should know. I was one of them.

And my life hasn't been the same since.

Trip and I met when we were teenagers, way back before anyone, himself included, could even dream he'd turn into the Hollywood commodity that he is today. This was back in 1990, and I cite the year only to avoid dumbfounding you when references to big hair or stretch pants are mentioned. Although, come to think of it, I am from Northern New Jersey, which may serve as explanation enough.

Make no mistake, I am not bashing Jersey. It is my home, where I was born and bred and is my absolute favorite place on God's green Earth. We have beautiful beaches, miles of shopping malls, the best food in the country and the world's greatest city only minutes outside our door. If you've ever been here, I don't need to tell you, you've already learned for yourself.

And if you haven't... Well, then please don't believe everything you've ever seen on TV.

It is this mindset that gets our scrunchies in a twist whenever anyone outside our garden state feels they have the right to make a negative comment about it.

Just to avoid any bodily injury when visiting, I've compiled a short list of rules for out-of-towners. We New Jerseyans do not find the following comments entertaining:

1. "Oh, you live in New *Joizey*? What exit?"
2. "Hey, let's all go *downthashaw*."
3. "Yo, fuggheddaboutit!"

Other commentary that can get your ass kicked quickly and efficiently:

Anything regarding the Turnpike, the smell, the toxic waste dumps or the swamps. This also includes, but is not limited to, references about the mafia, gobbagool or the Bada Bing, even though we all secretly love The Sopranos.

The vast majority of us are nothing like the people you've seen on "Jerseylicious" or "The Real Housewives of New Jersey", and please don't even get me started on those knuckleheads from "Jersey Shore".

But obviously, I'm getting ahead of myself.

In 1990, Jerseyans didn't have to deal with such negative representation. At that time, we were West Orange's Thomas Edison and Paterson's Allen Ginsberg. Sayreville laid claim to Bon Jovi, Elizabeth was home to Judy Blume and Freehold was all about Springsteen. Hoboken is where Frank Sinatra hung his hat, and Metuchen is where David Copperfield first pulled a rabbit out of his. Back then, even Martha Stewart was only just starting to show off all the "good things" she'd learned as a crafty adolescent Jersey Girl from Nutley.

And even in boring old Norman, we had a brush with greatness, even if we didn't know it at the time. These days, we can take credit for churning out the most sought-after leading man in Hollywood. Because today, Norman is the place that Trip Wiley always refers to as "home".

PART ONE
1990

Chapter 1
LISA

Lisa DeSanto and I have been friends since she moved here when we were both seven. Her family originated from Atlantic City (which seemed incredibly exotic and worldly at the time) to head north and plant roots in the forgettable little suburb of Norman. Thank God they just happened to buy a house on the same street where I had lived my entire life.

I remember being so excited when I first heard that a girl my age was going to be living only three houses away! Until that point, I was relegated to hanging around the neighborhood with my little brother and the four McAllister boys next door. The only other girls on our street were Flora and Phoebe Kopinsky who were just babies at the time.

It's not that spending my formative childhood years around all those boys was all bad. I am an excellent kickball player and have been known to throw a mean whiffleball curve from time to time. To this day, I still retain the ability to scale a fence without breaking a sweat and I think my tolerance for pain is probably a little higher than most girls I know.

Looking through the family albums, I can count on one hand the number of pictures of me that don't include scraped knees or a Band-Aid somewhere on my body. Even my First Communion photos show an otherwise unassuming little girl, hands folded innocently in prayer, dressed in a frilly, white dress... and wearing a cast on her forearm. I won't get into the whole story here, but the particular circumstances in which I broke my wrist that spring involved a Wonder Woman costume, an invisible airplane and the roof of the McAllisters' garage.

Lisa, on the other hand, was always more of a "real girl" than I was. I hadn't realized I was such a tomboy until I went to her house for the first time.

Upon entering Lisa's room, I was immediately informed of the fact that her mother had let her decorate it almost entirely by herself. It was actually painted pink and there were white, eyelet curtains at the windows and a rainbow comforter on her wicker bed. My only attempt at decorating at that time involved a Scooby Doo blanket that I had won on the boardwalk. The pictures on her walls were of David Cassidy and Scott Baio and Donny Osmond, a bit of a departure from the Burger-King-issued, 1978 Yankees and Sgt. Pepper's Lonely Hearts Club Band posters that hung on mine.

In spite of our differences, or maybe because of them, Lisa and I have been best friends ever since. It seems that it was within ten minutes of our first meeting that she taught me how to feather my hair, make braided ribbon barrettes and draw a proper unicorn, necessary survival traits for any girl in the late seventies.

Over the years, she has dragged me to the mall repeatedly, making me buy Jordache jeans, parachute pants, Guess denims and ultimately, to my enduring mortification, ZCavaricci's. She ran me through the gauntlet of makeup and clothes enough to help me get my act together in time for high school.

Prior to that, I was sort of clueless. I used to play football with the guys at recess and spent more time climbing trees than playing dollies. That tomboy stuff was fine during elementary school, but by sixth grade, my body had begun to sprout boobs and that's when all the boys started looking at me a little funny.

All the boys except the one I'd started to really like, however.

I had the hugest crush on Brian Hollander during that time and I just couldn't understand why my superior athletic ability wasn't helping to catch his eye. Lisa stepped in and gently explained that boys liked girls who were, well... more like *girls*, and I'd have more of a fighting chance if I started acting like one right quick.

It was the summer between seventh and eighth grade when Lisa went into full-on Frankenstein mode with me. She armed me with a bottle of Love's Baby Soft and a tube of Zinc Pink lipstick and gave me a complete beauty lesson, showing me how to put on makeup to suit my "season", and went clothes shopping with me to find outfits that would best show off my new boobs without making me look trashy. When all was said and done, I was surprised to find the girl looking back at me through the mirror. Until that moment, I had no idea that I ever wanted to be... *pretty*. But there I was, all made up, hair done and dressed like a real, live girl, and I realized that Lisa's description actually held some truth.

The makeover did wonders for my self-esteem. Not that anyone would have mistaken me for the most popular girl in school (that distinction belonged exclusively to Lisa), but I was confident that I was going to be able to carve out a nice little social status on my own, even without the fact that I had hitched my wagon to her star.

I couldn't wait to run into Brian and his friends at the lake or the park or something, envisioning myself making a smash as big as Sandy's at the end of *Grease*. I would walk onto the playground or someplace where all our friends would be hanging out and I'd snub a cigarette out with my high-heeled shoe. Every guy's jaw would drop and then we'd all break into "We Go Together".

That fantasy was squelched, however, when my father refused to let me buy a pair of black spandex pants that I'd found at the nearby Clothing Town. Plus, there was a slight problem with the perm that I had gotten, because it made me look more like Little Orphan Annie than Olivia Newton-John.

Lisa spent her allowance that week to buy me a home permanent kit, explaining that if we just brushed it straight through my hair and let it set for a few minutes, the afro on my head should relax.

She turned out to be right, because the treatment ended up giving me a decent head of soft waves. Thank God, because otherwise, I would have spent the summer looking like Weird Al Yankovic.

Throughout our relationship, Lisa has always loved the challenge of introducing me to a new movie. She's responsible for some of my all-time favorites, including the aforementioned *Grease* and *The Outsiders*, where my girliness finally kicked in enough to swoon over Danny Zukko and Sodapop Curtis, before

3

graduating to actual *films* like *A Streetcar Named Desire* and *A Place in the Sun*, where our crushes matured enough to include Marlon Brando and Montgomery Clift on our wishlists.

She knew everything about everything and tried to impart her all-encompassing wisdom to me on a daily basis. Such relevant bits of knowledge on topics ranging from fashion to mascara to French-kissing etiquette. The latter of which led to my first real kiss with Brian Hollander in the basement of Lisa's house during a game of Spin-the-Bottle.

It was a setup, for sure, because lucky Brian was the only boy in the room at the time she suggested the three of us play. We agreed, and Lisa, ever the best friend, argued the direction of the pointed bottle any time it landed in her vicinity. On the two times she wasn't able to dispute the call, she merely pecked old Brian on the lips, allowing me to be the only one to swap actual spit with him. Of course, Brian's joy in the revelation that I was the easier conquest prompted him to lead me into the bathroom for a real makeout session. I even let him put his hands into the back pockets of my jeans! It was quite a memorable afternoon.

Even though kissing Brian should have been unforgettable enough on its own, there's another reason that notorious day sticks out in my mind.

It was the day my mother left us.

After all these years, it's still difficult for me to flat-out make that statement.

When you're a child who's been abandoned, it's the very center of who you are as a person. It's like having a parent die, but without any sort of finality. You suddenly turn from being a regular, everyday person who nobody blinks an eye at into That Girl Without A Mother.

To make matters worse, while there are the multitude of questions swirling around in your own head, there are the inquiries from friends and acquaintances and people you barely know. You try to be polite and accommodating toward anyone who asks about the situation, but really, you just want to slap them and tell them to mind their own business.

4

But worst of all are the people who don't bother asking anything at all. They are the ones who think they've got it all figured out and don't need to bother finding out the real story. They're the ones who will say pitying things behind your back like "Oh, that poor, little girl" or "The man aged ten years overnight when that woman left him". Sometimes, I'd overhear someone say something about "that Kate Warren woman", which always made the hairs on the back of my neck stand up.

There was a lot of talk that summer but mercifully, I wasn't privy to the majority of it until my teen years. I think I was so caught up in my own feelings on the matter to have been aware, or to have even cared, about what anyone around town may have thought. I was too busy dealing with it myself, trapped in my own head for the weeks following her absence.

Ultimately, I had a pretty bad spell at one point that summer, and I credit Lisa as being the one who brought me back from the edge. It seems she has been there for every single moment- whether epic or trivial- throughout my entire life.

One of our more monumental moments was that I was due to turn seventeen about a month into our senior year, lending even more distractibility to my mind on that particular September day back in 1990.

It was a beautiful, sunny day outside and my head was consumed with thoughts of my impending vehicular freedom.

Therefore, I was ill-prepared for the bomb that was about to hit my English Lit class on an otherwise unremarkable Monday afternoon.

Chapter 2
TRIPWIRE

I was sitting in Mrs. Mason's fifth period English Literature class when it happened.

It was only the second week of the new school year, my senior year (finally!) at über-prestigious St. Nicetius Parochial High School- since it was the only Catholic school in town, it was less formally referred to as "St. Norman's"- and already I was counting down the days until graduation. Five down; one-hundred-and-seventy-five to go.

It's not that I didn't like school. It's just that the weather was still perfect in September and it was hard to get back into institution-mode with the sun shining so maliciously through the open windows of my butter-yellow concrete cell; the warmth of a sunbeam against my skin taunting me with an almost audible ticking as the end of summer counted down its final hours.

I was staring outside, catching the scent of warm, cut grass and thinking about taking a dip in the pool at the end of the day. The pool was my haven, my one place I could go whenever I wanted to block out the world. Living in New Jersey only allowed about a five month window to indulge in that activity, but my father would sometimes take mercy on me during the winter months and splurge on a day pass for the pool at the Jewish Y. Being that it was September, however, I knew I had at least a couple more weeks before it would become an issue. I'd managed the rare task of getting in a few laps before school that day, waking up before my alarm even went off, allowing a few extra minutes to grab a quick swim. I turned my face into my shoulder and breathed in, picking up a hint of chlorine through the shield of Aqua Net in my hair, offering a small promise of the lazy, floaty afternoon to come.

I'd had a bad run-in with the Sun-In a few weeks back which streaked my dark brown hair the nastiest shades of burnt orange. My best friend Lisa, after laughing hysterically at my predicament, came over and helped me dye it back to my natural color. I would have considered that very helpful if it weren't for the fact that Lisa was the one who insisted I be the guinea pig for that particular brand of hair lightener in the first place.

I'd been staring wistfully out the window at the sunshine, daydreaming about working on my tan, driving around in Lisa's beat-up old LeBaron with the top down or getting in a few more laps once I got home from school.

The second bell hadn't rung yet and already I was zoned out, slouched in my seat, waiting for Mrs. Mason to get on with Part Two of *Romeo and Juliet*. I had gotten through the entire book over the weekend, a fact I was forced to keep to myself considering Mason's explicit instructions that we not read ahead.

My ears perked up when I heard Mrs. Mason speaking over the din of a not-yet-settled classroom. "Thank you. You can take the desk over there behind Miss Warren, by the windows." Teachers always tried to convey some illusion of respect by calling us by our last names.

My parents had saddled me with the unfortunate *first* name of Layla. My father has always explained that my mother was in the middle of a pretty heady rock-and-roll phase in the years surrounding my birth, which explains, but doesn't excuse, the fact that my brother's name is Bruce Springsteen Warren. I shit you not.

In any case, I hadn't been paying much attention to Mrs. Mason until I heard her say my name. I looked up and saw some new kid hand her a slip of paper then turn toward the direction of her pointed finger. The sight that greeted me was enough to stop my heart.

If I were living in a movie, the opening strains of *"Crazy Train"* would have piped in, creating a background for this gorgeous boy who was walking slow-motion toward me. Our eyes met for a second before I realized I'd been staring and suddenly looked away.

7

I tried to look engrossed in my book, flipping pages and avoiding eye contact as he sauntered down the aisle and slipped into the seat behind me.

I normally loved that the seating arrangements were done alphabetically. Most of the time, I wound up with a seat near the windows and I almost always got the last desk in the row. I couldn't imagine being someone like Sonny Aetine, who normally got stuck in the front seat right next to the classroom door. It always pissed me off whenever I was in a class with Art Zarelli, because that was the only time I ever had to deal with anyone sitting behind me. But now here was this new guy occupying a desk at my back, and suddenly, the idea didn't seem so bad. No sooner had he gotten himself settled when the bell rang, signaling the start of class.

Mrs. Mason stood and announced the obvious. "Good afternoon, everyone. You may have noticed that we have a new student today and I'd like to invite him up here to introduce himself."

God, what kind of sadism seminar do teachers attend that encourages torturing the new kid? If I had to get up in front of the whole class and offer some condensed biography of my life, I'd probably die. But New Kid strolled right up to the front of the room without the slightest bit of self-consciousness. And then, because *all* eyes were on him, I had the excuse to look right at him.

He had sun-streaked, sandy hair which he wore long on top, but short enough in back that Sister Jean wouldn't drag him by his ear into her office to shave his head as she'd been rumored to do. I hoped he'd keep on top of it, because it would have been a crime to shave off a beautiful mane such as that.

He bared a smile of gleaming, white teeth as he slid a hand into his back pocket, making the muscle of his arm strain against the sleeve of his white Oxford.

My God.

He mussed the back of his hair with his free hand as Mrs. Mason introduced him to the class as Terrence C. Wilmington *the*

8

third, which prompted him to immediately correct her with, "Everyone calls me Trip."

The smooth tenor of his voice caught me by surprise. Mrs. Mason must have been a little affected too, because she didn't bristle at being disputed, and merely smiled back at Trip's direct gaze and charming grin.

He turned back to our class and started in with the ease of someone who'd had to endure this barbaric ritual many times before. "My name's Trip," he said again. "My family just moved here from Indianapolis."

I don't know why, but the phrase *cornfed Indiana farmboy* came into my head at that moment. Indianapolis is hardly farm country, but I didn't count anyplace as a city except New York. Everything west of here was amber waves of grain as far as I was concerned. But even though he had the look of someone who'd have been perfectly cast in the role of sexy stableboy, he was way too polished to have been mistaken for a mere farmhand. Regardless of a rural upbringing.

"Before Indy, we lived in Seattle, Phoenix, L.A. and Chicago, where I was born."

Ah, okay. More "cities".

Mrs. Mason interrupted his schpiel then. "Is your father in the military, Trip?"

"Uh, no. He's in hotels. But I guess I could see why you'd get the impression that I'm an army brat. According to my sister, the brat part sums me up pretty good, though."

A few girls started giggling at the little joke which probably would have gone over like a lead balloon if it were told by anyone less gorgeous. I snickered at that thought and hoped it wasn't loud enough to hear.

Trip continued with, "My father likes to oversee construction when any one of his new hotels is being built. We normally spend a few years in each city until the grand opening and then we move on to the next one."

I felt my heart sink inexplicably, thinking that Trip's days here were already numbered. I didn't even know the guy, but I'd been

9

excited by the promise of someone new in this town, someone who hadn't lived here since birth like the rest of us. Someone who wasn't in every class picture of mine since kindergarten. Someone, let's face it, who was pretty easy on the eyes.

Mrs. Mason asked, "You named a bunch of big cities, there. How is it that you wound up in Norman, New Jersey? We're hardly a mecca for tourism."

That brought a few chuckles from the class as Trip flashed another amazing grin and answered, "Actually, the hotel's being built in New York. My father says this is his last hotel and he wanted to save it for when he was ready to retire, so I guess we're here for the long haul. The city's close enough to Norman and my dad spent his teen years here. I guess he wants that for me, too."

My stomach did a quick flip of rejoice. At the time, I was trying to convince myself that all I cared about was an improvement to the scenery of boring old Norman. Trip was like a one man beautification committee just by existing.

"Well, Trip, welcome to our town. I hope you'll like it here."

I guess Trip took that as his cue to escape, because he started walking toward me, back to his newly assigned desk, but not without saying, "Thanks. I have a feeling I will." Then he gave my desk a quick tap with his fingertips- which knocked me out- before sliding into the seat behind me.

I hoped I didn't have some noticeably embarrassing shocked look on my face, but my mouth had certainly gone dry and I swallowed hard. This, with my life, led to a very noticeable coughing fit which just got worse the more I tried to stop it. I raised my hand to be excused and Mrs. Mason just wagged her head in the direction of the door. I made a break for it, almost tripping on Mary Ellen Simpky's oversized Gucci purse on my way out of the room. I high-tailed it down the hall to the water fountain outside the girls' room and slugged down about a gallon of Norman's finest before the sputtering fit subsided. Without the luxury of long sleeves to swipe my face (Oh, please. Like everyone doesn't do it), I cruised into the bathroom in search of a paper towel.

Penelope Redy and Margie Caputo were standing together in the same open stall amidst a swirl of smoke. They both jumped when I walked in before realizing it was only me and not some teacher coming in to bust them for cutting class and sneaking a cigarette. Damn. I was so distracted that I forgot the cardinal rule of the Girls' Room, and didn't say "It's okay" upon entering.

We exchanged quick hellos before I turned toward the towel dispenser and they turned back to their conversation.

"I heard he's from Indiana," Penelope said through an exhale.

Margie spat back, "They don't make them like that in Indiana. Mount Olympus, maybe. But not Indiana."

Clearly, the hot topic of gossip for the next millennium at St. Norman's High School was going to be about the new kid.

"Do you think he has a girlfriend, like back home or whatever?"

Margie threw the butt into the toilet with a sizzle and flushed the incriminating evidence away. "Guys like that always do. Why? You think *you* have a shot at him? As if."

Penelope huffed at her friend's assessment and made her way over to the sink next to me. "That's *not* why I asked. I already have a boyfriend anyway. I was just curious, is all." Then she directed her next words to me. "Layla!"

I turned toward her all innocence, as if I hadn't spent the past minutes chafing my face and hands on the scratchy excuse for a paper towel just so I could eavesdrop.

Penelope asked, "What do you think? Have you seen him yet?"

"Who's that?" I asked unconvincingly.

She rolled her eyes. "The new kid. Terrence C. Williesomething."

Before I could stop myself, I found myself saying, "His name's Trip," and then probably blushed twelve different shades of red.

Penelope raised knowing brows at me as she pumped the dispenser lever of the paper towel holder, tearing off a three-foot length of recycled brown sandpaper.

I added quickly, "He's in Mason's class with me right now."

Penelope said, "Yeah. I had him in Biology."

"You wish," Margie piped in.

Penelope threw her towel in the trashcan, asking, "I wonder what the *C* stands for."

To which a quick-witted Margie shot back, "Hmm. Crumptious?"

* * *

When I got back to class, I avoided all eye contact as I tried to slide unnoticed back into my seat. I opened my book to the current page and was trying to concentrate on Capulets and Montagues when there was an electric shock against my shoulder blade; a finger poking me in the back. Trip was apparently trying to get my attention. Like he hadn't already.

I snuck a quick glance to make sure Mason was still at the blackboard before twisting around sideways in my seat. If I were Lisa, I could have come up with the perfect thing to say to him. But I was me, so the wittiest remark I could come up with was, "What is it, New Kid?"

At first, this brought a staggered look to Trip's face, but then he rewarded my jab with a smirk. Seeing his lip curl into a crooked smile while getting a close-up view of his gorgeous blue eyes for the first time made my composure slip just the slightest notch. I guess he didn't notice, because he simply asked, "You okay?"

I supposed it shouldn't have been a big surprise to find out my coughing fit hadn't gone undetected. "Yeah. Fine, thanks. How about you?"

Trip furrowed confused brows at me, compelling me to clarify. "The dog-and-pony show Mason forced you into, making you get up there and introduce yourself to the class. Was it awful? It didn't really seem to bother you."

Trip leaned back in his seat, tapping a pencil across his unopened notebook. "Yeah, well. Third time today. Guess I'm getting used to it."

I thought about what a nightmare this poor guy's first day had been. Although, he didn't seem too fazed by it. I guess it would have just been a nightmare for *me*. I gave him a sympathetic smile which was interrupted by Mrs. Mason saying, "Layla! Eyes up here, please."

I turned to face front, registering the few, sly glances I received from my classmates, busting me for ogling the cute new kid.

Kill. Me. Now.

The class's attentions went back to Mason's chalk diagrams, but my thoughts were entirely elsewhere. It didn't help matters when I heard Trip give a snicker and whisper, "Layla... *Nice*."

* * *

I met up with Lisa in the halls on our way to the gymnasium. Before I could even fill her in on the day's drama, she launched right in. "Oh my God, Layla! I can't believe I haven't talked to you all day. Did you see him?"

With the girls in the bathroom, I felt the need to play it cool. But this was Lisa, my best friend in the entire world, so there was no need to be coy. "Yes. He's in Mason's class with me."

Lisa pulled the heavy wooden gym doors open. "Holy crap. He is sooo cute. Damn. I wonder what the *C* stands for. I hope he's in our gym class, I'll bet he looks great in a pair of gym shorts. You know how I just love a guy that has strong legs and a gorgeous guy like that has just got to have strong legs. I mean, when I saw him walk into the cafeteria, I just about spit up my Diet Coke. Where were you? You totally missed it. I overheard Rymer and those guys sizing him up from the lunch line. They were all talk, of course, because as soon as he walked into the room, they were making a spot for him at our table. Which, you know, is good, because I guess we'll see him around a lot if he's going to be hanging with our guys. Oh, you know what?"

I was trying to keep a mental log of the twelve different topics my friend had just brought up in order to respond accordingly once she finally broke for air. Most of the time, Lisa is pretty high-strung to begin with. But forget about getting a word in edgewise when she's *really* excited about something. Although, I guess I was getting a little excited, too. I didn't realize Trip had our same lunch period until Lisa just told me about it. I had grabbed a soft pretzel and a soda on my way down to the art room, skipping lunch period that day like I sometimes did in favor of some extra studio time.

"Hellooo, Layla. You in there? Are you even listening?"

No.

"Yes. Hanging around our guys. Got it."

Lisa sat herself down on a bench in the locker room and slipped her blouse off over her head. "No, Dippy. I said Rymer's having a party this weekend because his parents are going down to Cape May for three whole days. Sargento's brother already said he'd get us a keg. Do you think he'll be there? What are you going to wear?"

This, of course, was a loaded question if there ever was one. I have learned over the years that whatever I said in answer would be met with Lisa's crinkled nose and unsolicited input. So, after a while, I just stopped answering it seriously. "MC Hammer pants and my *Schoolhouse Rock* T-shirt. You?"

Lisa had finished getting her gym clothes on and was checking out her hair in the mirror. I couldn't imagine why she'd feel the need to make adjustments considering the amount of gel, mousse and hairspray keeping that bouffant in check. A mere costume change wasn't going to be enough to ruffle that 'do. I mean, we all had big hair, but Lisa's was usually tornado-proof.

She turned from the mirror and retied the shoelace on her pink, Reebok hightops before answering. "Very funny."

Before Lisa could offer her opinion on a more appropriate party ensemble, Coach Lorenzo started blowing her whistle, signaling the start of class.

Chapter 3
GOODFELLAS

The next day, I woke up earlier than usual. I had set my alarm to go off twenty minutes before my normal wakeup time so that I could piece together an appropriate job-hunting outfit to change into after school. Had I not procrastinated the night before (I couldn't put *Catcher in the Rye* down and passed out sometime during Holden's duck fixation), I could have lain something out ahead of time. As it was, I was determined to make the right first impression on any potential employers and I didn't think my uniform was going to cut it.

Once I was satisfied with the results of my closet foray, I grabbed a towel off the doorknob and started to head off into the bathroom. I took a quick peek out my window toward the front of our house... and right at that very second I saw Trip jogging by! My heart slammed into my stomach, but I immediately turned off my bedroom light and continued spying from behind the safety of my mini-blinds. I was just able to catch him as he turned off my street and made his way up Cedar Drive.

When Lisa picked me up an hour later, I was still feeling a little flustered. I slipped into the passenger seat, listening to her babble about lordonlyknows when I guess the look on my face made her stop mid-sentence to ask, "What's with you?"

I just turned to her and said. "You were right."

She crinkled up her nose and asked, "About what?"

I bit my bottom lip in anticipation of the reaction I was about to provoke and replied, "About Trip in a pair of shorts."

* * *

I spent my morning going about my usual routine, counting down the minutes until lunch. Sitting in World History and

16

listening to Mr. Sasso drone on and on tried my patience more than usual as I watched the clock barely ticking away the time. Who could concentrate on Tiananmen Square when the promise of sharing a lunch table with Terrence C. Wilmington III was only minutes away?

After an eternity, the bell finally rang. I shoved my way through the throng of students rushing to their next class and ducked into the ladies' room for a quick hair check and lipstick application. I knew I was being ridiculous, but I also knew that my confidence always shot up a couple notches whenever I felt like I looked okay.

Inside the cafeteria, Lisa was already at our table. My shining red lips didn't escape her notice, but best friend that she is, she didn't call me out for it and merely smirked as I sat down. She patted my shoulder as she got up, explaining through a smile, "I'm going to grab us a couple sodas. Be right back."

I sat there and concentrated on trying to look cool and unaffected, hoping to strike just the right note of blasé for when Trip finally sat down.

Greg Rymer and Mike Sargento sidled down with their lunch trays completely piled with food as usual. Rymer ripped half the paper off his straw and blew the remaining wrapper off the end of it toward me, jolting me out of my trance. "What's up, Warren? Not eating today?"

Shit. I forgot about having to eat in front of Trip. I'm no Scarlett O'Hara or anything, but the thought of chewing like some common cow in front of the cute new guy was beyond horrifying. But sitting there sipping demurely on a Diet Coke like some salad-eating girly-girl was not the image I was hoping to portray either. Besides, the last thing I needed was for my stomach to start growling in the middle of English Lit. I resigned myself to the prospect of having to eat *something* as I joined Lisa in the lunch line.

Eyeing up the prospective meals offered in your average, high-school cafeteria is daunting enough. The menus aren't exactly

17

being considered for worldwide culinary acclaim. But trying to find something edible *and* dainty was like navigating a minefield.

Meatball sub was too sloppy, spaghetti was right out. Oh, curse you, Italian Tuesday!

I settled on my usual mid-day selection: a big, soft pretzel with yellow mustard. Normally, I'd grab an apple or something, too, but I was feeling self-conscious enough as it was. I figured whatever tidbits I managed to scarf down my throat would have to provide enough sustenance for the day.

I bypassed a tray and pulled a few napkins out of the dispenser on my way back to the table.

Lisa was already there, sitting with Rymer, Sargento, Cooper Benedict... and Trip. I slid inconspicuously into the seat next to Lisa and cracked my can of soda. The guys were busy talking about their plans for the weekend.

"So, Coop," Rymer started in, "Tell your hot sister to come to my party on Saturday night."

Coop gave Rymer a warning look. "Dude. If you fuckin' say one more thing about my sister..."

Rymer ignored the threat and continued by twisting the knife. "What? She's hot. I think she's got a little crush on me, too." He elbowed Sargento before continuing, "You see the way she was sweatin' me last week when she picked us up from practice? Man, I thought she was gonna kick you two out of the car and jump me right there in the parking lot." He took a huge bite out of his sub before adding, "Trip, you gotta see this girl. Total bitch, but black hair, great ass and tits bigger than DeSanto's." This earned Rymer a shove from Coop and a meatball to the chest from Lisa, which made us all crack up.

I'd been ripping little pieces off my pretzel and trying to pop them unnoticed into my mouth. I was mid-chew when Rymer reached across the table to grab my stack of napkins. Cleaning sauce off his Oxford, he suddenly decided to switch subjects. "Oh, hey Warren! You meet Trip yet?"

I was caught off guard enough to almost choke, but luckily, I caught myself. I still had a mouthful of food, so I shielded my lips with my hand and answered as best I could. "Uh huh. We're in Mason's together." Then, I swallowed and was able to nod in Trip's direction to add casually, "How's it going?"

The guys were still laughing at the big, red stain that Rymer was unsuccessfully trying to wipe off his shirt, so Lisa and I were the only ones to absorb the full force of Trip's lazy grin when he replied, "It's good, *Layla*. How's it going for you?"

I almost died at the way he said that, looking right at me with half-lidded eyes and those perfect, full lips smiling out my name. I felt Lisa kick me under the table, so I knew she caught it too. Oh my God. Was he *flirting* with me? As intrigued as I was, my survival instincts quickly won out. The guys would never stop busting my chops if they caught me flirting with the new guy. I smiled politely and offered evasively, "It's good."

Just making courteous small talk, right?

Soon after, the bell rang, so we all grabbed our garbage from the table and ditched it in the trash on our way out the door. My locker was right outside the cafeteria, so I pit-stopped there to get my English notebook. When I stood back up, I was surprised to see Trip standing right behind me.

"Oh! I didn't see you there!" I said like a complete tool.

He looked a little taken aback. "I just thought..." and then he nodded his head in the direction of the hallway and I realized he was waiting to walk with me down to English class.

I laughed to save face and said, "Yeah, sure. Duh."

He was teasing me when he asked, "You alright there, pal?" He threw an arm around my shoulders and gave me a quick squeeze against his side, which, had he added a noogie, would have made the platonic gesture complete. To this day, I have no idea what compelled him to do something like that. It's not as though I'd never been treated as one of the boys before. In fact, it's how I'd spent the first twelve years of my life, and hell, I could still hold my own with my guy friends. But Trip barely knew me and besides, I thought I'd shaken off that persona years before. Had he picked up my tomboy vibe even though I was sure I hadn't been putting it out there? Dear God. Was it Brian Hollander all over again?

The thought made me so flustered, so determined, that I did something so completely out of character. Just as we were approaching the classroom, I noticed some random kid at his locker. I saw the mirror hanging on the open door and inspiration struck. I whipped my lipstick out of my purse, telling Trip, "Hey, hold on a sec, huh?"

I uncapped the lipstick, leaned into the mirror and applied a swipe of Bing Cherry across my slacked lips, making sure Trip could see my every move. Very Marilyn Monroe. Very *not* tomboy.

I tossed the weapon into my purse, smacked my lips together and asked Trip innocently, "You ready?"

I caught a glimpse of the poor, unsuspecting freshman staring at me like he had just won the lottery. I guessed it wasn't every day that a senior girl dropped by his locker. I couldn't get a read on Trip, but I hoped his blank look was a good thing. "Uh, yeah. Yes."

Hmph. Take *that*, "pal"!

Chapter 4
GETTING LUCKY

After final bell, I ran into the girls' room with my bag of clothes. I'd settled on a pair of flat-front black slacks and a pale pink silk blouse. I ditched my Wigwams and slipped into a pair of black ballet slippers before taming my hair down a bit with a brush. I had to be careful not to overdo it, because too much brushing would cause that armor of Aqua Net to start flaking, making me look like I was The Dandruff Queen. I took a final look in the mirror and decided that I looked professional. At the very least, I looked respectable. And definitely a little older.

By the time I stepped outside, most of the kids had already cleared out, which was a good thing. It wasn't a long walk over to the strip mall, but it really sucked to be a senior without a license and risk getting caught hoofing it around town. The first four weeks of school were turning into the longest of my life. I suppose Lisa could have driven me, but she already had a job working at the bakery right around the corner from where we lived and I didn't want to make her late. She wouldn't have had enough time to schlep me in the opposite direction, fight through the mosh of cars at the mall and still make it to her job by 3:00. No big deal. It was a nice day out and I didn't mind the walk.

I got about ten steps away from the parking lot when a black Bronco pulled up beside me. The windows were tinted and only cracked an inch, enough to allow me to hear some creepy old dude ask, "Hey, little girl. You need a ride?"

I'd been in these situations before. The best thing to do when confronted with a pervert is to simply ignore them. Just pretend not to hear them. Which is exactly what I did as I kept walking, hoping the freak would just go on his merry way and find some other, more stupid girl to lock in his basement.

But this pervert wasn't going to be shaken so easily. "Hey! Little girl! Do ya want some candy?" I started to slide my hand into my purse, fishing around for my mace keychain just in case.

21

But then, something about the way he started laughing made me do a double-take and turn on my heel. When I did, the Bronco's window slid down, revealing Trip in the midst of cracking himself up.

"You idiot!" I yelled, laughing and smacking the door of his truck. "I thought you were a creepy old man, you jerk!"

Trip could barely contain himself. "I know! I thought you were gonna start running. Holy shit that was funny."

I gave him an "oh really" look.

"Running, huh? You should have been so lucky." I pulled the keychain canister of mace out of my bag and held it up for him to see.

That sobered him up pretty quick. "What the? Is that *mace*?"

I gave him a smug smile and said, "Yes. And I would have used it, too." When he looked impressed, I decided to lose the false bravado. "I'm really glad I didn't have to, though. Jeez, you scared the hell out of me."

He winked at me, calling a truce. "Sorry. Hey, where you going? I'll drive you."

Truth was, I *really* wanted to get in Trip's truck. But I also really didn't want him to think that I really wanted to.

"Um. Actually, I'm just headed over to the mall."

"Doing some shopping?"

"Nope. Looking for a job."

Trip nodded his head in approval. "Good for you. Hey, c'mon. After scaring the hell out of you, the least I can do is give you a ride. C'mon. Hop in."

Well, when you put it that way...

I rolled my eyes then stepped up into the passenger seat.

"Where to, Miss Daisy?"

Cute.

"I figured I'd start at Totally Videos and work my way down. I guess you can just drop me there."

He put the car in gear. "As you wish."

I don't even know what I wish, I thought.

22

I mean, I probably should have just been content to ride out my good fortune.

Sometimes, when you're part of the popular crowd, there's a ton of pressure on you. Everyone is always aware of what you wear, or do, or say. Sometimes, it feels like you're being scrutinized with a fine-tooth comb, any flaws magnified tenfold. You're always expected to be "on". You're always expected to act a certain way. It can be draining in a way I never felt when I was just plain old Layla Warren, blending in with the wallpaper.

But sometimes, there were perks.

Here was this great-looking guy, fresh from the farm and plunked right into my very own high school. Out of some instinctual, unspoken law of the universe, it was just assumed that he would be part of our group. I was sure most of the girls in school were drooling at Trip from afar. And yet, lucky me, I was afforded actual *access*.

Yet somehow, it felt a little vapid. I wondered if he would have bothered offering me a ride if I was just some random classmate as opposed to a girl who was part his new circle. I supposed I'd never figure it out, but what I really wanted was for Trip to *want* to be around me, not just hang with me out of default.

Not that I was complaining. At that moment, I was just happy to be where I was.

Bolstered by that, I asked him, "How did you do that with your voice?"

He asked, "Do what? Trick you into thinking I was someone else?"

"Yeah. You were pretty convincing back there. If I wasn't so freaked out, I might have actually been impressed."

This earned a laugh from him. "You're pretty funny, you know that?" Then, in answer to my question, "I was just goofing around with you. There was this guy who used to work at the hardware store back in Indy. He was actually a decent old guy, but he had the creepiest voice, like Lurch from The Addams family. I guess inspiration struck when I saw you. I didn't even realize I knew how to impersonate him until I did it!"

23

He laughed again and then, out of the blue, added, "You look nice, by the way."

I started to get fidgety and OCD, like I sometimes do when I'm feeling a little nervous. And sitting next to Trip in his truck- idly making small talk and then hearing him toss a compliment my way- was making me *very* nervous. I made myself stop playing with the zipper on my purse and stowed it away at my feet before diverting his comment with, "Thanks. Do you have a job?"

He took his hand off the wheel to scratch the back of his neck. "Yeah. I do some work for my father down at his office every now and then. This one's over in the industrial park, off Main? Just phone calls and filing and stuff."

"Oh, so you're a secretary," I teased.

That made him smile. "Yeah, good one, I guess I am."

"Do you like it?"

He gave me a stock answer. "Uh... I guess so. I mean, it's a decent job and all and I like making my own money, even if my father is the one who's signing my paychecks."

He took a sharp right, causing me to grab the holy shit bar over the window as he continued, "Actually, you know what? It kinda sucks, actually. I absolutely hate it. I really, absolutely, freakin' hate working there."

That made me laugh. "Wow. Why don't you tell me how you really feel! But hey, I guess acknowledging your problem is the first step toward recovery, right?"

"The problem," he snickered out, "isn't mine." His laugh had an edge to it, but I didn't know him well enough to discern what that meant.

Had I known him better, I probably would have asked him what was wrong. But I thought it would be rude to go playing pop-psychologist with a person I'd only known for one day, so I let it go.

By then, we were already at the mall anyway. Trip pulled up to the side entrance and threw the car in park. His bitter tone was gone, replaced with a playful voice as he said, "That'll be eight-fifty."

I made a big, phony show of digging through my purse. "Damn. I left my wallet in my other bag. I'll have to owe it to you."

He smiled as I got out of the truck, and because I knew he was watching me, I made extra sure not to slip and wind up face-down on the sidewalk.

I was feeling a little elated from the time I'd just spent alone with him, while simultaneously feeling let down at the thought of it coming to an end. I knew I was stalling, hoping to drag a few more seconds out of our time together, but I couldn't stop myself. "Hey, thanks for the ride."

He leaned over toward the passenger side to talk to me out the open window. "No problem."

I tapped my toe against the tire as I asked, "See you tomorrow?"

He winked and repeated, "See you tomorrow."

Short of throwing myself across the hood of his truck, there was really nothing else to do at that point but say goodbye. I had just turned and was starting to walk inside when I heard him yell, "Hey Layla!" which made my stomach do a little flip.

I looked back at Trip, still leaning out the passenger window with a wide grin playing at his lips and answered, "Yes?"

His grin turned into the full-force smile, the one that stopped me dead in my tracks at lunch.

"Good luck."

At that, he threw the truck in gear and took off.

Chapter 5
BRAIN DEAD

The rest of the week went by in a blur. I did remember to start waking up about ten minutes earlier than usual so that I could catch Trip during his morning jog. Sitting off to the side of my window in the dark and peeking through the blinds was risky, but even feeling like a stalker and losing a few minutes of sleep was worth the payoff. I mean, there were worse ways to start a day, am I right?

Trip and I still walked from the cafeteria down to English every day, and sometimes, we even managed to carve out a few moments of conversation during class. Riveting commentary such as, "What page are we on?" or "Do you have an extra pencil?"

But even still, it was the part of day that I most looked forward to, those few stolen moments when he'd be sitting just inches away from me. It was unnerving and exciting... and totally self-destructive. I spent the entire day preoccupied with waiting to see Trip, then spent the class so distracted by the mere proximity of him that I was starting to turn into quite the space cadet. At the very least, I consoled myself with the knowledge that English was my best subject, so it's not like my studies were suffering from any daydreams during that class. But still. I didn't know how much longer that would be the case and I already seemed to be slipping everywhere else.

By Friday, I'd fallen behind on my silk-screening project, so I opted to cut lunch and head down to the art room instead. It was slightly devastating, knowing I was skipping out on some major social time with him, but I had to take control of my life. I couldn't spend every waking moment thinking about Trip Wilmington.

By the time I beat the bell to Mason's class, Trip was already at his desk and a note was waiting for me at mine. I slid into my seat and unfolded it.

Where were you?

My stomach did an involuntary flip, appreciating that he'd noticed my absence from our lunch table. I gave a "Hi" over my shoulder and started to say, "I went down-" but before I could finish, Mason called attention to the front of the room and I was forced to shut up. Trip mimed writing in the air with an imaginary pencil, so I scribbled

I went down to the art room

and passed it low behind me for him to grab.

A few seconds later, as Mason was explaining our Shakespeare outline or something, a folded wad of paper was tossed over my shoulder.

What for?

I decided to bust his chops:

To do art, dummy.

I heard him snicker behind me. A minute later, I felt his hand tuck the paper into the waistband at the small of my back. I turned just long enough to shoot him a look and catch him raising his eyebrows at me.

I kind of figured that out already on my own. And who are you calling dummy, dummy.

I made sure Mason wasn't looking before tossing back my response.

YOU!

27

Then I threw a second piece of paper over my shoulder, where I had written:

...Dummy.

I heard Trip stifle a guffaw, choking back the laughter as he spent an exorbitant amount of time writing a reply.

At that point, we were asked to work on our "Mind Ramble" exercises, a little task that Mason utilized to get our creative juices flowing. She'd give us a subject- in this case, *Romeo and Juliet*- and ask us to keep it in the edges of our thoughts as we scribbled whatever the hell our minds told our hands to put on the paper. I really tried to let my brain wander and produce an effective Mind Ramble, but I couldn't get past the idea that Trip was apparently "mind rambling" right then about *me*.

I made a mental note to rip out a new sheet of loose-leaf for my reply to his manifesto, once he finally finished and handed it over. I was going to make damned sure I'd be the last one of us to get possession of his note, because there was no way I was ever letting that paper out of my hands at the end of this. Hell, I'd probably frame the stupid thing when all was said and done.

Near the end of class, Mason told us to put our pens down- Trip never stopped writing- and she did a quick review of the work we'd done on *Romeo and Juliet* to prepare us for the project we were going to be working on.

Then she passed out little stapled booklets that she had run off on the copier and collated, saying, "Rather than bore you by going over what I've already compiled here, I'll ask you just to follow the directions in the booklets. I'm expecting great things from each and every one of you."

The bell rang and she added loudly over the noise of a dispersing classroom, "Have your partners picked out by Monday! Enjoy your weekend!"

I got up and turned to give Trip his booklet and saw that he was still writing. "Hey Dummy," I prodded. "The bell rang."

I tried to peek over his hands to catch a glimpse of anything he'd written down just as he swiped the pages off his desk and folded them out of my sight.

"That for me?" I asked.

He grabbed his books and tucked the note in his shirt pocket. I couldn't interpret the look on his amused face; kind of embarrassed, but still lighthearted. "Maybe. Someday. Just not today."

I was just dying inside. Somehow, some way, I was going to get my hands on that thing. I didn't even care if it wasn't the love letter I was delusionally hoping it was, even though he'd started writing it long before our teacher asked us to Mind Ramble. I figured maybe he'd just gotten caught up on a tangent and rambled on endlessly about it. But the thoughts flying around the head of Trip Wilmington, whatever they were, were just too enticing a mystery not to be explored. What I wouldn't have given for just the slightest glean into that brain of his. The key to unlock that particular treasure chest was folded right there in his pocket, yet he wasn't handing it over. It was like offering a starving person a cookie, but holding it just out of their reach.

Of course, I couldn't ever convey my overwhelming obsessions to him. So, I gave a casual shrug and said, "Whatever floats your boat, *pal*."

Chapter 6
WHERE THE HEART IS

I had absolutely nothing to wear. The thing was, from Monday to Friday, getting dressed for school was a no-brainer. Grab an Oxford, choose a skirt, out the door. I know the public school kids probably wondered how we could possibly wear uniforms every day without wanting to jump off a bridge. But the truth was, I kinda liked it. There was no fashion show to compete with from day to day. We all looked the same from our necks down to our ankles.

Until the weekend.

My entire annual school-clothes budget went toward replenishing Oxfords, maybe replacing a skirt or two and restocking my undies drawer. The rest went toward shoes.

When you wore a uniform every day, the only place left to express yourself was with your shoes. You'd be surprised how creative we could get with our footwear while still keeping within the guidelines of "hard soles, nothing above the ankle". And trust me, there wasn't a girl at St. Norman's that didn't push those parameters right to the edge.

But blowing the majority of my school-shopping allotment on shoes constantly left me scrambling on Saturday nights. After all, unlike the public school kids, I couldn't very well hit a party in my weekday clothes.

I'd already torn through my closet, dismissing every garment I owned as unsuitable, more determined than ever to get a job and earn some wardrobe money.

My father had already left for the evening- poker at the VFW- so I took advantage of his absence and raided his closet.

The closet in his bedroom was a huge walk-in which I was normally forbidden to enter. Though I suspected it had less to do with my father's desire for privacy and more to do with the indefensible fact that my mother's side had remained virtually undisturbed since the day she left us.

One time in fifth grade, we took a class trip to Thomas Edison's laboratory. It was so cool to see his workspace with all the long tables set up, awaiting his next stroke of genius.

I remember thinking that his office was so cool. All those books! And in the corner of the library, there was a cot for his erratic sleeping needs. The story was that he'd work for endless hours, pass out for ten minutes and then wake up and get right back to work again.

But what sticks with me most is his desk. A beautiful rolltop plunked right in the middle of the expansive room, fitted with a piece of plexiglass across the opening. Apparently, upon his death, his wife had the desk sealed up. Stopped in time, exactly as he last left it, posthumously honoring the work that would forever go unfinished.

That was my father's closet.

Despite the fact that his side was crammed with clothes and shoes and boxes of godonlyknowswhat, my mother's side was left completely untouched.

I ran my hand across the racks of clothes, the remnants of what she left behind, neatly aligned, undisturbed and awaiting an owner who would never release them to the light of day again. I pressed my face to a row of blouses and inhaled the familiar scent of my mother- Chanel No. 5 mixed with lemon- and it brought tears to my eyes for only the briefest second.

Sometimes, like at that moment, it was easier to make believe that my mother had died. It gave me permission to mourn her loss, appreciate the person she was while still allowing myself to be sad that she was gone. Because how was a person supposed to feel when their mother *chose* to leave? Was I supposed to love her less because of it?

I pushed those thoughts aside, again, and remembered why I was in there in the first place. Emotionless, I rifled through the hanging clothes, most of which were pretty outdated. My fingers grazed a butter-soft cotton, so I shoved the hangars aside to get a better look. I found myself staring at a flowery whisper of a blouse with flowing hippie sleeves. I stripped off my Bon Jovi T-

31

shirt and slid the blouse over my head. I hopped up onto Dad's bed to check myself out in his dresser mirror and felt a slight pang when I realized it fit like a glove. I'd finally grown into my mother's body.

I had a brief glimpse of an alternate life- one in which my mother and I could have shared this moment, giggling about having just doubled our wardrobes- and then dismissed the thought realizing that that scenario was never going to happen. I wondered if she'd feel violated that instead, I was just swiping something out of her closet without her knowledge.

Screw her. I'm wearing it.

I blew my hair out poker straight, but braided a random strip down one side. I threw on some jeans and a pair of strappy sandals- thanking God for my awesome shoe collection- because the look wouldn't have been complete without some hippie footwear.

I assessed the final product of my work and was happy with the end result. Although, I was going out on a limb there with the retro duds. I figured I'd have to endure a few jabs from the guys, but nothing too traumatizing. I'd gotten used to their relentless ballbusting over the years. Growing up in a neighborhood full of boys helped me to form a thicker skin than most girls I knew. Hell, one night I saw Francine Mentozzi reduced to tears over a pair of zebra-print stretch jeans when Rymer took one look at her and suggested she head back to the zoo. She didn't hang out too much after that.

That's something I never understood. How anyone could feel "victimized" by "the cool kids" just because they weren't a part of them. Unless someone was really asking for it, none of us went out of our way to pick on anyone. We were too busy doing our own thing to care.

But from the outside, did that seem excluding? Did our goofing around come across as bullying? Didn't those kids know that *we* got *our* chops busted every day, too? Maybe that was the difference between the "cool kids" and the not-so-cool ones. Maybe we were just better able to laugh at ourselves and not take

32

any negative comments so seriously. Maybe that was the only line separating the people who enjoyed their school years from the ones who were scarred by them.

I'll give you an example: Junior year, Roger Vreeland and I were paired up on a science project. We'd meet at his or my house after school a couple times a week to work on it. Now Roger is someone I'd known since kindergarten, but never really hung out with or anything. He was kind of quiet and spent most of his time with the Audio/Visual crowd. But we actually hit it off fairly well during that project. We were surprised to find that I was smarter and he was funnier than we both had previously thought. We ended up getting some good work done in spite of a lot of joking around.

One day, I showed up to his house with a replacement bag of Munchos, because I had demolished the last of his during our previous work session. I mean, it's just what you do, right? A person would have to be pretty rude not to at least replace a bag of Munchos.

But you know what he said? "Wow. Thanks. You know, it's funny- I never realized you were *nice* before."

I'm sure he meant it as a compliment, but I was all, "What's *that* supposed to mean?"

And he actually said, "Well, you know. You were always too cool to talk to me."

Can you believe that? What the hell? I should have said that the reason we never talked was because he never opened his mouth in my direction, which was the truth. But did I go and jump to the conclusion that we never spoke because he was "too cool" to do so? No. I couldn't imagine going through life with such a huge chip on my shoulder like that.

I mean, it's not like we were such a mutually exclusive group who spent our days trying to find ways to torture and alienate our fellow classmates. If anyone ever wanted to be a part of things, all they ever had to do was show up.

That's the thing about popularity that no one ever tells you. *It's all about confidence.* That's it. That's the magic formula, boys and girls. Speaking as a person with experience on both sides of popularity, I can tell you that that's all it takes. If you can mind the slight angular shift between holding your head up high and sticking your nose in the air... If you can strike the right balance between conformity and originality... If you can be friendly but not perky, optimistic yet unaffected, lead instead of follow... you're in. It may seem like a tightrope-walk to be sure, but you just gotta fake it until you make it. After a while, you won't even be that conscious of the fine line you're walking all the time.

I was anxious to get over to the party, but until I got my license, I was at the mercy of Lisa's time schedule. I sat down at the top of the stairs where I'd have a good line of sight into the driveway. Not that I needed to keep watch for her. That girl normally started honking the horn from her house. This night was no exception.

I bolted out the front door, simultaneously fumbling with my keys to lock it behind me while flapping my hand down to shush Lisa, who started beeping even more incessantly upon my presence.

When I finally opened the passenger door, I snipped, "Shut up already! I have neighbors you know!"

Lisa just laughed and said, "I know! I'm one of them, Dippy!"

Chapter 7
HOUSE PARTY

Greg Rymer lived in Norman Hills- the "rich neighborhood"- on the northern side of town. Back in the seventies, the land developer who had the area bulldozed was eventually sent to prison for bribing a bunch of government officials in order to get the zoning rights. Prior to his arrest, however, he was responsible for building some gorgeous homes.

Rymer's was a sprawling ranch nestled into a copse of trees, with huge sections of wall made up almost entirely of glass. I guess the secluded property allowed for them to live in a fishbowl without feeling like exhibitionists. Sometimes, it freaked me out to hang there at night, though. When just a few of us were there watching a movie or something, I always thought that there could be some murderer creeping around out in the woods spying on us. Seriously, the alienated house was the perfect backdrop for a slasher film. There wasn't another home within earshot. No one would hear your screams.

On the other hand, that's why it made such a perfect party house.

With the number of cars crammed around the front yard, I rest assured that any potential murderers would be outnumbered by party guests. Besides, all the real creeps were already inside.

I remember hearing once about the correct way to enter a room. A person should stroll in with confidence and head straight for a familiar face. The worst thing you could do was linger like an insecure little wallflower, fumphering around two steps inside the door. Lisa knew this, too, which is why we gave a quick knock before heading right on in. We kissed a few people hello on our beeline to the back deck where we knew the keg would be.

Cooper and Sargento were standing around the boombox, fighting over DJ duties. Rymer was sitting on the railing, using the keg as a footstool and holding a stack of red Solo cups.

He saw Lisa and me walk out and said, "Five bucks."

I went for my wallet, but stopped when I heard Lisa say, "Rymer, you pantywaste. Are you seriously going to try and pull this shit again? Asking *girls* to kick in for the keg? No wonder you never get laid."

The guys snickered into their sleeves which put Rymer in the position of having to retaliate. "Alright, DeSanto. I'll give you and Janis Joplin here both a cup, no charge. But you're gonna have to pay for it later, if you know what I mean."

We all knew Rymer was full of shit, but the guys stopped laughing at the suggestive comment and turned toward us, waiting with anticipation to see how we'd respond.

Lisa didn't disappoint. She got right up in his face and said, "Rymer, if I actually believed you even *had* a dick in those pants, we could talk. As it is-"

"Oh, you want to see it?" He hopped off the railing and started making a big, phony show of unbuttoning his jeans. We knew he was bluffing about dropping his drawers, but thankfully, we weren't forced to test that notion. Because just then, Trip came out the door and stopped him in his tracks with, "Jesus, Rymer. Can't you ever keep your damn pants on?"

We all started laughing as Trip made the rounds of hellos and handshakes.

Rymer gave Trip a high-five, then handed him a cup. Lisa just went ballistic. "Oh, so you give your buddies beer for free but charge the girls five bucks? Nice racket you're running here."

Trip was busy getting a beer from the keg as he said, "Dude. You can't charge the girls for beer, man. That's just stupid."

Lisa chimed in, "I know, right?"

Trip handed her his filled cup and dug a fold of bills out of his pocket. Lisa and I tried to protest as he peeled off a twenty and slapped it on the railing before grabbing three more cups off the stack and filling them at the tap, passing the first off to me as he finished. Lisa and I shrugged at each other and started drinking.

Rymer tried to save face. "Trip- No way, man. Take this back. I wasn't really gonna charge them and what kind of asshole would I be if I didn't cover your cup?"

36

Lisa cut in with, "A huge one!"

Rymer shot her a dirty look, then turned and started jabbing the twenty back in Trip's direction. "Seriously. It's your first night hanging with us. Take it."

By that time, Trip was almost finished filling the fourth cup. "Not gonna happen, dude. Just take it off my tab the next time."

Then he clinked his cup against mine and gave me a wink which almost made me spit up my mouthful of beer.

"By the way," he added, "Who the hell tapped this thing? They foamed the hell out of it."

We all started laughing again because it was a great slam on Rymer, who obviously must have tapped his own keg. Poorly.

Normally, having been shown up in front of his friends, Rymer would have gone on the rampage. I don't know why Trip was given a free pass. Maybe Rymer was trying to be welcoming to the new kid. It's possible he may have just realized he was being a jerk. Then again, maybe he thought he'd finally met his match and just didn't want to get his ass kicked.

The thing was, Trip managed to put Rymer in his place without completely tearing him to shreds. Hell, Rymer actually had a *smile* on his face! I'd never seen anyone get away with that.

Just as we were pulling it together, Cooper pointed out Trip's two beers and asked, "Yo. What's with the double-fisting tonight?"

Trip didn't miss a beat and answered him with, "Double fisting? What, is your sister around?"

We all lost our minds cracking up. Even Coop was forced to crack a smile as Rymer gave Trip another high-five. While we were catching our breath, *Tess Valletti* walked out onto the deck.

She walked right over to Trip, who handed her a drink in an unmistakable gesture that said they were together.

Unbelievable. The guy was in town for less than a week and he'd already managed to start dating *Tess Valletti*.

Here's the 411 on Tess: She was a year older than us, so she'd graduated the previous June. During her four years at St. Norman's, she was drooled over by every straight male in the vicinity. Tall, blonde and funny, she was not only gorgeous, but popular, too.

She used to only date college guys, much to the average high-school-girl's relief. The fact that Trip- a senior in high school, mind you- was able to get her to go out with him was pretty impressive. The fact that she let him drag her to a high school party was nothing short of *miraculous*.

She and I were in the same typing class the year before, so we actually knew each other pretty well even though we didn't really hang out too much or anything.

"Hey, Layla!" she said.

"Hi Tess. How's it going?"

She took a sip of her beer. "Great. Really great. Well, you know, aside from the fact that I'm here at *Rymer's* and all."

Everyone thought that was just hysterical, of course.

Lisa would never admit it, but I knew she was euphoric once Tess finally graduated, giving her the chance to ascend to her rightful and long-awaited position as Queen Bee. Yet here she found herself back in Tess's shadow only two weeks into her reign.

Lisa couldn't allow herself to take a backseat any longer and decided to pipe in. "So, Tess... How the heck did you wind up here tonight?"

Tess shot Trip a sly look and joked, "Oh, you know. The usual, boring old story. I was on my way to meet some girlfriends out tonight when I got hit on by some random guy at the convenience store."

Trip threw an arm around her shoulders and added, "Yeah. Last time I was at the 7-11, all I picked up was a Slurpee."

Lisa and I laughed, but I was feeling pretty torn up inside. Seeing the two of them together was just the slightest bit devastating. They looked like a page ripped out of a magazine, standing there with their dazzling good looks and their suggestive smiles. They gave off the vibe that they were part of some secret club the rest of us would never be asked to join. What, do beautiful people have radar or something for one another?

Chapter 8
NIGHT OF THE LIVING DEAD

I spent the next couple of hours hanging out with some girls from my art class. Just as we decided to start a game of Quarters, Lisa grabbed my arm and pulled me over to a more private corner of the kitchen. "Oh my God, Pickford's here!" she managed to whisper-scream in my ear.

Pickford was Penelope Redy's twin brother, but I didn't really know him too well. Lisa had been eyeing him up since the first day of school. He'd shot up about six inches and apparently spent the entire summer vacation lifting weights, because he showed up for senior year looking like a completely different person. Tall, dark and lean, with just enough muscle to not appear lanky. He wasn't really my type- I'd recently been displaying a particular affinity for *blonds*- but he was definitely cute. It wasn't easy to transition, but Pick was always a well-liked guy and with the new abs and attitude, Lisa figured it wouldn't be long before he sidled on in to our group. That he'd shown up at Rymer's was an encouraging start.

I asked, "Where is he?"

Lisa nodded her head in the direction of the living room. "In there, I think. Peek out casually and see if you can see him. But don't be obvious!"

I leaned out the doorway and scanned my eyes across the living room for Pickford. It didn't take long to find him as he was a full head taller than the rest of the kids in the room. "Yep. There he is alright. I'll call him over so you can smooch him. Hey Pick!"

Lisa threw her hand over my mouth, saying, "Shut up, you retard!" and dragged me back behind the kitchen wall.

She still had a hold on my mouth, so I licked her palm.

She pulled away quickly, wiping her hand on her jeans. "Ewww! You're so gross! What's your damage, anyway?"

"Um, okay, *Heather*. Did you just seriously ask me what my damage is?" I cracked up, then added, "That's what you get for trying to smother me with your freakish paws."

Lisa held a hand in front of her face, inspecting it for flaws, saying, "Maybe they're not *dainty*, but they're not freakish. *You're* the freak."

"You are."

"You are, Jerk."

"Don't call me Jerk, Oven Mitts."

"Don't call me Oven Mitts, Janis Joplin."

"Yeah, well, up your nose with a rubber hose."

"Ha! Up your ass with a piece of glass. You'd love it."

"Yeah? Well, *you* love Pickford Redy."

Lisa stopped laughing and looked at me wide-eyed. "Shit. Yeah, I totally do," which cracked me up all over again.

* * *

Most of the time, the purposes of a high school party were to socialize, drink and hook up. The latter of which I was reminded of while waiting in line for the bathroom as Coop Benedict tried to stick his tongue in my ear.

Cooper and I had been close friends for like, *ever*. He was really cute and we'd gone out a few times, but we'd realized we weren't destined to be the next Bruce and Demi. Sometimes, we'd get drunk and make out, but that night, he was just *too* drunk and I wasn't digging his sloppy proposition.

Thankfully, Sargento came out of the bathroom just then and I told Coop he could get in there ahead of me.

He wobbled on his feet for a second and said, "Why don't we *both* go in?"

I told him no, that was alright.

He put a hand against the door frame and slurred his next words. "C'mon, Layla. You looso hot in that hibbie shirt. Come in w' me."

And then, like I knew he would, he started singing.

I'll give you one guess what song it was.

"Oh, for crying out loud, Coop. Just take your damn turn in the bathroom so I can get in there. I really gotta pee!"

He finally gave up and closed the door behind him, adjusting the lyrics and singing loudly, "*Lay*-la... She's really gotta pee! *Lay*-la..."

Just as I was shaking my head at that, Trip appeared around the corner. I'd spent the past few hours avoiding him and Tess like the plague. I just didn't think I could handle seeing them being shmoopy all night.

"This the line?"

"Yep."

"Who's the songbird in the can?"

"That would be Cooper Benedict."

Trip could hear the altered version of my song and asked, "How many times has someone sung *that* to you?"

"If I had a nickel."

That made him laugh.

He leaned a shoulder against the wall, crossed his arms and nodded at me. "You know, I almost didn't recognize you when I first saw you out there. You look really different with your hair like that."

I didn't know if "different" was a good or a bad thing. I resisted the urge to check my flat hair in the hall mirror and took a sip of my drink instead. I'd had more than a handful of conversations with Trip already, but I still felt nervous talking to him, wanting to make a good impression, even though I knew it was really stupid to develop a crush on a guy that nine hundred other girls were practically in love with, too. A guy that dated older, beautiful and more experienced girls like Tess Valletti. A guy that was only talking to me at that moment because I happened to be standing there at the time. In my head, I knew this. In my stomach, the butterflies did not.

"So... How are you liking your first Norman party?"

Trip jammed his fists into the front pockets of his jeans and rocked back on his heels. "It's cool. Everyone's being really cool."

"It must be hard to constantly have to go through the trouble of making new friends just to up and leave them all the time."

"Yeah, you'd think so. But I keep in touch with a few of them. Every now and then, I'll hitch a ride on the jet with my father when he goes to check on his properties and we get to hang out. Me and my friends, I mean- not my father."

There was a bite to his last sentence, but I figured he was just trying to make sure I didn't think he spent his free time hanging out with his dad or something like that. Remembering his family owned hotels, I said, "Well, at least you always have a place to stay!"

He chuckled and said, "Yeah, that's true. I normally get my own suite... and room service doesn't suck."

That sounded so grownup and worldly to me. I couldn't imagine hopping on a plane whenever I wanted and staying in my own hotel room. The only time I'd ever been on a plane was flying coach to Disneyworld where I was crammed into a double room at the Ramada with my father and brother for a whole week. Jeez, I remember thinking *that* was so cool!

Trip brushed by me and gave a knock on the bathroom door. "What the hell is taking him so damn long?"

When he got no response, he knocked again. "Yo, Coop! Whadja drown in there?"

Still no answer.

Trip gave me a concerned look before trying the knob. It was locked. "Coop! Hey, Coop, open up." *Bambambam!*

Nothing.

We both started to worry. Trip took a step back and I half-expected him to pull a *Cops* and kick down the door. But he thought better of it and instead ran his fingers along the top of the door frame, coming down with a key. He jabbed it into the doorknob and within seconds, we were in.

There was Coop, on his hands and knees, with his face hovered over the bowl. He gave a groan and Trip breathed a heavy sigh. "Dude! We thought you were dying in here!"

Coop barely lifted his head. "I am. I'm dying. Ohhh..."

It sounds kind of mean, but we both started laughing. I think we were probably just relieved that Coop was okay. Besides, he did look pretty pathetic.

Trip crossed his arms over his chest and asked, "Alright, so what are we supposed to do with this sorry bastard?"

"Do you want to lay him down in one of the back bedrooms and then try to find out who his ride is?"

"Good idea."

Trip leaned down behind Coop, put his arms around his chest and heaved him to his feet.

"Wait," I said. "You think he's, you know... empty?"

Trip peeked over Coop's shoulder into the bowl. "Yeah, I think so. From the looks of it, the only thing he's got left in here are his kidneys."

"Ohhh. No, man. I puked out my kinees. Ohhh..."

I closed my eyes and flushed the toilet while Trip maneuvered Cooper out the door. Between the two of us, we were able to zombie-walk him down the hall into Mr. and Mrs. Rymer's bedroom and get him flopped across the huge four-poster bed where he instantly fell asleep. He was lying on his back snoring away when I suddenly realized that save for a comatose third party, I was practically alone- in a *bedroom*- with Trip.

He ran a hand through his hair, trying to put himself together after the ordeal, looking at me as if he was just realizing the same thing.

Like an idiot, I said, "Um... I still need to use the bathroom," and darted off into the adjoining master bath.

When I came out, the last thing I expected to see was Trip still there, hunched over Coop with a black Sharpie marker.

I peeked over his shoulder to check out his handiwork: Coop was sporting a new handlebar moustache and unibrow.

I clamped my hand over my mouth and chastised the artist. "You're awful."

Trip capped the marker and tossed it on the nightstand. "No, I'm funny. Awful would have been if I used the razor."

I had to agree with him.

We were both standing there, looking down at Coop- passed out and scribbled on- when Trip asked, "He your boyfriend?"

I stammered out, "Uh, no. God no. Why'd you think that?"

Trip raised an eyebrow. "I don't know... Maybe because I saw him tonsils-deep in your ear a few minutes ago and yet he still has his balls."

Crud. He saw that?

I don't know where he got the impression that I was some kind of Amazon who would rip the scrotum off of an over-amorous seventeen-year-old boy, but maybe he falls into that group of every non-Italian outside of the tri-state area who thinks all Jersey girls are mafia princesses.

Just for the record? We're not.

I ignored his "tough-chick" assessment and blurted out, "So, where's Tess?"

Duh.

"She had another party to get to. Why?" His lips curled into a smirk after he said that and it was all I could do not to jump his bones.

"Oh, no reason. I just haven't seen her. Hey, um, did you start that report for Mason's class yet?"

That made him smile, probably because I'm the only girl to ever find herself alone in a room with Trip Wilmington who decided to use the opportunity to discuss homework.

But he answered my stupid question anyway. "No. You?"

"No."

Then he said, "You think maybe we should work together on it?"

And I know I answered, "Yeah, sure. That'd be okay." But I know I was thinking something more like, *Yes! Of course! That'd be awesome!*

"Great. I figure a girl's perspective would be really helpful on it, you know? I never understand what the hell Shakespeare is talking about but girls always seem to get it. All that love story crap."

"Crap? It's not crap, it's *Shakespeare* for godsakes! How can you say that?"

"Look. Just because some dude wrote stories a million years ago doesn't mean he's not open to some criticism. What's so great about him anyway?"

"Well, for starters, he's *Shakespeare*. Trip, are you serious? He wrote stuff like nobody'd ever read before."

"Big deal. Nobody'd ever *written* anything before. It was probably cake to become famous back then."

I rolled my eyes but realized he had a point. "You're nuts. Let's just go find Coop's ride."

We were still smiling as we began the search for Coop's designated driver. Working as a team, first by taking care of our drunken friend, then by playing detective together, was actually a lot of fun.

It was weird, the way I was starting to feel comfortable around Trip. I hadn't lost sight of the fact that he was still gorgeous and how it was completely unsettling, but he also had this... *way* about him. He just had this way of making people around him *want more*. Want to know him, figure him out, be around him. I couldn't describe it at the time, but I suppose what I was recognizing, even way back then, was his Star Quality.

If such a thing exists, then Trip Wilmington had it in spades.

Chapter 9
OPPORTUNITY KNOCKS

The following Monday was my first day of work at Totally Videos. I scoped the store for Martin, the twenty-one-year-old, pasty and pimply afternoon manager who, obviously impressed with my non-existent resume and sub-par interviewing skills, called me on Sunday to offer me a job.

He was behind the counter when I walked over, gave him my best salute and said, "Hola, Señor Martino. Yo soy Layla Warren. Yo trabajo aquí."

I suppose I should mention here that Martin is not Latino *at all*, and I, obviously, only had the most rudimentary understanding of the Spanish language even after two years of having taken it as an elective.

Martin looked at me as if he was sure I'd suffered a major head injury on my way to work that day, but proceeded to ask one of the other "associates" to mind the store while he dealt with me.

First on the agenda was to take me into the back office so he could print me up a new nametag. While it was running through the laminator, he went to a storage locker and grabbed me a navy blue vest. Along with my khaki pants and light blue Oxford (would my body never escape from a button-down shirt?), I was to wear my vest "at all times".

"Even when I'm not here?" I joked as I put it on.

Martin didn't get it. "Uh, no. Just while you're working your shift."

Detract one point for the sarcastic new employee.

I didn't really think it was necessary for Martin to actually pin my nametag on my vest himself. I mean, I have arms and all. But I figured that was the closest his hands had actually ever been to a real live boob before, so I didn't make a big deal about it. Hell, why not give the poor kid a thrill? Besides, if I even dared to make a joke (which he wouldn't have gotten anyway), he'd have

46

probably blushed twelve different shades of red before passing out from embarrassment.

We left the office and Martin gave me a quick tutorial on the register before showing me around the store. Most of my "training" was pretty ridiculous and unnecessary.

Here's a sample conversation:

Martin: "Okay, see the wall, here? This is where we keep our New Releases."

Me: "Oh, you mean you keep the new releases along the wall under the HUGE SIGN that says 'New Releases'?"

Martin (not registering my sarcasm): "Yes, that's right. A new release is any video that has come into the store recently. Mostly, it's the category for movies that are less than a year old."

Me (bored): "Uh-huh."

Martin: "So let's give you a pop quiz. Say I'm a customer-"

Me: "You're a customer."

Martin (seriously): "Uh, yes. I'm a customer and I ask you where I can find *Lethal Weapon*. What do you do?"

Me: "Call the cops?"

Martin (finally realizing that I was screwing with him): "C'mon, Layla. You need to know this."

Me: Martin, look. Don't worry about it. It's pretty self-explanatory. I know how to read and I'm sure I'll be able to steer any customers in the right direction." And then, to toss him a bone and make him feel all managerial, I added, "What I really need is another lesson on the register. Think you could go over that again with me?"

This made Martin puff up a little with authority. "Sure, no problem."

He spent a good twenty minutes going over checkout with me and I knew I should have been hanging on his every instruction so as not to look like a big dummy later on. But instead, I became mesmerized by the patterns of zits on his cheek. I was mentally connecting the dots to form The Big Dipper... and that's when Trip walked in... with Tess.

47

They didn't see me as they giggled over some private joke on their way over to the Comedy section.

I was planning on busying myself behind the counter checking in the pile of returned videos, but Martin asked me to set up a cardboard display of *Back to the Future Part III* instead. I took the stack of cutouts from him and sat down in the middle of the store to put it together.

So it was in the midst of attaching a "Coming Soon" sign to Christopher Lloyd's kneecap when I heard Trip say, "Hey, Layla! There you are."

I put down my project and tried to look surprised to see him. Had Tess not been standing right there, I would have thrown out a flirty line like, "Why, were you looking for me?" but I figured it probably wouldn't have gone over too well in front of the girlfriend.

Instead, I went for, "Hey, Trip. Hi, Tess. Renting a video?"
DUH.

They both said, "Yeah," and Trip added, "So, I guess you got the job. Cool."

I tucked a strand of hair back into my banana clip and countered, "It's really not, but thanks."

Trip smiled as Tess checked her watch. He said, "No, it's cool. Working here's gotta be better than my dad's office. Are you guys hiring?"

I raised my eyebrows. "*Here?*"

"Yeah, why not?"

I shot a quick look at Tess, but she didn't seem to have any opinion on the matter. "Umm, let me check."

I mentally crossed my fingers as I went into the office to ask Martin. I made a huge point not to mention that the potential employee was a friend of mine and simply said, "Some guy out there was asking about a job opening?" Martin didn't say whether they were looking for more help or not, but dug out an application for Trip to fill out.

Tess wandered around the candy display looking bored as Trip met me at the front counter to fill out the form. He had his license out- copying the numbers onto his application- and that's when I saw it.

Terrence C. Wilmington III's middle name was *Chester*.

Chester! This was just too good. But I made the decision to keep it to myself for the time being. It was awesome enough just having the inside scoop on him, knowing something NO ONE else knew about the infamous Trip Wilmington, so I didn't want to call him out on it right away. As trivial as it was, his middle name was something only *he* and *I* knew about. Even though he was unaware of it, there was some tiny little unspoken bond between us now, some inherent bit of information that even Tess Valletti wasn't privy to. It was like I had a piece of him all to myself.

It took me a couple tries, but I was finally able to get the register working properly. I scanned their chosen movie *(Spinal Tap- nice)* as I asked, "Are you sure you want to work here? I've only been here for two hours and I'm ready to quit."

Trip didn't look up from his writing. "Baby, that's half the reason I'm applying here. You *need* me."

I rolled my eyes, but he didn't see. I leaned way over the counter and whispered my best horror-movie warning, *"Ruuun."*

Trip laughed as he signed his name to the bottom of the page. "Too late now, sweetheart. Here you go."

He handed me the completed application, which I put in a top drawer for safekeeping. "You're sealing your fate here, you realize that, don't you?"

He gave me a dirty look out of the corner of his eye, and I was expecting some sort of witty retort. Instead he asked, "What do I owe you?"

"Three-eighteen."

He slapped a ten down on the counter. I was counting his change when out of nowhere, he came out with, "So, hey- I was thinking- You want to get together tomorrow?"

At first, my heart leapt out of my chest, until I realized that he was only trying to arrange a brainstorming session for our Shakespeare thing. "Oh, for our report. Yeah, sure. I'm not working tomorrow, but-" and I hated having to say this aloud, "I don't get my license for another two weeks, we'll have to do it at my house."

Oh my God. Did I just say "do it at my house"?

Trip gave a shrug. "No problem. I'll just drive you home after school." He turned and called out over his shoulder, "Hey, Tess, you ready?"

At that, she sauntered over, they offered their goodbyes and then they were gone...

...leaving me trying to think about *anything* other than the fact that I was going to be spending an entire afternoon alone with Trip Wilmington.

Chapter 10
...ALMOST

There was never a longer Tuesday in my entire life. Lisa didn't settle my nerves any with the way she kept talking about it *all day long*. She was confident that Trip and I were going to be spending most of our study session groping each other on the couch. I wasn't so sure.

I'd avoided talking to him at lunch and made sure he didn't get the chance to walk me down to English. I couldn't escape him during class, but I kept the conversation to a minimum.

It seems stupid now, but I didn't want to do anything that would jinx our plans for the afternoon. I thought if I said or did the wrong thing, Trip would realize I was a total dork and wouldn't want to partner up with me for the thing after all. All I needed to do was get through that one afternoon with him in order to show him how indispensible I'd be as an assignment buddy. Then I could relax knowing that by then, he'd realize how much he needed me, if for no other reason than that he wanted a good grade.

By the time school let out, I had already decided that I was good to go. This was confirmed when Trip actually showed up to meet me on the front steps. In front of everyone, he plucked me out of the crowd and *put his hand at the small of my back* for the walk down to his car.

Let me tell you, it felt *amazing* to be seen with him. I hoped everyone noticed it. Maybe rumors would get started that we were carrying on some sort of secret relationship. People would say things like, "I heard that Trip Wilmington dumped Tess Valletti for Layla Warren."

And if anyone actually had the balls to ever ask me outright, I'd only give them the satisfaction of a mysterious smile while saying something classy like, "I never kiss and tell, *dahling*."

While I was picturing who was going to play me in the movie version of my life story (Alyssa Milano, maybe?), Trip unlocked the passenger door of his Bronco and held it open until I got inside. I thought it was so cool how he did that. Maybe it was a common thing to do where he came from, but in Norman, the guys were always too aloof to treat any of us like actual ladies. God, didn't they realize how easy it was to impress us?

Trip cruised over to his side of the truck and slid himself behind the wheel. As he put the key in the ignition, I made the decision that whatever song was playing on the radio at that moment would be burned forever into my brain as "our song".

He turned the key... and New Kids on the Block came blaring out of the speakers singing *"The Right Stuff"*.

Okay, fine. The *next* song would be the one.

"What the hell is this crap?" Trip asked as he popped a Guns N' Roses tape into the cassette player.

I watched as he loosened his tie over his head and unbuttoned his blue Oxford so that it hung open casually over his thin, white T-shirt, stretched taut over the contours of his chest. He shifted over to fix his hair in the rearview mirror, his arm pressed against mine as he leaned across the center console. I could feel the heat of the day just emanating off of him and smell the crisp, clean scent of his skin just inches from my own body.

And that, ladies and gentlemen, even to this very day, is why I completely fall apart whenever I hear even a single note from *"Paradise City"*.

I was trying to play it cool- tapping my hands against my knees to the music, looking absently out the window- but I was actually a trembling mess inside. I mean shit! I was riding shotgun in Trip's truck! For the second time in less than a week! But this time, I had him all to myself for the next two, maybe three, hours. How the hell was I going to hold it together all that time?

I grabbed my purse off the floor and started rifling through it, looking for nothing in particular except a way to occupy my hands.

"Damn, you're fidgety."

That caught me off guard. "What?"

Trip turned down the radio and said, "I don't think you've stopped bopping around once since getting in my truck."

I always fidget when I'm nervous. Not really the smoothest habit, but at least it was better than Charlene Henderson's nervous cheerleader tick. You could always tell when she was feeling even slightly uncomfortable when the poor girl started in with regimented clapping.

"Oh. I was just looking for... some gum! Here it is. Wanna slice?"

"Slice?"

"Yeah. It's Juicy Fruit." I held a piece in his direction. "See? It's a slice. Want one?"

This made Trip smile. "Yeah, sure. Unwrap it for me?"

So I did. I thought about sliding over to the driver's side and feeding it to him all *9 1/2 Weeks*, but then wimped out and just passed it over.

"Thanks."

I was such a dork that I found myself sneaking looks at him as he chewed a stupid piece of gum. But just watching his jaw clench up with every chomp was enough to make my palms all sweaty. I tried to look inconspicuous as I wiped them against my polyester skirt.

As we pulled up in front of my house, I realized that I had never even given Trip the address. It was pretty cool that he had obviously done some recon and found out on his own. Then again- and I got the worst, most panicky feeling in my chest when I thought this- maybe he knew where I lived because he'd seen me spying out my window at him every morning. Could God be that cruel?

My fears were laid to rest when Trip said, "This *is* your house, right? Funny. I run through this neighborhood sometimes."

And I thought, *Yes, you do. Every day so far except Sunday.*

But I said, "Oh yeah? Guess I'll have to alert the Neighborhood Watch. They don't appreciate riffraff roaming around on their streets."

Trip grinned as he let me out of the truck. "Yeah. Just try it, Dummy."

I gave him a light backhand on his arm in answer.

Before I led him up our front walk, I jumped up and grabbed a leaf off the tree at the curb. It was something I'd done a million times, but I couldn't believe I hadn't thought to skip that little ritual for one, stupid day. I was a little embarrassed as I shrugged and offered a brief explanation to Trip. "Sorry. Superstition."

He laughed. "You do that often?" he asked. "Maul trees in your spare time?"

"Just that one," I answered, before playfully admitting, "Every day, actually!"

Even though I was laughing, I was feeling pretty skittish at the thought of being alone with Trip for the next few hours. My father usually didn't come home from work until dinnertime and Bruce had freshman football practice every day. Knowing this, I had made a point to do a quick cleanup before leaving for school that morning in order to make sure the house would be presentable in the afternoon. Living with two men is a constant study in maintainable hygienics. My father wasn't so bad, but Bruce was an absolute slob. After he split for the bus stop, I was met with a destroyed bathroom- soaking wet towels and clothes all over the floor. Hello? Ever hear of a hamper?

Thank God I'd taken care of Bruce's discarded boxer shorts, however, because Trip hit the bathroom the second we were inside the door. I utilized the time during his absence to pull a couple of Cokes out of the fridge and settle myself at the kitchen table.

I had my English notebook lain out and was tapping my pen against the page in front of me as I read the booklet of requirements for the project. Basically, we were supposed to give a report on our assigned scene in a "style of our choosing". We were to focus on the motivations of each character and interpret Shakespeare's language into our present-day vernacular.

Here are the questions we needed to answer in our report:

- What do your characters want? What are they trying to say? How do they go about achieving their goals?
- How are you like/unlike your assigned characters? What traits do you share? What traits are completely opposite from you? Would people who know you agree with your assessment?
- How would your characters like living in Norman, NJ? How would your characters dress and speak differently if they were living here today? (Please utilize a visual aid for this portion of your project.)

I was pondering investing in some posterboard for the visual aid aspect of our presentation when I realized Trip was taking an awfully long time in the bathroom.

Oh, dear God. Please tell me he's not pooping in there.

My suspicions turned out to be unfounded when I heard a noise coming from down the hall.

I moved down the hallway to my bedroom where I saw Trip standing at my dresser, giving the once-over to all of my things.

Thank God I made my bed that morning, but what if he'd gone snooping through my dressers or something? I had a brief recollection of the set of pink, flowery, days-of-the-week cotton panties that were shoved to the back of my undies drawer. I never wore them, but couldn't bring myself to throw them away. They were a gift the past Christmas from my Aunt Eleanor, who always used the excuse of having four sons to buy the cutesiest, girliest things possible for me. They were so, so, so very uncool. My reputation would have been destroyed.

"What are you doing?"

He looked up just then and smiled. "Just checking out your room. It's the best way to get to know someone, don't you think?"

"Yeah, I guess. Or, you know, maybe you could just ask them stuff."

I watched as he ignored me and picked up one of my glass atomizers. He gave a quick squirt of *Anais Anais* in the air and took a sniff. "Nice." He put the bottle down and rifled through a dish of change, coming up with a guitar pick. He held it up, impressed. "This yours?"

Yeah, right. My cousin Jack tried to teach me only a million times, but I was a total sped. I could never get my fingers to bend just the right way and it got so frustrating that I decided it just wasn't worth it. "Nope. My cousin's."

He tossed the pick back into the dish before noticing my jewelry box. He ran a finger across the intricate lid, saying, "This is pretty awesome, all the carvings. It looks old."

"It is." I don't know what prompted me to continue, but I added, "It was my mother's."

Trip's hand stopped over the engraved surface. He didn't look up as he asked, "Was?"

God. It had been so long since I had to talk about this. Everyone I knew at sixteen had been in my life at twelve... I'd already been through the story with anyone who I considered a friend. Everyone else just made it up. I didn't think I wanted my mother's desertion to be the first thing Trip found out about me.

I tried to sound casual as I shrugged and offered, "She died a few years ago."

I wondered if he was fooled by my attempt at nonchalance or if he could actually hear the lump in my throat. In any case, he pulled his hand away from the jewelry box as quickly as if it had burned him. I hoped he wouldn't ask too many questions- it was my first attempt at lying about the situation and I didn't really like how it felt. But he didn't even raise his head as he simply offered, "I'm sorry."

Again I shrugged, trying to seem unaffected. "It was a long time ago."

He refocused his attentions on the photos taped around the perimeter of my mirror as I tried to ignore the knot of guilt growing in my belly. He was pointing to a picture of me as a little kid; Dorothy Hamill haircut, sitting on a Big Wheel, wearing a white karate uniform and an American flag draped across my shoulders. "Is that you?"

I leaned over his shoulder, pretending to get a better look. My arm grazed his back, which caused me to shiver. And I may have imagined it, but I swear he flinched a little from the touch as well.

"Yeah. That's me, all right. I was pretty obsessed with Evel Knievel back in those days."

Trip started laughing. "That's hysterical."

"I was kind of a tomboy."

"No way. I'm not buying it."

Then in one fell swoop, he grabbed my snowglobe off the dresser and flopped down backwards onto my bed. He propped some pillows behind his head and crossed his feet at the ankles, shaking the thing like it owed him money.

You'd think I would have been a nervous wreck having Trip first in my room, then in my *bed*. The sight was definitely surreal, but more phenomenal than terrifying.

"Make yourself at home."

"Oh, no. I couldn't impose."

At that, he flashed me a devastating grin and held up the globe for me to see. We both watched as a blizzard overtook New York City, before the storm subsided into harmless flurries.

"It makes music, you know" I said. I walked the few steps over to my bed and sat on the edge. I wasn't even self-conscious as I overlapped my hand around his and turned the globe over to wind up the bottom.

Trip gave it another good shake, instigating another snow storm as the plucky strains of *"New York, New York"* filled my room.

I remembered the Christmas my mother bought it for me. We'd taken a trip into the city, just the two of us, to see the tree at Rockefeller Center. I felt so cosmopolitan- even if I wasn't able to put that description to it at the age of eight- walking around amongst the noise and excitement of New York with the crisp, winter chill all around us. She was wearing this phenomenal green velvet coat with fur-lined trim. I loved the way it felt against my cheek whenever I'd lean into her throughout our sightseeing. It felt special to have her all to myself for the whole night, a rare event that didn't occur too often after my baby brother came along. Even before then, I remember the feeling of always wanting to keep her close so she wouldn't just slip away.

I watched Trip balance the snowglobe on his chest with one hand and tuck the other one behind his head. He had such a contented look on his face that it made me feel calm, too. Maybe a little *too* relaxed.

"She didn't die."

"What are you talking about?"

"My mother. I lied. She didn't die, she moved out. When I was twelve."

"Oh."

"I'm sorry. I don't even know why I lied about it. I guess you asking about her just caught me off guard. I thought it would be easier to just say that she died. Not that you wouldn't have found out eventually anyway. It's just... I never had to actually *tell* anyone about it before."

"What do you mean?"

"Well, everyone around here already knew everything. Or thought they did. I never had to *explain*, you know?"

"Why's that?"

"Small town."

"Oh."

The song ended and Trip looked up to meet my eyes. I couldn't really discern the expression on his face, but I hoped it wasn't pity. He broke the silence when he asked, "You want to talk about it?"

I reached over and grabbed a scrunchy off my nightstand and started playing it with my thumbs. "Not really. Is that okay?"

"It's *your* life, Layla."

In that shared moment, he continued to lock my gaze to his, holding me prisoner with his eyes, and I suddenly realized he was going to kiss me. *Oh my God this is it!* My heart slammed against my ribcage, probably so violently that Trip could actually see it. The seconds of quiet seemed to stretch out into eternity as I sat frozen, staring into that beautiful face, waiting for him to move first.

Without another word, he bounded off the bed and returned the snowglobe to my dresser, breaking the moment. "Hey, I'm starving. Whaddya got to eat around here?"

Okay, then!

I resisted the urge to nudge the snowglobe a half inch into its rightful place and instead led Trip back to the kitchen.

He sank into one of the chairs and cracked his Coke while I called out an inventory from the pantry. After much deliberation, he finally settled for some regular Doritos, lamenting the fact that they weren't Cool Ranch. Through a mouthful of chips, he started, "So, I was thinking... this assignment we have to do."

"Yeah?"

"Well, I figure most everybody is gonna get up there and give some stupid report, you know, just read off a piece of paper or something."

"That's normally how one gives a report, yes."

"Yeah, but we're supposed to do a visual, too."

"Uh-huh. I was planning on picking up some posterboard or-"

"Well, I was thinking of doing something a little different, maybe."

I watched Trip lounge back in his chair with a mischievous little grin on his face and realized I'd be submitting to whatever scheme he was cooking up.

I was in no position to deny him anything when he looked at me like that.

Chapter 11
THE GRIFTERS

As it turned out, Trip's scheme entailed the brilliant idea to film our own version of *Romeo and Juliet,* set in Norman, New Jersey, circa 1990.

We spent the rest of that first afternoon deciding on how we were going to answer some of those questions in Mason's booklet and outlining our filming schedule.

The plan required me to "borrow" a video camera from work, which I did without guilt. It's not like I was going to keep the thing, but at the cost of renting it for the next couple months, I may as well have bought one of my own. At the pathetic minimum hourly wage Totally Videos was paying me, that thought wasn't even a possibility. Because they paid me such a lousy salary, I decided to justify my liberation of said camera as an early holiday bonus. It just happened to be three months ahead of the holiday, is all.

The next day, we found out that Trip had gotten the job at Totally Videos and was scheduled to start on Monday!

Our thoughts on that news were that it was best to keep our association under wraps in order to remain employed. But Martin, sleuthing genius that he was, became hip to the fact that we were friends on that very first day. I suppose we weren't necessarily as stealth about our relationship as we had hoped to be.

Trip had become easily bored with register duty, a detail compounded by the fact that the store was having a slow day. He decided to make better use of his time by hiding behind the display racks of the drama section and flinging Skittles at me.

I tried to ignore him until the candies started coming by the handful, causing me to drop the pile of tapes I'd been returning to their proper spots on the shelves.

I grabbed the empty box of *Terms of Endearment* off the shelf and chucked it at him, just narrowly grazing his head as he ducked out of the way, knocking over a bin of rolled movie posters.

That prompted him to hurl the entire, theatre-sized bag of Skittles in retaliation, sending a rainbow of tiny projectiles pinging off the shelves and scattering across the floor.

Martin had been in his office during our little war, but he must have been watching us on the security cameras, because he chose that moment to come storming out the door. Upon seeing the two of us laughing our asses off amidst a pile of videos, posters and candy, we guessed the jig was up. He commanded us in a booming voice to, "Clean up this mess before any customers come in and see it!"

At first, I thought that Martin could have refrained from jumping down our throats. I mean, obviously we were planning on cleaning up our mess, and we sure didn't need some dorky kid just out of high school chastising us like he thought he was actually some sort of authority figure. I thought that maybe if he slathered on some Oxy every once in a while and got himself a decent haircut, he could find himself a girlfriend and lighten up a little.

But then suddenly, I kind of felt bad for him. The poor guy was only trying to do his job while having to deal with us two idiots all day.

Trip must have been thinking the same thing, because neither one of us busted his balls and just went about the chore of picking Skittles off the carpet.

But even scouring about the floor on our hands and knees was actually pretty fun. Trip made working there bearable for the first time, even if from then on, we toned it down a bit for Martin's sake. Having him there proved to make work less of a trial and more of an adventure.

Who am I kidding? If I'm going to be honest, I'll admit that Trip proved to make my *life* less of a trial and more of an adventure!

Week Two of our film collaboration had us trying out the pilfered camera for the first time. It took us a little longer than expected to learn how to use the clunky thing, a task that probably would have been made much easier had I thought to grab the accompanying User Guide during my heist. But after affixing the camera to my father's tripod (also "borrowed"), we managed to get off some very educational test shots of Trip doing cannonballs in my pool. It was at that point that I realized Mason wasn't going to be grading me on my ability to watch Trip Wilmington strut around my backyard in his swimming trunks. I wouldn't have traded that sight for a 4.0 if my life depended on it, but I knew we'd eventually be expected to do some actual work.

Week Three, we decided we were going to need to learn how to edit our film (that we had yet to start shooting). It was my brainchild to "borrow" Bruce's VCR and rig it up to mine. With some advice from Roger Vreeland at the AV club, we (legitimately) borrowed some of his cable wires and spent the better part of our afternoon getting the primitive editing station set up and running. We'd practiced splicing our films by playing the raw footage in one VCR while recording selected scenes in the other. But after about an hour of this, Bruce came home from football practice and confiscated his VCR from Trip and me, leaving us back at square one.

Before I could risk the implications of "borrowing" another tape player from my father's room or the den, Trip came up with a way to hook the camera directly into my VCR. That system turned out to be way better than our original one, so we thanked Bruce for his inadvertent help by spending the rest of the afternoon in the kitchen, baking him some chocolate chip cookies.

The following Thursday was my birthday.

Chapter 12
POSTCARDS FROM THE EDGE

I woke up before dawn, a bundle of nervous energy, and hopped right into the shower. My appointment at the DMV wasn't until ten o'clock, but I didn't want to be a minute late. My father had agreed to let me play hooky from school so that I could go down and take my driving test. I'd waited seventeen whole years to get my license and there was no way I was going to wait an extra minute.

My dad knew that I was excited, but he was still surprised that I had gotten up as early as I did. I met up with him in the kitchen, where he was sitting at the table with a coffee and hidden behind the *Star Ledger*. He lowered the newspaper just enough to peek over the top.

He gave a quick glance toward the clock on the stove and said, "Well, if I didn't know any better, I'd think it was someone's birthday."

I kissed him on the cheek and said, "Not just any birthday, Dad. It's someone's *seventeenth* birthday."

He pretended to have forgotten. "Is that so?"

I grabbed a glass from the cabinet and answered, "Yep."

As I was pouring juice into my glass, Dad said, "Well, then I guess it's a good thing I bought this."

I looked over my shoulder to see him sliding a small, square box toward the center of the table.

The box was black velvet and sporting a little pink bow on top. I didn't know if it was on purpose, but pink and black were my favorite colors.

I pulled out a chair and joined him at the table. "Is that for me?"

Dad folded the paper and laid it next to his coffee mug. "Nope. It's for Bruce. You know how much he likes the color pink."

I rolled my eyes at his teasing. "Can I open it?"

"I don't know. Can you?"

"Dad..."

"Yes, of course. Go ahead."

We were both giggling as I cracked open the velvet jewelers box. Inside was a small, gold medallion on a thin chain.

"Oh, how pretty! Wow, Dad. Thanks."

I started to lift the necklace out of the box as Dad said, "It's a St. Christopher medal. The patron saint of travel."

I could already tell where this was going as he added, "I was hoping he could watch over you every time you get behind the wheel and keep you safe."

I don't know why, but I started to well up. I was able to hide my teary eyes under the guise of lowering my head to put the necklace on. I rubbed my fingers over it and said, "It's perfect. Thank you, I love it." And then, to avoid getting too sappy, I added, "Wow. You must have some pretty strong faith that I'll pass my test today, huh?"

Dad shook his head. "Don't need faith today, Layla-Loo. You've got this one in the bag all on your own."

At that, we high-fived and I got up in search of some breakfast.

After Dad left for the office- assuring me that he'd be back to pick me up by nine thirty- I was left to eat my cereal in silence.

The Thought came then, as it did from time to time, but always at my birthday or at Christmastime. The Thought- the one I'd played with in my mind for the better part of nearly five years- The Thought that maybe my mother, wherever she was, was thinking about me that day.

I wondered if even though she left us to start some big, new life, that maybe, just maybe, she hadn't completely forgotten about her old one. Did she remember that it was my birthday? Did she know that Bruce had started high school? Did she even think about us at all?

I had this delusional fantasy that my father was in possession of a stockpile of letters and postcards from my mother. That he'd intercepted a mass of correspondence that she'd penned over the years and hidden it away under a floorboard in his closet or something, thinking that he was protecting Bruce and me. That one day, maybe even my birthday, he'd come to the realization that we were entitled to read what our mother had written. He'd hand over a stack of unopened envelopes, tied with a ribbon as if they were a gift.

The postcards would be brief but witty, with pictures on the front of exotic places that she had visited. She'd write how she was always thinking of us, how we were with her in every corner of the world, and how she missed us terribly. The letters would be long and flowery, explaining why she left and letting me know that she loved me.

I'd find out that even though she left us, it wasn't because her life with us wasn't good enough. Maybe she had left *because* she loved us, because she didn't think *she* was good enough.

I swiped the tears from my cheeks as I threw my empty cereal bowl into the sink. Bruce staggered in just then, grumbling to himself about something or another.

Bruce wasn't much of a morning person, so normally, I steered clear of him until he was fully awake and could act like a normal human being. But that day, I interrupted him on his way to the fridge, said, "Good morning," and wrapped my arms around him for a hug.

We weren't normally so touchy-feely with each other, so his first reaction was, "What the...?" But then, it came to him as he hugged me back. "Oh, hey, happy birthday."

I pulled back to give him a kiss on the cheek. I had to stand on my tiptoes in order to reach his face. When did he get so much taller than me?

I gave him a big smile and a punch in the arm. "Thanks, Bruce. I'm glad you remembered."

* * *

65

That night, Dad let me borrow the car so I could drive myself to work. It was so liberating, to finally be behind the wheel *on my own.* No Dad, no driving instructor! I immediately reprogrammed all of my father's radio stations, but then set them all back to his original choices, thinking that if I ever wanted to borrow the car again, I'd better not push my luck.

I parked in the employee lot and went in the rear entrance to Totally Videos, where Martin was in the storeroom ready to greet me.

"So?" he asked.

I couldn't contain my smile. "Yeah. I passed."

He offered a pat on the back and, "Well, congratulations. And happy birthday!"

"Thanks, Martin."

"Now help me unpack these boxes."

And at that, my birthday party was over.

I spent a good hour unpacking the new shipment of movies, re-packaging them from their original video covers into barcoded clear cases, then stuffing bricks of Styrofoam into a few of the empty covers before shrink-wrapping them. I knew that in a few months, I'd be expected to reverse this process, returning the videos back into their original covers for sale in our "Previously Viewed" bin. It was a vicious cycle.

It wasn't until about seven o'clock or so when Trip showed up to surprise me. It was a pretty slow night and I had just been daydreaming about him from behind my post at the front register. I was envisioning a *Sixteen Candles*-type scenario; Trip and me sitting on his dining room table, sharing our first kiss over my birthday cake. And suddenly, *poof!* there he was, right there in the flesh. Okay, maybe I spent *a lot* of my time thinking about him, so it's not like he just happened to show up at some fluky moment or something, but I still like to think that I psychically willed him to manifest at that exact instant.

I watched him stroll in wearing black jeans, a grey jacket and a shit-eating grin. "Happy birthday!"

I must have been smiling ear to ear when I told him, "I knew you'd come."

He came over and leaned his forearms against the counter I was standing behind. "So... Do I even need to ask?"

I dug underneath the shelf into my purse, coming up with my father's keys and jangling them in front of his eyes in answer.

"Awesome! You passed! I knew you would."

I couldn't keep the smile off my face or the satisfaction from my voice when I replied, "Thanks. Even aced parallel parking."

"Thatta girl."

He reached into the pocket of his jacket and pulled out a twin-pack of Twinkies. He tossed them on the counter saying, "I baked you a cake."

It was no Jake Ryan move, but it was damn near close enough for me. I exaggerated my reaction when I said, "Oh, Trip! You shouldn't have."

He grinned. "Oh, don't pretend like Twinkies aren't your favorite. I went to a lot of trouble to get those for you."

I said, "Oh, I'll bet," but he was right. I freakin' *loved* Twinkies. I opened the cellophane wrapper and handed him one. "My father always taught me it was bad luck to twink alone."

"Oh, that was bad."

I giggled, clinked my cake to his and took a bite. *Heaven.*

"So, you had nothing better to do with your evening than come in here on your night off and fatten up an old lady?" That was only funny because I was officially the youngest member of our entire class.

He polished off the last of his Twinkie in his second bite and said sheepishly, "I just thought it would suck that you had to work on your birthday. Does it?"

I don't know how I managed to get the words out, but I leaned forward and replied, "Well, it did... until now."

He gave me a smirk and drummed the counter before saying, "Hey, look. I gotta go, but I'll see you at school tomorrow, okay?"

"Yep. I'll be there."

He stood there for an extra second, just locked onto my eyes, and before I could ask him what was up, I watched as he leaned across the counter toward me. I was a statue as his hand slipped around my neck, his rough fingers at my nape, his knuckles brushing under my hair. As if that weren't thrilling enough, the next thing I saw was his face coming closer to mine before his lips offered a sweet, slow kiss on my cheek. Just that small contact was like a lightning bolt through my body, a splash of ice water in my veins. I couldn't breathe very well at that second, but I managed to catch the warm scent of him, all sugary and soapy and sending shivers down my skin.

He pulled back, looking almost as stunned as I felt, and I knew I wasn't imagining things when I heard him actually stammer the slightest bit as he said, "H-happy birthday, Layla".

He regained his composure quickly enough, because in the blink of an eye, his wide grin returned as he offered, "See you tomorrow."

I stared as he walked out the door, hating to see him go but loving the view as I watched him walk away.

* * *

The next night, Trip and I punched out at Totally Videos around ten and he offered to drive me home. I was exhausted- Fridays were a big night for movie rentals- and all I wanted to do was crash for the next twelve hours. Football season was well under way and I was looking forward to watching our Lions kick a little Butler Bulldog ass the following afternoon.

On the way out to the parking lot, I took a shot and asked, "Hey, can I drive?" but Trip just looked at me like I was nuts and replied, "Nobody drives Beverly but me."

So, I was sitting in the passenger seat of Trip's Bronco, flipping through the radio stations, almost missing the fact that he'd turned in the opposite direction from my street.

I looked up from the stereo controls and asked, "Umm, what's going on?"

Trip just pasted a smile on his face and said, "Don't worry about it. Just shut up and let me drive."

Once he turned down Trestle Ave, I knew exactly where we were headed.

The Barrens was an old, abandoned field in an area of town known as The Mud Hole. The lot was formed in a large C shape from a bend in the river, abutted by the nearby railroad tracks. Supposedly, there was once an actual house on that godforsaken property, but it had long since been torn to the ground. All that remained was a concrete slab, fractured and uneven, weeds growing through the cracks and covered in four decades' worth of graffiti. Everyone in Norman affectionately referred to the spot as "The Patio", and it was the most popular destination at The Barrens for hanging out. For any underage kids who dared to cross the tracks, it was as good a place as any to sneak some beers or make out with their not-so-significant others.

Trip parked his truck amidst the trees behind the rusted-out cargo container, where I could see Coop's Audi and Lisa's LeBaron. I shot a look at Trip, who was grinning at me shamelessly before getting out. I walked around to the other side of the hold to The Patio, where Lisa, Pickford, Cooper, Rymer and Sargento were sitting in lawn chairs arranged in a circle. It was too early in autumn to need a fire, but they had one going anyway. It was just one of those things that you did at The Barrens.

Lisa spied me first, her eyes lighting up as she yelled, "Hey! Happy birthday!"

Everyone else turned toward Trip and me then, offering their own hellos and birthday greetings. Lisa got off her chair and ran over, welcoming me with a big hug before whispering in my ear, "I came here with Pickford!" She handed me a pink plastic bowler hat covered in glitter and looped a black feather boa around my neck. My birthday suit, apparently.

For a half-baked surprise party, my friends didn't do such a bad job. They had a decent fire going, which we appreciated more for the light and to keep the bugs away than for any actual heat we'd hoped to garner. Someone brought a boombox, there were a couple cases of beer in actual cans and Lisa had even baked some peanut butter brownies. She'd put a few candles in the cake pan and lit them, but I wasn't delusional enough to wait for anyone to start singing before blowing them out.

Amidst the swirling smoke, Trip asked, "Whadja wish for?"

And obviously, I couldn't tell *him*!

So I said, "Won't come true if I tell, right?" which was the expected response anyway, so no one pressed me on it.

I watched as Rymer shotgunned his Budweiser and I asked, "Hey, don't you guys have a game tomorrow?"

Rymer tossed the empty can over his shoulder before responding. "Yep. But Coach won't allow us to get laid during football season. Drinking's all we got."

I looked wide-eyed at Cooper and Sargento for confirmation. They were both nodding their heads, Coop saying, "It's true."

"Get out of here!" I said, appalled. "How can he- why would you even *agree* to that?"

Before Coop could even answer me, Pick piped in with, "That's why I play basketball!" and Trip added, "And that's why I play hockey!" the two of them high-fiving above my head and laughing hysterically.

"Holy crap, I can't even *imagine*," I said, realizing a second too late how that must have sounded. I didn't mean I couldn't imagine having to abstain from sex for four whole months- I meant I couldn't imagine letting anyone lord that much control over my life.

But Trip grabbed hold of the setup I provided. He raised his eyebrows at me and said, "You know I play hockey, right?" which just set everyone off on a laughing fit.

I knew he was just joking around, but having Trip flirt with me even a little bit helped to make my seventeenth the Best. Birthday. Ever.

70

Chapter 13
ROMEO.JULIET

Over the following weeks, I spent so much time with Trip Wilmington that it was ridiculous. At Totally Videos, our schedules lined up so that we were together two out of the three days a week that I worked there. Even though I had passed my driving test and gotten my license, I still didn't have a car yet, so Trip offered me a ride to and from work every Monday and Friday.

In school, I saw him every day in between; hanging out at lunch, walking with him through the halls and then sitting near him during English class.

On the weekends, we'd normally bump into each other at parties, and sometimes, Lisa, Pickford and I would carpool with him to go to the football games on Saturday mornings.

On top of all that, I had him all to myself every Tuesday afternoon while we worked on our English project. It was my favorite day of the week, because for all the time that we spent together, the Shakespeare thing was always just the two of us.

It's not as though I could report some romantic version of our film collaboration. I wish I could tell you about the passion-filled hours spent rehearsing the balcony scene between Romeo and Juliet, or, better yet, the "morning after" scene where they're all spoony and basking in the glow of Romeo's proposal having just spent the night screwing like a couple of bunnies.

No. The fact of the matter is that our assigned scene was Act 3, Scene 3. Which, if it's been a while since you've brushed up on your Shakespeare, means Trip got to play the charming, dashing, lovesick and romantic hero, Romeo. I, on the other hand, was cast in the role of... the nurse. Yep. The ugly, old, obnoxious nurse, who was nothing more to the story than a third wheel, the comic relief, and eclipsed in every scene by the beautiful object of Romeo's affections. Basically, that's how I felt anywhere in the vicinity of Trip's girlfriend, so let's hear it for method acting!

Tess wasn't making too many appearances, but I knew that they had to still be dating. At least I assumed they were. It sounds weird, but for all the talking that we did- and we talked a *lot*- we never really discussed it.

Preferably, I would have bypassed some of that riveting conversation for a little more making out, as it would have been nice to be more to him than just a "buddy".

But the way I saw it, I was happy enough that Trip and I kind of had this unspoken *thing*. I don't mean like boyfriend/girlfriend, but when we were together, we were just... *us*. He was a different guy with me than the one he was at school or at parties, and I knew I was the only one to see that side of him. And he knew that I knew.

But even barring any romantic inclinations, our relationship was pretty great. I think the Tess thing was always there in the background, keeping us just friends. It didn't stop me from looking for hidden meaning in the fact that he never discussed her with me, however. It had to mean something that he never wanted to ruin *us* by bringing up *her*.

I liked to think that Trip really liked me a lot, and maybe under different circumstances he would have even made me his girlfriend. But it was understandable that he wasn't about to trade in a Tess Valletti for a Layla Warren.

I still found my knees going weak sometimes (okay, *always*) whenever I was near him. But it wasn't like some all-consuming anxiety for me anymore. The more time I spent with him and got to know him as an actual person (you know, as opposed to a Greek God), the more comfortable it was to be around him. Funny thing was, we actually made really great friends.

Lisa chastised me for accepting a "consolation prize", but truth be told, it turned out I really liked the guy. And not just "like" liked, but genuinely was able to get past the pretty face- somewhat- to see the great person behind it.

Here's why:

For one thing, he was funny. And I don't mean he was funny, like some annoying comedian, always on, always delivering a punchline. He was funny in the way you can drink too much Kool-Aid as a kid and get "drunk" and giggly and silly with your best friend across the kitchen table on a random rainy Thursday. He was funny in the way you can crack up watching your little brother try to win a battle with a bag of gumballs, seeing how many he can fit in his mouth, laughing while grey gum juice runs down his chin. He was funny like that. Unexpectedly goofy. And silly. And dare I say it, even a little dorky. Not Anthony Michael Hall, *geeky* dorky... More like Rob Lowe guest-hosting Saturday Night Live *pretending* to be dorky. You know, dorky... but still incredibly hot.

Secondly, he was smart. For all his talk about not understanding Shakespeare, he actually seemed to grasp it almost better than I did. Which was impressive, but also a little unsettling. After all, *he* was the one to come to *me* for help. I was supposedly the straight-A student (well, in Mason's class, anyway) who had already consumed our entire year's suggested reading list in the first month of school. A fact that Trip found fascinating, given that I went to school, had a job, and yet I still managed to get out of the house every weekend.

"When do you find the time?" he'd asked one day during a break from filming.

I had answered back, "I don't know. I was always a big reader. I guess I just *make* the time."

Truth was, I only became a big reader after my mother left. I mean, I always liked to read, but after Kate flew the coop, I started to *consume* books. Two or three entire novels over a weekend, bleary-eyed and exhausted, bypassing sleep in order to just finish one more chapter, and then break down and read just one more after that.

Fiction, autobiographies, true crime... it didn't matter. As long as I had something in my hands, something that would grab me, suck me in and hold my attentions for a few hours.

I had always kept a book in my purse. Still do, even to this very day. You never know when you're going to find yourself in a traffic jam or a waiting room or something. Back in Junior High, however, there was always an indoor recess or crappy TV night where I could devour a few dozen pages.

Our family counselor at the time- a horrid, tiny woman who smelled like chicken soup- had said that I was simply looking for an escape from my reality. Well, *DUH*. What teenage girl doesn't want to escape from her reality? Combine that analysis with my borderline OCD and you've got an existential dual diagnosis dilemma on your hands. (Did I mention I read Freud at thirteen?)

All in all, I'd have to say that becoming an avid reader was probably the healthiest thing I could have done, given the circumstances. My father seemed to think so, too. It wasn't long after Dr. Chickensoup's contemptuous assessment of such "troubling obsessive behavior" that Dad decided we'd had enough therapy. He told Bruce and me in no uncertain terms that we were going to be just fine and we believed him. I've worked hard to prove him right every day since.

I mean, jeez, it could have been worse. I could have channeled all of that hurt and anger and obsessive behavior into drugs or violence or sex. The fact is, I had only ever tried pot a few times, gotten into one fistfight in my life (with Bruce) and let's just not get into my complete lack of experience with that third thing there.

Speaking of sex, however...

Lisa and Pickford had been going pretty hot and heavy all through the fall. Part of the reason I had so much free time to spend with Trip was because Lisa was spending most of *her* free time with her new boyfriend. I knew it was only a matter of time before her virginity status became a thing of the past. I'd started to feel like she and I had been travelling toward the same destination, but that she had found a short cut. Truth be told, I envied her for that.

We'd still drive to school together every day, but we weren't hanging out as much as we usually did. Even when we'd hit a party together, she'd spend the whole night wrapped up with Pickford. More often than not, I'd bypass the ride as third wheel in the backseat and just find someone else to drive me home.

A lot of times, that "someone else" was Trip. It was purely innocent- most of the time we'd do nothing more scandalous than hit the King Neptune Diner before he dropped me off- but people did start to talk. Well, Lisa did, anyway.

* * *

We were scheduled to give our Big Report on the day before Thanksgiving. Trip had been an absolute nervous wreck leading up to it, spending the last days beforehand adjusting the color and sound obsessively and reediting parts that I thought we'd already finalized. We stayed up late on that last Tuesday "fixing" our film, finally wrapping it up at midnight in order to get some sleep for the next day's presentation. I didn't know why he was making himself- and let's face it, *me*- so crazy about the thing. It was just an English report. Because we were last on the schedule, we'd seen all of the other presentations in the class already and knew we were the only ones to have made a film. That right there would have ensured us a good grade, if for no other reason than that we'd shown some originality. Creativity went a long way in Mason's class.

I walked into the classroom that Wednesday to find Trip already sitting at his desk, chewing on a thumbnail and bouncing his knees. He looked like a heroin addict and I told him as much.

"How the hell can you be so calm about this?" he asked.

I shrugged and answered, "I'm not, really. I don't want anyone to laugh at us for our terrible acting, but other than that, I know we'll get a good grade. Mason'll see how hard we-"

"Who cares about the grade, Layla? What if everyone thinks it sucks? What if we put ourselves out there and it turns out to be absolute shit? What if-"

"Trip! Chill. It's *not* going to suck. You made sure of that. I would have been happy enough just to turn in something passable. You're the one that treated it like *Citizen Kane* for godsakes. It's gonna be great, you'll see."

He took a deep breath, gave me a high five and said, "Okay, okay. You're right. Where the hell is Vreeland with the damned TV?"

Soon enough, Roger showed up with the Audio-visual cart and I popped the tape into the VCR.

...And that's how only a handful of people know that Trip's first film was actually an amateur adaptation of William Shakespeare's *Romeo and Juliet*, opening to mixed reviews in the fall of 1990 during Mrs. Mason's fifth period English Lit class at St. Nicetius Parochial High School in Norman, New Jersey.

Chapter 14
REVERSAL OF FORTUNE

Thanksgiving was at my Aunt Eleanor's, as usual. I always had a good time with my cousins, even though all four of them were way older (like, in their twenties) and all of them were boys. Lisa always had the worst crush on my cousin Sean, but then again, so did a lot of girls. My aunt must have had the patience of a saint, dealing with the constant stream of girls coming and going through her sons' lives.

Aunt Eleanor was my mother's sister, but the two of them were complete opposites in practically every way; from their hair color to their personalities to their commitment to their family.

Needless to say, I thought the world of Aunt Eleanor.

I always thought it was pretty spectacular that my father had been able to maintain a relationship with her after my mother left. I can't imagine it was easy for either of them to have to face one another; their one, big, shared grief hanging over them like a cloud. It's not like we all got together every day or anything, but we'd always try to celebrate the big holidays in one way or another, and we'd manage to see each other a few additional, random times throughout the year.

After dinner, I sacked out on the couch with my cousin Jack, the two of us groaning about how much we'd overeaten. I thanked God that I didn't have to go to work that night, grateful that the store had been closed for the holiday.

The next night, however, was my Friday shift with Trip.

We were almost through with our night, breaking down boxes in the freezing storeroom, when he pulled out a miniature bottle of champagne from his jacket pocket. He'd swiped it from his parents' liquor cabinet, assuming they wouldn't miss the party favor from "Bebe and Eric's Wedding Extravaganza", the gold and white label informing us of the bottle's origins.

I grabbed a couple Dixie cups from the sink in the breakroom, we did a quick perimeter check for Martin, and Trip unscrewed the bottle.

I laughed, "You know champagne is good when there's a screwtop."

He poured some into my cup and said, "Only the best for you, Miss Warren."

He filled his cup, clinked it against mine and I asked, "What's the occasion?"

He answered, "I just figured we should toast the success of our award-winning film."

"Yeah, Trip? We haven't won any awards."

"Yet."

I laughed as he downed his drink in one shot, grimacing and staring at his cup as if it had offended him. I was no connoisseur, but I didn't think it tasted that great either.

"Oof, that's bad." He shook his head, trying to rid himself of the awful aftertaste. Then he poured another cup.

"*And*," he started in, and I didn't like the tone in his voice, "I also wanted to give myself a proper sendoff."

Oh, God! Was he moving again already?

"What do you mean? Where are you going?" I asked, trying to sound merely curious instead of completely devastated.

He tried to hold back a grin and look properly humble. "Well, I made the team."

I knew he was referring to the travelling hockey team that he'd tried out for weeks before. He didn't allow himself to talk about it too much, but I knew it was a really big deal for him.

"You made the team! That's great! Congratulations. When did you find out?

"Wednesday night. The coach called and asked me if I was available. Can you believe that? Am I available, like I'm Wayne Gretzky or something and might not be able to fit his team into my busy schedule."

"Wow. That's awesome."

"Yeah, yeah it is. I'm pretty psyched. Although..." and his expression turned shamefaced as he tried to break the next news to me gently, "Tonight's my last night working here. I already talked to Martin."

I tried not to deflate too visibly, but damn! He was quitting! Work was going to suck without him there. I realized that things were drastically changing between us; no more Tuesday filming, no more Mondays and Fridays at Totally Videos. "Well, that sucks," I finally stated, before throwing back the rest of my drink.

Every last bit of my designated Trip Time was slipping away. All that was left was the last Saturday football game, because the very next day was homecoming.

Chapter 15
CROSSING THE LINE

I'd started to notice Lisa's increasing frustration with me over the previous weeks, but it wasn't until the day of the homecoming game that I perceived actual disappointment on her face.

Trip had shuttled Lisa, Pickford and me to the field that day. It was a particularly grey and drizzly afternoon, even for the end of November. As we started our walk toward the bleachers, my sneakers kept getting sucked into the mud. Rather than let me try to make the journey by tiptoe, Trip offered a passage by way of piggyback. He was doing an exaggerated slip all over the mud puddles, pretending that he was going to drop me any second. I was cracking up and threatening his life when I happened to catch the disapproving look Lisa shot my way.

I knew something was about to go down as she was getting dropped off afterwards. Trip would normally save me for the last stop, but that day, Lisa asked me to get out at her house instead. I knew we'd been building up to some Big Conversation over the past few weeks, but I guessed she had finally decided it was going to happen right then.

We said goodbye to Trip and made our way into the house. She didn't say a single word to me until we were locked safely away in the sanctuary of her room. "Okay, Layla. This has really got to stop."

I was sitting on her bed Indian-style, picking at the chartreuse marabou pillow in my lap. "What has?"

She rolled her eyes at me for that. "This!" she shouted, sweeping her arms in a wide arc, "This whole, stupid thing with you and Trip! What the hell is going on with you two?"

Her abrupt words caught me off guard. "I don't know" I stammered, while still trying to maintain an air of smugness. "Why don't you tell me?"

I knew Lisa well enough to expect a full-on assault for that, but rather than the verbal tirade I was anticipating, she said, "I know I've been spending a lot of time with Pickford. But he's my boyfriend. What's going on between you and Trip... is just... well, it's *disturbing*."

That made me puff up a little in defense. "What's so *disturbing* about it? We're friends. We hang out." And then, just to throw a little salt in the wounds, I added, "You know, kind of like how *we* used to."

She bypassed opening that can of worms for the time being and stuck to her original argument. "Oh, please. Friends my arse. It's so obvious you're in love with him. Everyone knows it. Just admit it. And seriously, what's the point?"

I didn't appreciate being backed into a corner, but it's not as though Lisa had the situation figured out completely wrong. It was just that it was a little embarrassing to find out that people other than my best friend were aware of how I felt. Shit. Did *Trip* know?

"It's not like that, alright? Like, okay, yeah, it would be great if he felt the same way. But it's more than that. I really, truly enjoy hanging out with him. We like each other. Why does it have to mean something?"

She joined me on the bed, sitting opposite me and mirroring my pose. "It doesn't have to mean something when two people are really and truly just platonic friends. What doesn't work is when one of you has a big, fat crush on the other."

What did she know? "Big wow. You had a crush on my cousin Sean for like, *ever*. Where'd *that* go? Nowhere, that's where."

"Sean Danner is like twenty-something-years-old and every girl within the tri-state area has had a crush on him at some point in her life! But I'm not so delusional that I'd stop living and pine away for some guy who barely knows my name. Crushing on Sean didn't stop me from dating other guys in the meantime."

"I date."

"You hook up. Big difference. But you haven't even done so much as that since Terrence the Third came to town."

81

"That's not true."

"Oh, please. Coop has been so hard up the guys are calling him Blue Balls Benedict, for chrissake. The poor guy's standing booty call isn't even picking up the phone anymore and everyone knows it. I'll tell you something else; everyone knows it's because you're too busy panting after Trip, following him around like a stray puppy. Face it, you're hopeless."

"Thanks a lot!"

"Oh, what? Tell me I'm wrong. Go ahead and name the last guy you went out with."

Lisa knew as well as I did that the last guy I could even consider classifying as an ex-boyfriend would be Cooper Benedict. And we had pretty much "broken up" over the summer.

"So, what? You're suddenly some big authority on relationships just because you've got a boyfriend?"

She bounded off the bed just then. "No, not at all. But I am an authority on *you*. And I'm trying to tell you, *as your friend*, that your little crush on Trip Wilmington is nothing more than a way for you to self-destruct. I'm trying to stop that from happening. Do I need to bring up The Live-Aid Incident?"

Looked like Lisa was going for the big guns.

"The Live-Aid Incident" was the name we had given to my little breakdown during the summer of 1985. It was a few weeks after my mother had left, and even though my father repeatedly tried his best to explain that she wasn't coming back, I secretly held the belief that at any moment, she'd come walking through the door.

I'd spent endless hours sitting up in the tree in front of our house, waiting with the best view down our street so I'd know the second she was on her way back home to us. I'd started collecting a leaf off that tree for every day that she was gone, storing them in a shoebox under my bed. I thought that if I wished hard enough, if I *believed* hard enough, she'd eventually come back. That's why, even to this very day, I can't walk by that tree without grabbing a leaf off it. I'd long since given up on thinking it was doing any good, but by then, my OCD had turned the pointless superstition into an obsessive ritual.

It wasn't until Mtv aired the Live-Aid concert that Lisa was able to coax me down from my perch in order to come watch it with her. It was practically a twenty-four-hour event, so I spent the night at her house so we could catch every minute of it.

The following day, the weirdest feeling overtook me like a tidal wave. I suddenly became paralyzed at the thought of going back to my own house. I'd finally begun to comprehend that my mother was really and truly gone, and couldn't bear to think of going back home, knowing she would never be there again.

My father had called over to the DeSantos, but Lisa's mother assured him that she didn't mind having me around and why doesn't he let me stay an extra night?

By the third day, sure that I had worn out my welcome, my father came over to walk me back home. I packed up my sleeping bag and got two steps out the DeSantos' front door when out of nowhere, a scream surged its way out of my throat; an inhuman sound that rocked my lungs and scared the ever-loving hell out of me. Before I knew what was happening, I launched into an uncontrollable temper-tantrum, just screeching bloody murder right there on the DeSantos' porch.

I must have thrown myself down on the ground because the next thing I remember is thrashing about on Lisa's front lawn, just screaming and screaming and screaming at the top of my lungs, my throat running raw from the effort. My poor father didn't know what to do and just wrapped his arms around me, trying to calm me down, saying, "It's all right, Layla! You're all right!" over and over and over again.

A few of the neighbors came out on their front steps, drawn out by the unyielding sound, but I was in such a state that I barely even noticed. Mr. and Mrs. DeSanto came running out to us, but I think I spooked Lisa so bad that she wasn't able to make it past her front door. Mr. DeSanto threw his arms around both my father and me, trying to help Dad get my thrashing under control as he yelled to Mrs. DeSanto, "Steph, call an ambulance!"

It must have only been a few minutes later when the emergency crew arrived. The whole scene from that point on is such a blur to me now, but I know the last conscious thought I had of the episode was seeing two female EMTs running over and yelling, "Hold her still!" before a white warmth spread throughout my entire body.

The next thing I knew, I was waking up in a hospital bed to the sight of my haggard and worried father leaning over me.

"Layla? It's Daddy, sweetheart. You're in the hospital, baby. Just relax, okay?"

I remember feeling so bad that I had put that look on his face. I was able to whisper out, "I'm sorry, Daddy," but even that small effort was like passing broken glass through my throat.

Then he called out the door for a nurse before I blacked out for the second time.

It felt like forever that I was finally let out of the hospital, the doctors offering Dr. Chickensoup's business card to my father upon my release. I spent the immediate days watching TV in my bedroom, trying to eat the meals Dad brought me on the tray that we'd always used for sick days or special-occasion breakfasts in bed. I had absolutely zero appetite, but did my best to clear my plate in the hopes that my father would lose that worried look on his face.

My third day home, I'd actually started feeling a little better. I'd never feel completely whole- I knew even at the age of twelve that those days were long gone- but at least I was feeling a strange sort of acceptance about the situation.

My mother was gone.

She wasn't coming back.

I could either let that destroy me or I could learn to live my life without her.

That same day, Lisa paid me a visit. She walked in with a handful of hydrangea for me, and I actually laughed when she told me that she'd stolen them from Mrs. Kopinsky's front yard.

I knew she had to be a little freaked out by the completely mental fit I'd thrown on her front lawn, and I started to try and explain.

She put her hand up in a halt. "You don't need to explain anything to me, Layla. If you want to talk- about anything- I'm here for you. But please don't feel like you need to explain. Ever. Okay?"

I was touched that Lisa had let me off the hook so easily. She was really the best friend in the world to me at the lowest point in my young life. She came over every day, nudging me back toward my old self a little more each time. She was the one who eventually got me swimming again. That first day back in the pool was like a baptism, cleansing and renewing. It became the one place I could count on to always make me feel somewhat normal.

For all the time Lisa spent that summer nursing me back to life, she never made me feel as though I should be committed to a rubber room. That was a blessing, because I'd spent enough time thinking that for the both of us.

The way I figured it was that my mother must obviously have had something wrong in her head to have left her husband and two young children behind. Over the years, I'd done some research on manic-depression, because that became the most reasonable diagnosis I could give to the mother who abandoned us.

After that, there wasn't a day that went by when I didn't worry over the state of *my* mental health, thinking that maybe my mother's crazy gene had been passed down to me.

Even though I still tended to be a little obsessive about some things- my compulsion toward reading, my neatness streak and my superstitious tree-mauling, for examples- The Live-Aid Incident was the only time I'd ever actually gone balls-out, cuckoo-for-cocoa-puffs crazy. As more time went by, I was able to write the whole scene off as a one-time episode. Even Dr. Chickensoup felt that my tantrum that day was most likely an isolated occurrence, due to the immediate stress of my mother leaving me at such an impressionable age. She actually told my father that it was practically a good thing, the catharsis of experiencing a loss so soon and so completely.

I'd relayed the highlights from that therapy session to Lisa, who took the information in stride. In the years since, Lisa never once brought up the subject of my breakdown as though it were a major personality flaw. She's never told another soul about it and had never treated it as though it were some recurring condition, waiting to jump out unexpectedly one day from under the bed.

Until now.

I sat there on Lisa's bed, gaping at her. I couldn't believe she was comparing The Live-Aid Incident to my relationship with Trip. "Are you *serious*? This is nothing like that!"

Lisa sat back down. "Layla, yes, it is. I know you. I know you're not just hanging around with Trip because you enjoy his friendship so damn much. You're hoping that if you just hang in there long enough, eventually he'll come around. I'm telling you, when it finally hits you that you're caught in The Friend Zone... you're going to lose it. You're going to implode."

Talk about going for the jugular.

"Who the *HELL* do you think you are?" I seethed at her, before jolting off the bed, cutting her off before she could say another word. "What kind of a thing is that to say to me? *WHERE THE FUCK DO YOU GET OFF?*"

Lisa opened her mouth to respond, but I stormed out of her room before she could see the tears starting to gather at my eyes. I stomped home, went right up to my bedroom and put my stereo on full blast until my father, one floor below me, started banging on the ceiling to turn it down.

Chapter 16
HOME ALONE

I didn't spend too many Saturday nights at home. I'd originally had tentative plans to attend the homecoming dance that night, but after my fight with Lisa, I wasn't feeling up to it.

By eight o'clock, Dad had already left the house, taking Bruce to pick up his date on their way to the school. He'd come into my room before leaving, supposedly to check on me, but more to try and convince me to go to the dance. I briefly explained that Lisa and I had gotten in a stupid argument, but I assured him that I was fine and that he shouldn't cancel poker night just because I was being a big mope. That made him smile before he kissed me and headed out the door.

It was pretty cool to have the house all to myself on a Saturday night. I didn't quite know what to do with myself, however.

I considered snooping around my father's closet, but with The Live-Aid memory fresh in my mind, I didn't have the strength to confront any of my mother's belongings.

I thought about reading a book, but I'd already read everything in the house. It was early enough that I could have hit the Barnes and Noble at the mall before closing, but Dad had taken the car. Even if Lisa and I weren't fighting, I couldn't have asked her to drive me. There was no way she would have missed out on one of the most important nights of our senior year of high school just to cart my ass to the mall.

I'd finally resigned myself to the prospect of watching the movie I'd liberated from work weeks before. Lisa had begged me to bring it home for her but we hadn't been able to coordinate a two-hour block of time to be in the same room together to watch it. I decided that I'd made every effort to try and find something else to do and screw her anyway I'm not waiting.

I made a huge bowl of popcorn slathered with extra butter and salt, twisted my hair into a knot on my head, threw on some sweats and hit the sofa.

If anyone else had been in the room, I would have probably spent my time watching *Pretty Woman* by completely tearing it to shreds for being a great, big, steaming pile of crap.

But by myself, I hadn't realized how mesmerized I'd been by the flipping movie until I was suddenly startled by a tapping noise outside. It had stopped raining hours before and it was still too early for Dad or Bruce to be home, and besides, I would have heard the car pulling into the driveway and the rattle of the garage door opening.

I grabbed the remote and hit mute so I could better listen. Sitting there in the silence of my empty house was pretty spooky. I could actually hear the sound of my own breathing and was acutely aware of my thumping heartbeat.

I sat there for no more than a few seconds, when *bam!* I heard it again!

That was all the excuse I needed to bolt up the stairs and lock myself in the relative safety of my dark room. I tried peeking outside just as the pattering sound hit again...

...and could just make out the dark, outlined figure of Trip throwing pebbles at Bruce's window.

I threw open *my* window and yelled, "You dick! You just scared the hell out of me!"

Trip's focus shifted from Bruce's room to mine. "Hey there, Lay-Lay. Whatcha doin'?"

I clicked on my nightstand lamp. "What am I doing? I'm trying not to have a heart attack! What are *you* doing?"

Trip dropped the handful of pebbles he was still holding into the shrubs and wiped his hands off on his pants. "Hey, did I guess the wrong window? I thought that one was your room."

"Hey Psycho," I jeered, "Instead of throwing boulders at my house, why didn't you just knock on the front door like a normal human?"

That made a wide grin spread across his face before he answered, "Now what would be the fun in that?"

I rolled my eyes and laughed at him. My sight was better adjusting to the dark and I could see that Trip was wearing a pair of khaki slacks and a navy blue sweater. He looked, as usual, incredibly handsome.

"So hey," he started, "How come you weren't at the dance?"

I could have given him the whole rundown of my fight with Lisa, but then I'd have to tell him the reason behind it. Instead of getting into all that, I just said, "I wasn't really into it. Why? Did I miss anything?"

"I'll say."

Oooh. Gossip.

"Why? What happened? Trip, spill it!"

He laughed at my inability to control myself and then said, "Well, you weren't there to accept your crown, for one."

"My crown?" I asked, incredulously. I mean, there was no way he was saying what I thought he was saying. But then... rationality returned. "You are so full of shit."

He laughed his ass off at that and said, "Yeah, you're right. I am. But I am also your homecoming king, so you'd better show a little more respect to me from now on."

That, at least, was a tad more believable. "You got king? Really?"

He was still grinning as he said, "Nah. Not really. Jesus, Layla, you're oh-for-two tonight. But hey- on a totally different subject- did you know that the word 'gullible' isn't in the dictionary?"

"Ha. Ha. Ha."

I was so relieved when it turned out that he was only joking about my winning homecoming. I would have died if it were true. It's not like I would have been there in person to endure the indignity, but even still, that's the kind of title that sticks with a person for their whole life, and it just wasn't really my thing. I'll never forget how my dad once came home from the office one day, laughing about some poor idiot who'd filled out an application to work there, actually listing "Homecoming Queen" on her resume. God. Can you imagine? Homecoming Queen. It's just so... *perky!*

I had a vision of head cheerleader Carolee Simcox, standing up on the stage crying, wearing her sparkly, plastic crown and princess-waving to the audience. "Hey, who really won?" I asked Trip.

"Lisa and Pickford."

"Wow! No way."

"Yeah, well, you and I came in a close second. I swear to God about that. I'm not bullshitting you this time."

"What? Really? That's weird." It was kind of mind-boggling to find out that people had lumped Trip and me together on some ballot sheet. It's not like we were some official couple or anything, despite my wishes to the contrary. I mean, Trip was born to be Prom King, but I couldn't see how anyone would actually think to write down *my* name when it came time to submit their vote.

He asked, "What's so weird about it?" but before I could explain, he got a wicked gleam in his eye and added, "Oh, hey. Lisa gave a speech."

"Trip, shut up, she did not!"

He must have been putting me on. No one actually *speaks* after being crowned, for godsakes! Lisa herself had made fun of many a cheesy high school movie for just that very thing. What the hell was she thinking? "Oh, God. I'm so embarrassed for her!"

He laughed. "No, it wasn't that bad. Just a quick thank you, not much else. It was fine."

I started to feel kind of sad that I wasn't there to share in my friend's big night. "Well, I'm glad she won. I'm sure it means a lot to her. She's got to be pretty happy right about now."

Trip stuck his hands in his pockets and tapped his toe at one of the shrubs. "But you wouldn't have been?"

"What? Happy to win Homecoming Queen?" I laughed. "You're joking, right? I mean, I'm happy for Lisa and all, but I can't imagine getting thrilled about something so... *superficial*."

That made him stop fidgeting with the landscaping and stand stock still, looking up at me with an expression I can only describe as... amused shock.

He floored me by responding, "You know that's my favorite thing about you, right?"

I couldn't breathe. *Trip had a favorite thing about me?*

Somehow, I managed to squeak out, "What's that?"

He grinned sheepishly and looked away for a second before raising his head and conceding, "Layla, you are completely different from any other person I've ever met in my entire life."

I'd have been less blown away if a bomb had been detonated right there on my front yard.

I couldn't speak. I was rendered defenseless, watching him standing there under my window, looking up at me with those beautiful, blue eyes filled with awe and hope as he added softly, "I *missed* you tonight. The dance wasn't as much fun without you there. I don't know. I thought, I mean, maybe I should've-"

"Trip?" I didn't mean to cut him off mid-sentence, but I'd finally found my voice. There was no way I was going to let him say such amazing things to me without us being together in the same room. I took a deep breath and asked, "Do you want to come in?"

It was more of an invitation than a question, and my heart just about slammed into my stomach at having asked it aloud.

I watched as his eyelids relaxed and his mouth curled into that lazy grin of his which never failed to kill me. Then he nodded his head almost imperceptibly as he breathed out one, remarkable, little word.

"Yes."

There was no misreading the way he was looking at me, or his words, or his intent. I was pretty sure that this was the night when *everything* was about to change between us.

It figures that there I was without makeup on, dressed in sweatpants and my hair all tied up in a ponytail. But none of that was about to stop me from finding out what promises awaited behind that look in his eyes.

"Okay, Lemme just come down and unlock the door."

I closed my window and started to turn toward the hallway, but just then, *at that exact freaking moment*, I saw the headlights of Dad's car coming down the street.

I thought, "Dear God, really, are you kidding me? Now? *Really?*"

It was positively shattering to realize that my life-altering night was being crushed.

After my initial devastation, I was able to recognize a bit of humor in the moment, however. As Dad's car had been pulling into the driveway, Trip had been diving for the bushes.

Even through my despair, I found it funny the way he felt the need to hide away like some fugitive just because my father had come home. Dad had already met him a handful of times and he knew that we weren't a couple or anything, but Trip was acting like he'd just been caught with his hand up my shirt and his pants around his ankles.

Maybe I should have let him in a few minutes earlier.

Chapter 17
AWAKENINGS

I knew that Trip and I had crossed over into some exciting new territory that night and I was just dying to find out where it was leading. I mean, a guy doesn't just show up outside his *buddy's* window late on a Saturday night to tell them how much they were missed at some school dance, right?

The minutes felt like an eternity, waiting for the phone to ring. I spent my wait trying to decide if I should play it cool when he called, maybe a little hard-to-get. But then I realized that was probably pretty stupid and he wouldn't buy it anyway. He knew me too well. And really, here was everything I'd wanted for so long unexpectedly dropping into my lap. I'd have to be an idiot to go and play games with it.

I figured I'd played it cool long enough. If Trip wanted to be my boyfriend, then I was going to let it happen, ecstatically, without toying with his head.

I stayed awake until midnight that night waiting for the phone to ring.

It didn't.

I stuck close to home all day on Sunday, because I wanted to be there when he finally decided to call, or better yet, maybe stop by. I'd made a point to shower and put on a decent-yet-casual outfit in case he made another appearance on my doorstep. I wanted to look a little nicer than I did the night before when he caught me without makeup and wearing a pair of sweats. I wasn't going to let him catch me looking like such a frump the next time he decided to spill his heart out.

By dinnertime on Sunday, I still hadn't heard from him and I started to wonder if I'd only imagined what was going on between us. I started to wonder if maybe there wasn't even an "*us*" to begin with at all.

I began kicking myself for being such an idiot, "panting after Trip like a stray puppy", just like Lisa had said. She said that everyone knew about my crush on him, and at the time, I thought she was just trying to be hurtful. But *did* everyone know? Was I the butt of some cruel joke, people whispering behind my back for being some pathetic, love-struck loser who was way out of Trip Wilmington's league? Is that why everyone voted for us at homecoming, as a big setup to put me in my place? Was there a bucket of undumped pig's blood hovering above the stage at that very moment? I mean, he was dating Tess Valletti for godsakes. Did I really think I stood a chance of stealing him away from a girl like that? Me. Layla Warren. Semi-converted wallflower and longtime tomboy.

Yeah. That's what a guy like Trip wanted. A fraudulently popular, obsessive-compulsive dork with a wicked jump shot.

I washed the makeup off my face and went to bed.

* * *

The next morning, I woke up late as the phone was ringing and nearly fell out of bed when I went to answer it. My head was dazed from sleep, but my heart was beating out of my chest as I fumbled for the receiver and choked out, "Hello?"

At first, there was a deafening silence as the clock ticked off the seconds, the *hours*. The anticipation was killing me. "Hello?" I said again.

And then at last, I was met with, "I'm sorry."

Lisa.

I sank back into my pillows and let out the breath of air I hadn't realized I was even holding in.

"Yeah, I know."

I could hear Lisa fiddling with the cord on her end as she laughed out, "You *know*? What the hell is that?"

I laughed, too.

It was great to have a best friend that didn't need to have the upper hand all the time. A lesser person could have used my blundering words to prolong the fight.

"I'm sorry. You're right. I want to apologize, too. It's just that *I know* you weren't trying to be hurtful when you said all that stuff to me the other day."

"Well, at least you got that right."

"But it did hurt, you know."

"I know, I know. That's why I'm sorry. I could have said things better."

"Yeah, maybe you could have. But it wouldn't have changed the fact that everything you said was true."

Lis gave a big sigh on her end. "Look. What the hell do I know? Maybe you're not wasting your time like I said. I was thinking about what you told me and maybe it's not so horrible that you and Trip are just friends."

Hearing his name out loud only compounded my humiliation.

"No. You were right. This thing between him and me is disturbing."

"Yeah, but maybe you only started spending so much time with him because I've been a bad friend. Maybe you were only put in this weird position because Pickford and me have been up each other's butts for the past two months."

"He's your *boyfriend.*"

"Yeah, but you're my *best* friend."

Lisa and I didn't normally wear our hearts on our sleeves, mushing up and telling each other how important we were to one another. Aside from the half-pendants we used to wear in fifth grade- she was BEFRI and I was STENDS- there weren't too many declarations of our BFF status. It wasn't something we felt the need to reaffirm all the time. It was just who we were.

"I know. You're mine, too."

"Pick you up in about an hour?"

"Yep. Oh, and hey- Congratulations, Homecoming Queen!"

"Oh, sweet Jesus, if you ever call me that again, I will strangle you with my satin sash."

By the time Lisa and I finally got off the phone, I had to rush to get myself ready for school, rallying my way through my morning ritual. I was really freaked out at the thought of having to see Trip. He'd officially left me hanging all weekend and I still hadn't figured out why. My stomach was in knots as I stepped out my front door to wait for Lisa in the driveway.

The weather had turned colder overnight, depositing a layer of frost over every surface and blade of grass on that Monday morning. It was the time of year when most girls would wear a pair of sweatpants under their uniform skirt for the commute to school. I tried it once, but stripping the pants off upon arrival left me feeling naked the whole rest of the day. It was better to just deal with icy legs for the few minutes every morning, so as not to feel self-conscious all day long.

Frozen nerve-endings aside, I always loved that time of year, right before the season turns into winter. Summer is always the best by far, but late Fall always runs a close second. I love the smell of the cold- crisp and brisk and smoky- crunchy, wet leaves under my feet and the scent of a wood-burning fireplace in the air. I loved the promise of wool sweaters, leather boots and corduroy jackets, knit scarves and fur-lined gloves. I loved seeing my breath as I talked and writing on frosty windows with my finger.

It's awesome to live in a place where the seasons change. Sure, a year-round warm climate might seem like a blessing at first, but after a winter or two floating around a pool, doesn't all that green just eventually become downright boring? I couldn't imagine looking up at Norman Hills that time of year and still seeing all the trees dressed in their summer greens. It would be a crime to miss out on such a fireworks show, oranges and yellows and the occasional red, splashing across the Earth in one last magnificent blaze of glory before succumbing to the inevitable, albeit temporary, Brown Blah.

By the time I made it to Lisa's car, I was feeling pretty nervous and pissy about having to see Trip, because I still didn't quite know how I was going to act toward him. I relayed all that to

Lisa, after filling her in with a few of the highlights from Saturday night.

"Wait. So he just came over after the dance? Just showed up at your window?"

"Well, yeah." Lisa didn't realize that that wasn't so out of the ordinary. He came by all the time. We hung out a lot. And we talked on the phone all the time.

Well, *almost* all the time.

"But why is it such a big deal that he didn't call you after? You didn't... you know..."

"Nope. Well, it's not like we weren't headed in that direction. He just... never made it inside the house is all."

"But you think he wanted to?"

That was the part that had me so confused. How was I supposed to describe not just what he said, but the way he said it? How was I supposed to describe the look in his eyes? The hope that I saw there? I thought he'd said all those awesome things in the expectation that it would ultimately lead us together, but then he just left me hanging all weekend waiting for confirmation which never came.

Lisa summed up my latest thoughts on the matter. "You think maybe he was just making a booty call?"

I'd started to come to the same conclusion, but just hadn't wanted to admit it to myself. But there it was.

I finally conceded. "Yeah. I don't know. Maybe. Probably."

"Well, screw him! What the hell is that?"

"Your guess is as good as mine."

"All the time you two spend together and he takes advantage of that to pay you a latenight? You're better than that! God, you must be so relieved that nothing happened."

I don't think "relieved" was even in the ballpark of what I was feeling. All morning, I'd been fighting the thought that Trip was possibly a big, fat user. I had spent almost three whole months completely infatuated with him, jumping at his every beck and call, wasting countless hours hoping for any sort of return on my investment.

97

And what had he offered? Nothing.

I was his buddy, his *pal*, someone whom he got a kick out of on occasion. He probably only came over after the dance to make sure I was still going to be his adoring little mascot. The one time I don't show up and fawn all over him, he has to swing by to test the waters. It was worse than a latenight! He was probably only stroking his ego, making sure that I was still in love with him.

The inescapable epiphany hit me like a Mack truck.

I finally realized just how completely pathetic I truly was over him. I saw myself from Trip's perspective and grasped what a truly wretched, ridiculous idiot I'd been all along. The revelation fueled my insecurities; but in an unexpected way, it also obliged me take stock of my assets, too.

I mean, maybe I wasn't Tess Valletti, but I sure as hell wasn't some complete loser that deserved to be treated like a runner-up, backburner consolation prize to be utilized at his convenience!

From then on, I made the conscious decision to stop being the butt of everyone's joke, stop making myself so available and most importantly, stop being so completely obsessed over Trip Wilmington.

I cracked the window and was met with an icy chill, snickering to myself at the thought that Trip's first winter in Jersey was going to be even colder than he could have imagined.

Bye bye, drooling puppy.

Chapter 18
THE RIFT

I readied myself all morning for The Big Production I was going to be putting on; the one-woman show entitled, "*Fuck You, Trip Wilmington.*"

By lunchtime, I was all fired up. Which, in my world, meant my Big Plan was nothing more than to give him the cold shoulder, letting him know that I wasn't going to be his hungry little lemming anymore, being so available to him in exchange for the few crumbs he'd deign to throw at my feet.

So, when Trip sat down next to me and gave me a big, grinning, "Hey there," I completely ignored him and turned my attentions across the table to talk to Cooper.

"It was such a good game on Saturday! I couldn't believe the score. What was the final? Twenty-eight to ten?"

Coop swiped the back of his hand across his chocolate milk mustache and said proudly. "Twenty-eight to *seven.*"

"Wow, seven! Even better. God, and that wasn't even counting your last touchdown that the ref ruled out!"

Trip, unwilling to be ignored, thought he was being funny when he nudged me in the arm. "Layla? Hellooo. What? You don't even say hi?"

I gave out a sigh, as if I thought him rude for interrupting. I turned my head to face him and used the most bored voice imaginable to say, "Hi," then went back to my conversation with Coop.

"It's so weird that that was the last game. I'm not going to know what to do with myself on Saturdays now!"

Cooper gave me a dirty look out of the corner of his eye, smiled and invited, "I'm sure we could think of something."

I didn't hesitate to smile back and respond, "I bet you could."
Game on.

I knew I was being overbright and more than a little flirty while talking to my ex-boyfriend right in front of Trip. He'd never seen me like that before and I'm sure he'd thought I'd gone schizo. But I wanted to show him that even though *he* didn't think I was all that and a bag of chips, there were plenty of other guys who did. Plenty of other guys who would be *honored* to have the full force of my attentions. Plenty of other guys that wouldn't make me feel like I was wasting my time.

I locked onto Trip with my peripheral vision, could tell he was intensely watching my conversation with Coop like it was a tennis match, a dazed look on his perfect mug. Good. He probably didn't know what the hell was going on, but at least I had the satisfaction of throwing him off balance.

Cooper took my response as motivation, leaned across the table and said matter-of-factly, "Well, okay then. We'll have to think of something to do on Saturday."

His tone made it clear that he was asking me out for more than just an ice cream soda at the corner drugstore, and that it was already a foregone conclusion that I'd agree.

I couldn't help noticing how his eyes flicked toward Trip for just the slightest second which was sort of weird in a pissing contest kind of way. But I was even more aware of my surprise at how willing Coop was to take the bait. Even though I'd been flirting like mad with him, I was still startled that he'd actually asked me out so quickly. I felt kind of guilty for leading him on, but I was too far gone to turn back now.

I gave a shrug, like it was no big deal that Coop had just propositioned me in front of our entire group of friends and said, "Yeah. Sure! Sounds like a plan. It'll be nice to hang with, you know, a *guy* again."

Rymer chimed in with, "So then why the hell are you making plans with Coop?"

Cooper gave him the finger as Sargento and Pickford joined in with Rymer's rowdy whooping, and I smiled so wide it hurt, trying to make it look like I was having the time of my life, all the while ignoring the disapproving glance I got from Lisa.

Everyone knew that I'd been spending a lot of time with Trip, but no one knew for sure just exactly what we'd been up to together. The rumor mill had probably assumed that Trip was only slumming around with me because he was getting some. In one fell swoop, I'd managed to let everyone know that my constant companion was more of a "girlfriend" to me than a boyfriend.

In other words, with one spiteful comment, I'd managed to completely emasculate him.

It wasn't exactly what I'd set out to accomplish- ripping him to shreds while simultaneously giving the impression that I was some sort of pent-up slut- and I realized for the first time how powerful the weapon of words could be. When you're popular, people listen.

Believe me, it wasn't a pleasant revelation.

Trip was uncharacteristically quiet after that, but after what I'd just done to him, what did I expect? I'd felt justified at the time, but I started to feel awful about tearing him down. Technically, Trip was still "The New Kid", coming to some strange town with all new people, trying to fit in, and there I was, treating him like a pariah at the cool kids' table. The pang of guilt ate away at me as I gnawed at my bottom lip through a fake smile.

When the bell rang, Trip followed on my heels across the hall, but I pretended not to notice. Just as I went to grab my books, he stepped in front of my open locker. He put his hand on my arm, did a quick scan to make sure we weren't being watched and leaned in to ask under his breath, "What the hell was that in there?"

I was trying to recover from the bolt of electricity that was running through me at the nearness of him, but I managed an innocent, "What the hell was what?" as I shook off his hand and squatted down to retrieve my books.

Trip stood to the side, allowing me access to my locker, which I was pawing through with abandon. "Come on, Layla. You *know* what. Why are you treating me like I'm some piece of garbage all of a sudden? Did I do something?"

Ha!

I shrugged off his question and said evasively to his knee, "Trip, I don't know what you're talking about. I'm just trying to get to class right now, okay?"

I stood up to leave, but he slapped a hand up on the wall next to my head, obstructing my path. I clutched my books to my chest as he backed me against the lockers, blocking my escape. His eyes were shooting icicles as he spat out, "Oh, really? You have no idea what I'm talking about? That's just an ordinary day for you, then, huh. Hanging all over Coop Benedict, treating me like a disease... Obviously, you're pissed about something."

My heart was beating like crazy, having him that close. His arm braced on the wall next to my head, the entire length of his body just inches from mine, from the tips of our noses right down to our knees. Kids were shoving their way through the halls, bumping into Trip's back every few seconds, pushing him even closer against me, his chest pressing against my book-laden arms in waves. My eyes were shooting up and down the corridor, trying to look anywhere but at his face, not an easy task considering it was only two inches away from my own. "Why would I be pissed?" I said like the fraud that I was.

"I don't know, Lay. Why don't you tell me?"

He looked so broken, so legitimately hurt, but I was determined not to get sucked in. All I wanted was to tear into him, make him explain what he put me through over the weekend, lay everything out on the table. But what would be the point? The only thing I could hope to accomplish would be to force Trip to say out loud what I'd already learned to be true: If I was in love with him, that was my problem to deal with. I didn't think I could bear hearing him say outright that he didn't feel the same.

I guess he took my silence for stubbornness, because the next thing I knew, he pushed off the wall and threw his hands up in the air. "Fine. You want to play games, go right ahead. I don't have time for this. You want to talk, you know how to find me." At that, he stormed off, throwing a punch at a random locker mid-stride on his way down the hall.

102

Chapter 19
DISTURBED

I'd spent the next few days after our big blowout retreating away from Trip. Not that I had to work very hard to do so; He had pretty much made it a point to avoid me, too.

The tension between he and I during that time was a tangible thing; a thick, heavy, syrupy smog that hung like a wet wool blanket in the air between us. But soon enough, we fell into a new normal; keeping things civil, simply pretending that our prior relationship never existed. It panged my heart sometimes, not having him there to joke around with or talk to, but I knew I needed to suffer the detox first before I could even begin to look forward to any sort of rehab later.

English Lit class- previously the highlight of my day- became so awkward and stressful that I would spend more of my class time concentrating on *not* thinking of the person sitting behind me than paying attention to the lessons being disseminated.

Then there was my job. As excruciating as it would have been to face work had he been there, it was even worse to face it while he wasn't. The job went back to being the same sucky chore that it was the first week I started. Without Trip, it ceased to be fun anymore, regardless of the fact that we were hardly speaking. Add to that the fact that Martin had hired some thirty-year-old degenerate as Trip's replacement who spent more time getting high in the parking lot and trying to sneak a peek down my blouse than actually doing any work. Thankfully, I only had to deal with Dirtbag Ray on Mondays and Thursdays.

The weekends were their own train wreck.

Lisa and Pickford were practically inseparable and therefore MIA at that point, leaving me to hit every party alone, or worse yet, with Coop, the poor guy roped unknowingly into my drama. I supposed I was only reaping what I had sown, but it was torture not only to have to look at a misled Coop every day, but to see Trip stroll through the door with a new girl on his arm every night. A circumstance made more agonizing by the revelation that he'd obviously not been exclusive with Tess Valletti for quite some time.

The first Friday, it was Barbara Vlajnik, whose reputation was less than pristine. I watched her sidle up against him throughout the evening at Rymer's, but was able to take some perverted sense of pride out of the fact that he barely even looked in her direction all night.

But then just twenty-four hours later, he showed up at The Barrens with Margie Caputo, where he proceeded to down about three hundred beers before nuzzling his lips against her neck and trying to shove his hand up the front of her sweater in full view of everyone sitting around the fire. Thankfully, Margie hadn't been so receptive to his exhibitionism, but we did all hear her try to talk him into the woods for a more private session instead. Soon after, they got up to take their leave- in Margie's car, however- where I heard later that she'd brought him home only to watch as he promptly passed out two steps inside the foyer.

The following weekend, Pickford and Penelope had a party at their house. Pick was going through a bit of a defiant phase toward his father and what better way to rebel than by defiling the old man's condo?

Trip came staggering through the door of The Redys' with a bottle of Jaegermeister in one hand and some skank from Norman Valley in the other. Lord only knows where he picked that one up. She was even more drunk than he was, taking digs at any girl within earshot about being "nuns in training" while she hung all over Trip, downing shots of booze straight from the bottle.

When I couldn't watch another minute, I asked Coop to drive me home. On the way out the door, Trip shouted at my back in the most *awful* voice, "Have a good time, you two!" Then out of nowhere, the skank decided to chime in by saying, "Hell knows we sure will!" before drooping a bony arm around Trip's neck and adding, "Right, baby?"

They both enjoyed a good laugh at that.

It was enough to turn my stomach.

My mind kept seeing that filthy waif hanging all over him, contaminating him with her skank spores. Even worse was the fact that Coop assumed I pushed to leave the party early because I wanted to be alone with him, leading to a very distracted makeout session in the back seat of his car. And no, the hypocrisy was not lost on me that I was unable to put my heart into making out with Coop while my mind was consumed with thoughts of Trip hooking up with someone else. But I knew I was only dating Cooper because I'd cornered myself into it, not because I had any desire to actually be with him, selfish witch that I was. Besides, old habits die hard. Being with Coop was easy. It was familiar and constant and held no surprises. Trip, on the other hand, was maintaining his impulsiveness. He seemed to genuinely be enjoying all the attention he was receiving from his multitude of clingers and the thought ate away at me that he might actually fall in love with one of them.

Lisa informed me the next day that Pickford had sent the skank home in a cab once he realized that Trip was about to pass outright in the middle of the entire party. Apparently, he spent the night on the Redys' couch but snuck out early the next morning. Pickford woke up to a twenty tacked to his bedroom door, where Trip had simply scribbled "Thanks. Sorry." across the front of the bill.

There was a huge part of me that was relieved to hear that nothing happened between him and the skank, but there was this irritating other part of me that wanted nothing more than to pick up the phone and call him. I hated the idea that he was headed down this self-destructive path and wanted to stop him before the Keith Richards impersonation went too far, mostly because there was a tiny little fragment of my brain- a miniscule, infinitesimal speck- that felt the need to take responsibility for kicking him down that road in the first place.

I managed to resist the urge, however, and by the time Christmas break rolled around, it had become much easier to pretend he didn't even exist.

Or maybe it was just getting easier to lie to myself.

Chapter 20
MISERY

The First Snow is always fun- especially if it lands on a school day- and you can either bundle up and go outside to goof around or curl up next to the fireplace with a mug of hot chocolate and a good book. The snow gets old pretty fast, however, especially when your dad forgets to get the snowblower fixed and has to recruit his kids to help him shovel out the car at six in the morning.

But most of winter is just... grey. Grey and wet and boring. After the excitement of the holidays is over, there's nothing left to do but watch your Christmas tree die as you stare at the walls in your house every night. Then there are the months of hibernation, no parties to go to because nobody bothers to throw one. It's not worth the risk of driving icy roads at night and everyone has Seasonal Affective Disorder anyway, so it's not as though my calendar was filled with an excess of socializing opportunities.

In other words, I hardly had to put any effort into avoiding Trip over the winter.

Of course I had to see him at school every day, but pretending he wasn't there had become almost as habitual as breathing by then. Hockey kept him pretty busy, so he wasn't able to make too many appearances on the rare occasions when there actually *was* a party or something going on, and I wasn't sure if his absence made the situation easier or harder to deal with. At least when we were ignoring each other, we'd have to be in the same room in order to do so, consciously aware of the other person at every moment. In a sick way, it allowed me to still think him a part of my life, even though the relationship- or lack thereof- was in tatters.

When he wasn't around at all, I couldn't keep tabs on him.

I knew I shouldn't have cared and scolded myself for being pathetic all over again. But at least this version of pathetic was a

106

far cry from the old one, as I was the only one to be aware of it. The tradeoff being that at least my misery was known only to *me* this time.

Lisa was the only one who knew me well enough not to buy into my act at nonchalance, but she also knew I wouldn't have been very receptive to her input on the matter. I'm sure she figured she'd already said enough on the subject of Trip Wilmington and to tell the truth, I'd have been inclined to agree. It's not that I harbored any bad vibes toward my best friend, but she *was* the one responsible for kicking this little birdie out of the nest a tad prematurely. Rather than be there to help pick me up after my fall, she just went on with her perfect life as if the matter was over and done with.

Maybe that's being a bit too harsh. *Nobody* has a perfect life and it's not like Lisa left me *completely* flat. I'd made it a point to put up the front that nothing was wrong anyway. I guess I just found so many things about her to be jealous about and I was feeling more than a little left behind. After all, she was Miss Popularity. She was the one with the great boyfriend.

She was the one who had a mother.

In addition to Christmas and Valentine's Day, my mother's birthday was in January, making winter even more unbearable. Dad, Bruce and I had gotten in the habit of "uncelebrating" the occasion with a pineapple upside-down cake every year. About a week before the actual day, Dad would start compiling the necessary ingredients on the kitchen counter without comment, the shrine of groceries standing sentinel for days until I finally caved and made him his miserable cake. It was an unspoken ritual between the three of us, maybe a downright masochistic one, but one we honored nonetheless. Like the swallows returning to Capistrano every spring, we all knew that my mother's birthday was rolling around the corner when the cans of Dole found their way back to our kitchen. As if we could forget.

Lisa knew that January was always pretty tough for me. Aside from July, it was the only other time of year when I relied a little heavier than usual on my surrogate mother, a woman who lived

107

three houses down and went by the name of Stephanie DeSanto. Having Lisa off spending every minute with her boyfriend, she was depriving me of my much-needed quality time with her mom. I missed hanging out at the DeSantos', having Mrs. D say things like, "There are my girls!" whenever Lisa and I came walking through the door.

I hated myself for feeling so selfish about everything, but once Lisa's virginity status had finally been relegated to the history books, it was as though she and I were officially living on different planets. There she was, relaying this Big News and all I could think about was how it affected *me*. Thankfully, I shut up about it and she was able to remain unaware of my self-centeredness in regards to her life. I could have done without hearing all the intricate details of their every coupling, however, but maybe I would have felt that way regardless. I'd never really been the kind of girl who was ever comfortable discussing such intimate events in such excruciating detail.

Or maybe it was just that I didn't have any intimate details to discuss.

I went out on a handful of dates with Cooper, but again, we found ourselves just kind of going through the motions. We were both aware that there wasn't some storybook, fairytale ending awaiting the two of us and managed to strike a mutual, unspoken agreement about our romantic status. Basically, we liked each other a lot, and since neither one of us was dating anyone else, we decided to kill some time together.

Cooper was a huge help to me over those months, even if he wasn't completely aware of it at the time. It was comforting to have a friend- a great-looking, charming friend- there to keep me from slipping down into a depressed, winter funk. Just the idea that an awesome guy like Cooper Benedict sought my company was enough to bolster my confidence.

Normally, after work on Friday nights, I'd bring a movie home, he'd come over and we'd stay in to watch it. Sometimes, we'd fool around a little, but only if the movie sucked so badly that it couldn't hold our attentions.

When I finally figured I'd saved enough money for a car, it was Coop who took me from lot to lot, helping me do my homework and kicking the tires of every used car in the Northern New Jersey area. By the time we narrowed it down to two different front-runners, Dad stepped in to make sure I wasn't being taken to the cleaners. I felt pretty proud that he'd stamped his approval on both cars, saying that I'd done good and was free to make my own choice between the two.

The first car was a Ford Mustang. It was candy-apple red, which was a little flashy for my taste, but it was also a convertible, which was a major check in the pro column. And each time I slipped behind the wheel, something just felt right. I loved the exhilarating grumble of the engine and the way I felt about myself when I had taken it out for a test drive. It would, however, also have sapped my entire budget, barely leaving me with enough scratch afterwards to buy a tank of gas. Plus, the leather seats had seen better days, the upholstery cracked all over and ripped clean through in a couple spots. I'd definitely have to use my next paycheck to invest in a couple seat covers.

Therefore, I'd been leaning heavily toward the Ford Taurus. Don't be fooled into thinking it was boring and dull. It was a really good car with low mileage and under my budget, allowing me to hang onto a nice chunk of my hard-earned cash. It was black, too, which made it look a little cooler than if it was Grandma Blue or something like that. I liked it. It was a good, solid, dependable car.

I had worked for months at a job I could barely tolerate, socking away enough money for a car of my own. I'd kept a lid on any frivolous spending just for the opportunity to be in that position, the one I'd dreamt about forever. Obviously, I wasn't planning to take the decision lightly.

All in all, I thought the Mustang was an excellent choice.

Chapter 21
STEPPING OUT

Spring came without fanfare at first, just a steady thaw of frozen earth, softening just enough to let the first crocus peek through and for a few birds to return to the neighborhood.

A few days after that, we were blessed with The First Nice Day.

There's nothing quite like The First Nice Day in Jersey. It's like we've all been released from cages or something, everyone jumping the gun on those opening rays of sunshine by wearing sunglasses and driving around with their windows down. I had taken advantage of my new convertible that day, taking the top down to drive around in barely sixty-five degree weather while pretending I wasn't freezing my face off. Everyone's music got played a little louder and their spirits got raised a little higher.

My spirits had certainly been raised; I'd received a few acceptance letters to some really good colleges- Swarthmore, Amherst... Dad's beloved Northwestern. I'd jokingly applied to Harvard purely as a shot in the dark, so there was no big surprise when I found out I'd been rejected.

But the day I opened the mailbox and saw a big, fat envelope with an NYU stamp in the corner, I just about exploded through the front door, excited beyond belief to show my father. He was happy for me, but couldn't see how I could turn down Northwestern for NYU. I made the case by reminding him that although I'd been drawn to Northwestern because of their creative writing program, there was no better place to get my artistic juices flowing than in the most amazing city in the world. Once I pointed out how much closer the commute home would be from the city than Chicago, I knew I had him sold. Dad dropped his subtle nudging for Northwestern once he realized I was sure I'd be happier in New York.

Besides, Lisa had been accepted to F.I.T., so we cooked up a plan to live in our respective dorms for a year or so, then go apartment hunting down in the village and move in together. Facing a big, strange city wasn't going to be so bad with Lisa by my side. I didn't think there was anything we couldn't do so long as we were together.

Speaking of being together... Lisa and Pickford had broken up over Spring Break. Turned out, he was taking his recent rebellious phase to new levels and Lisa got caught in the maelstrom. Apparently, Dr. Redy had had his heart set on a Columbia education for his son. (Funny, but I don't remember ever hearing about him pushing for Penelope to live up to any grand expectations.) In any case, Pickford decided to take UCLA up on their scholarship offer and play basketball for the Bruins rather than lay the groundwork for a career in medicine. The announcement had the intended effect of infuriating his father, who couldn't even threaten to withhold tuition money anymore now that Pick had been offered a free ride.

The fallout, however, was that he'd be moving to the completely opposite end of the country from Lisa. She just went bonkers when she found out about the "stunt" he had pulled, and I'm sure her tirade even gave Dr. Redy's anger a run for its money. Pickford tried appeasing her with promises of a long-distance relationship and by reminding her that they still had months together before they'd both be expected to go off to school, but Lisa wasn't having any of it. She told him she didn't see the point in staying together if they were just going to break up in a few months anyway.

Pickford really made a go of it, sending her flowers almost weekly and leaving love notes in her locker every day. I felt really badly for him, but my loyalties needed to lie squarely with Lisa. Don't get me wrong, I felt just as awful for her. Probably more so, since I had to watch her fall to pieces every day. She never let anyone see how upset she truly was, but when it was just the two of us, she would totally let herself go, bawling like a child; red face, puffy eyes, runny nose and all.

I was more than willing to be the rock for my best friend, since usually our dynamic worked the other way around. Without seeming too detached or self-inflating about the situation, I gotta say, it was actually kinda nice to have the opportunity to return the favor.

I tried everything I could think of to get her mind off the breakup; renting cheesy movies, frying up some Elvis sandwiches (her favorite), taking her to the bowling alley where we were always able to con a few beers... I even went so far as to dig out my old sticker albums from the attic so she could take a whiff of my much-coveted popcorn scratch n' sniff.

Nothing worked.

I figured she'd get through it in her own good time and that the only thing I could really do was just be there for her.

So, it caught me by surprise when one day in May, she just up and announced that we were going to the school's Spring Musical. Bizarre, because normally, Lisa wouldn't be caught dead at a school event that didn't revolve around some sort of gladiatorial-type sporting affair. And the kids in the theatre group couldn't possibly be at a more opposite end of the spectrum from the jocks.

But what I soon learned was that Penelope Redy was playing the part of Adelaide in the selected production of *Guys and Dolls*. Lisa and she had gotten pretty chummy over the past months, being that Penny was Pick's twin sister and all. I thought it was a bit sadistic of Lisa to purposely put herself in the same room with not only Pickford, but most likely his entire family as well. I knew she blamed Dr. Redy for indirectly causing the breakup, and it's not like he'd ever been the biggest fan of hers to begin with. But seeing as it was the first time she'd suggested leaving the house, I didn't hesitate to agree to go with her.

Imagine my surprise when the first people we saw at the school's entrance were Coop, Rymer and Sargento.

I walked right up to Coop. "Hey! I didn't know you were coming to this thing!"

Coop looked a little uneasy when he answered, "Yeah, well. I didn't talk to you today and these guys just decided we were coming about an hour ago."

I didn't know why he seemed so uncomfortable spilling the news that he'd made alternate plans without first consulting me on the matter. It's not as though he owed me The Big Check-In. Whatever romantic relationship he and I were in had pretty much completely fizzled out before Easter. We were still pretty close, though, and I knew he'd been feeling a little ashamed about leaving me to deal with Lisa twenty-four-seven. We'd had a big talk about it the week before, Coop expressing his guilt at not being there for me more, stepping in to give me a break while I was consumed with the task of caring for her.

We all found seats together (on the opposite side of the auditorium from Pickford and the Redys, Lisa pretending not to notice the way her ex-boyfriend's eyes followed her all the way down the aisle) and settled in. Rymer made some crack about "the theatre fags", not too loudly, thank God, but noisily enough that I felt the need to reach over Coop and smack his arm to shut up.

Leave it to the big, burly football player to assume everyone else in the school was second-rate. I didn't think he was being fair. Everyone has different interests. And maybe the theatre group was having just as good a time on stage as the meatheads were having on the football field. High school was a bumpy enough road to begin with. If you could find a group of people willing to have you come along, it made the ride a lot more fun. Just because this particular group had chosen a creative outlet as their vehicle didn't mean they were losers. But I guessed Rymer's attitude was that if you weren't part of the cool crowd, you weren't anything. No wonder so many kids hated us. Besides, what the hell was he doing at the damned play if he thought it was so beneath him?

About ten minutes after the curtain opened, I got the answer to my question.

Ladies and gentleman, the part of Sky Masterson was being played by the one and only Terrence C. Wilmington III.

Chapter 22
TOTAL RECALL

To say I was floored would be an understatement.

I stared at him from the safety of my seat, buried in shadow where I could watch without fear of being seen.

It was weird seeing Trip up there, perfectly at home, strutting from one edge of the scene to the other. I sat there, transfixed by the sight of him onstage. He looked so gorgeous in his suit and fedora that it almost put Brando to shame. And my God, the guy could actually act! He even managed a dead-on New York accent. Not bad for a kid who'd only been living here for little more than half a year. By his second scene, you could just feel the audience tuning in, holding their breath with anticipation, engrossed by the performance he was giving.

Once he started singing *"I'll Know"*, I realized that not only could he act, but he could actually sing, too. I watched enviously as he kissed Heather Ferrante, but laughed along with the audience when she slapped him. How many girls would've loved to have done that to him over the years?

I had the most ridiculous guilt, not even knowing what Trip had been up to the past months, hard at work, obviously pouring himself into such an endeavor. Knowing how much of a perfectionist he'd been over our stupid Shakespeare film, I couldn't imagine how obsessed he'd been while preparing for something like this. I kept thinking that I wasn't there to help him with it, wasn't able to be his comic relief during the endless drudgery of rehearsals, wasn't there to encourage him through the frustrating moments that I knew he'd encountered along the way.

I made myself let go of my remorse, at least for the next hour or so, in order to enjoy the show. I decided that it was his big moment and I didn't want to ruin it by letting my overactive brain distract me from it, so I pushed the self-absorbed thoughts aside and focused solely on what was happening onstage.

I smiled as he danced with Heather/Sarah and laughed when he had his huge fight scene with Big Jule. By the time he broke into "*Luck Be a Lady*", he had won me over; I'd been captivated by his every move, infatuated at his every word.

It was heartbreaking just to look at him.

There was something so beautiful about him, a glow that came from more than just the stagelights, and the more I watched, something deep inside me started to ache.

I felt Coop give my hand a squeeze, and until that moment, I hadn't realized I was crying. I became conscious of what Coop must have already noticed, the few traitorous tears dampening my cheeks.

I knew then that in spite of my denials, despite whatever brave face I'd been presenting to the world, no matter how much I tried to pretend that Trip didn't exist... I'd never stopped loving him.

I gave Coop a quick look of gratitude and squeezed his hand right back, registering why he hadn't told me about his plans to come see his friend in the play that night. Even the mere mention of Trip's name would have hurt me; even though I'd put up a good front, he knew I'd never truly gotten over him. That it should have been Cooper that recognized that- and taken pity- touched me in a way I can't describe.

By the time the play had ended, I was emotionally spent, but at least my eyes were dry. The guys immediately made their way backstage, giving me a moment alone with Lisa.

She was sifting through her purse, trying to find her chapstick, when I asked the million dollar question. "So, am I right to assume you didn't drag me here tonight just to see Penelope in a supporting role?"

Lisa abandoned her search to reply, "No, not 'just'. Penny's been telling me for weeks how good Trip was in this thing. I didn't think you'd want to miss it. Are you mad?"

I thought about how she had suffered through an evening in near proximity to her ex-boyfriend and his family in order to let me have this experience. It was a gamble, but I was grateful she'd taken it.

"No, I'm not mad."

"He was really good."

"Yeah, I know." Good didn't quite cover it, but I didn't want to seem all sappy and crushy.

As we were getting our things to leave, I saw Pickford make his way over. I gave Lisa a nudge, and when she turned and saw him, her whole body went stiff.

In the brief, awkward second of silence, I said, "Hey, Pick."

He barely looked at me to reply, "Whatsup, Layla," his eyes locked onto Lisa.

I didn't know whether I should take off and give them some privacy or if Lisa wanted me to stick around for moral support. So, I just kind of tried to blend into the background while those two continued to stare at one another.

Finally, I said, "Penelope did a great job tonight."

That broke Pickford's trance enough for him to reply, "Yeah. Yeah, she did. I was just heading backstage to congratulate her. You guys want to come?"

There was no way I was going to be responsible for making the decision on that one. Lisa finally spoke and answered, "Yeah, sure, why not?" But she grabbed my hand in an iron vise, letting me know that she wasn't going back there alone.

We grabbed our jackets and purses and followed Pick backstage, where there was a crowded frenzy of about a million people, all the actors talking animatedly with their friends and family. We had to plow our way through the crowd to find Penelope, who was in the process of kissing Dr. and Mrs. Redy goodbye. Just as we approached, they departed, and I was relieved that Lisa wasn't forced to make nice with them. Having to deal with Pickford was probably enough for her at the moment.

I was able to get in a quick, "Congratulations, Penny, you were great!" before I heard Rymer's big mouth behind me.

I turned involuntarily at the sound and saw that Trip was standing only a few paces away, looking right in my direction. Lisa was busy hugging Penelope, so she didn't see him nod his head at me in greeting. With Lisa distracted, I was flying solo on that one, so I took the path of least resistance by politely smiling and giving a quick wave.

I turned my attentions back toward my little group and saw that Lisa and Pick were trying very hard not to look at one another as they excitedly discussed the play with Penelope, but I did notice that they were, in fact, holding hands. I was so stunned by that that I hadn't noticed the tap on my shoulder was coming from Trip.

I turned, startled to see him there, smiling at me as if the past five months of our standoff hadn't occurred at all. Before I could think of how I was going to handle that, he directed my attention to the older couple standing next to him, by way of making an introduction. "Mom, Dad, I want you to meet Layla. Layla, these are my parents."

I wasn't about to snub the guy on his big night while his parents were standing right there, so I held out my hand to them both. Plastering a smile on my face, I said, "Nice to meet you."

Mr. Wilmington was a hulking, stern-looking man, but a smile cracked his façade when I did that. He gave my hand a good shake as Mrs. Wilmington just prattled on about how proud she was of Trip. Something about the way she was lavishing on the compliments made me think she was the type of mother that would have been just as indulgent in her praise had he just taken out the garbage extraordinarily well. But it was actually kinda cute.

Mr. Wilmington finally cut in, saying, "Okay, Maddie. You're going to embarrass the boy in front of his friend." He was almost laughing, sliding an arm around her shoulders and trying to get her to make with the farewells. At last, she gave Trip a final hug and they said goodbye to the both of us.

There we were, alone in the middle of a roomful of people. I wasn't quite sure why Trip had broken our silent treatment, but he looked so elated that I figured he'd have been busting with excitement toward anyone he encountered that night, even me.

I was glad to have been given the chance to tell him in person, "Trip, I gotta say... You were... *so good*!"

117

That made him grin even wider than he already was, and I could tell he was puffing up with pride even as he tried to downplay my compliment. "Thanks. But I think you're being too kind. It was no big deal, I was just okay."

I wasn't going to gush all over him, but he deserved to know what a great job he'd done. He deserved to know how he'd mesmerized the audience. How he'd mesmerized *me*. "Trip, stop. You blew the roof off this place tonight. Everyone loved you."

"Everyone?" he asked, without even missing a beat, looking at me like he expected me to answer him with unconditional adulation, answer him like the old Layla who idolized him and harbored a big, fat crush on him.

But New Layla wasn't biting.

"Truly, Trip. You could just *feel* how much the audience enjoyed themselves whenever you were on stage. I swear."

That seemed to please him immensely. He grinned ear to ear and immediately wrapped his arms around me for a hug. I'm sure he had only been trying to thank me for the nice words, but the gesture was startling enough on its own.

But then suddenly, the embrace turned into something much more.

Before I knew it, I was hugging him back, my heart leaping out of my chest, the electricity passing between us like lightning. Trip felt it, too, because the hug went on for much longer than necessary. I could feel his hands smoothing against my back almost imperceptively, his lips turning toward my neck ever so slightly, breathing me in, sending shockwaves through my veins. He pulled back slowly to look me in the eyes and I'm sure I must've looked as stunned as a deer in the headlights. His smile was gone, replaced with a seriousness I'd never seen on his face before, his heavy lids focused on my lips... and as he leaned in...

...Rymer jumped on his back, almost knocking my teeth out.

"Heeey, Brando! You believe this guy, huh? Warren, can you get a load of this guy or what?"

Rymer noogied Trip's head quickly before releasing him from a full-nelson and giving him a high-five. It was as though he were going for gold in the Cliché Eighties Jock Triathlon. Coop and Sargento opted for a simple handshake instead, announcing that they were splitting for the Barrens.

"You gonna make it over there later?" Cooper asked, and I didn't know if the question was being put to me or Trip.

Trip answered, "Nah. Probably not. I have to hit the wrap party tonight. Hey, you guys wanna come?"

Rymer looked at him like he'd grown a second head as he laughed out, "Party with the Theatre Fags? Thanks, but I think we'll take a pass, dude."

Coop and I just rolled our eyes at each other as I leaned in to kiss him goodbye.

Lisa popped over just then, letting me know that *she and Pickford* were ready to leave. She gave me the bug-eyes, silently willing me not to offer commentary while whispering, "Can you believe this?"

No. No, I couldn't. But she seemed happy, so I shut up and figured I'd get the whole story once we were alone.

Before I could say my goodbyes to Trip, he piped up and said, "Lis- I'll drive Layla home." He looked at me and added, "If that's all right with you, obviously."

I was stunned and confused and didn't know what to say. Lisa wasn't waiting for me to make my own decision on the matter and cut in with, "Yeah. That's fine. Hey, Trip, you were great tonight!" Before I knew it, she was kissing me on the cheek and chirping, "Okay, guys, see you later!" Then she grabbed Pick's arm and led him out the door.

That just left Trip and me standing there by ourselves again, recovering from our near miss. Trip took my hand and said softly, "Hey. Come to the party with me tonight, Lay."

I looked down at his fingers threaded through mine, not quite believing what I was seeing. "I don't know, Trip... I don't want to crash..."

"You're not crashing, I'm inviting you. C'mon, it'll be fun."

I didn't know what brought about the change in him, but the last time I'd seen that look on his face, he was standing under my bedroom window after the homecoming dance.

That was the last good night between us, the unofficial end of our affiliation. I'd spent months after that trying to maintain my distance from him, convince myself that I was better off without him. It seemed impossible, but I had done it. I had purged Trip Wilmington out of my system and gone on with my life. After all that, would I really even consider putting myself in a position to go down that same road all over again?

You'd fucking better believe it.

Chapter 23
THE INNER CIRCLE

The party was at Heather Ferrante's house. I think I can count on one hand the number of times she and I had ever been in the same room together, much less held a conversation. I felt like a complete intruder walking through the front door of her home.

Obviously, everyone else at the party felt so, too.

I'd been hanging with the "in-crowd" for so long, I'd forgotten what it felt like to be an outsider. Two steps inside the living room, I was reminded.

I couldn't help but notice the unwelcoming looks I was receiving from the Preppy Girls, who didn't even have the social grace to hide their disbelief at my presence. One of them (they all looked alike to me and I couldn't remember anyone's specific name) went so far as to singsong, "Hiii, Trip!" in a misguided, possessive sort of way, while completely bypassing even a polite hello to me. She was obviously the alpha female in her clan- her ballsy attitude instantly reminded me of Lisa- and I figured the rules of hierarchy held true for every clique; nerdy, cool, preppy or otherwise.

"Hey, Shelly. Hey, girls," he remarked in their direction. "You know Layla, right?"

Shelly just gave me the once over and turned back toward her group of lemmings.

I couldn't believe it. Was that loser nobody seriously snubbing me? Where did she get off? I didn't even know her name until a minute ago, and she was acting like *I* was the social disease?

It was times like these when I wished I were more like Lisa. She would have instantaneously come up with the perfect zinger to put that little Ally Sheedy right in her place. But because I'm me, I knew I wouldn't come up with something until thirty seconds after I'd walked away, then have to wait for the chance to use it in retaliation at a more opportune moment. Until then, I could just ignore her.

Kind of like I'd done for the past seventeen-and-a-half years, I guess.

I'd been about to write her off as just another jealous nobody with a self-imposed chip on her shoulder...

...when I realized that maybe her only problem was that she was just tired of being ignored for so long.

The rest of her little entourage stifled their giggles after my public snubbing, and I decided coming up with the perfect comeback was unnecessary. I was taken aback by why she would have even cared enough to bother trying to get one over on me- I mean, seriously, who the hell was I?- but it obviously meant a lot to her to have gotten the best of Layla Warren, so I let her have her triumphant moment. If she was going to live such a small life, it wasn't my problem to deal with.

Trip seemed oblivious to my Martian status and ushered me toward the back of the house to say hello to our hostess, who was busily setting out some paper plates and napkins along her kitchen counter. Heather practically blushed when Trip kissed her hello, which was pretty funny, considering she'd just wrapped up months of rehearsal as his costar in order to play his love interest onstage.

Thankfully, she was a bit more gracious than her friends in her greeting toward me. I took the opportunity to let her know that I thought she'd done a great job as Sergeant Sarah Brown. She smiled prettily and asked me if I'd like a drink, her kindness enabling me to loosen up a little and start being myself. I was expecting a dry party, something along the lines of soda and chips, so I was surprised when Heather directed my attentions over to a table set up with bottles of beer, homemade wine and champagne.

Who says we were the only ones who knew how to party?

Trip grabbed a bottle of Bud, while I opted for some red wine. He clinked his bottle against my glass (I was dumbfounded to be at a high school party where I could use actual glassware) and we headed out onto the deck.

Nathan Detroit was on his way back into the house, but stopped to shake Trip's hand and offer his congratulations. He proceeded to prattle on about the performance, hardly acknowledging my presence. Since I hadn't taken part in the play, I didn't have much to offer by way of conversation, and spent my time sipping from my glass. After a few minutes, I was surprised to find that it was empty and excused myself to go refill it.

I bumped into Roger Vreeland from the AV Club and I was grateful to see a somewhat familiar face. "Hey, Rog," I said.

He gave a quick glance over his shoulder before answering, "Oh. Hey, Layla."

I took a swig of my drink and asked, "What are you doing here? You weren't in the play, were you? I'm pretty sure I didn't see you up there."

He kept shifting from one foot to the other, and it appeared that he was embarrassed to be seen speaking to me. "No. I, uh, I helped with the set."

I started to get the impression that the whole theatre club had enjoyed having Trip all to themselves the past months, and the general attitude seemed to be that they didn't appreciate having to share him with someone from his old crowd again. I was being nice enough to everyone, but apparently, only Trip was being treated like an actual human, probably because he had temporarily become one of them.

Even though I thought Roger was being uncharacteristically rude, I decided to let him off the hook. "Oh, that's cool. Everything looked really great. Okay, see you later!"

I went back out onto the deck, giving Trip the excuse to wrap up his conversation with Nathan, who departed without incident. He headed back inside, leaving Trip and me truly alone for the first time in five months.

I leaned against the railing, took another swig of wine and tipped my head back to take in the night air. It was a gorgeously balmy night and I was with a gorgeously elated companion. Trip was practically floating all evening, high on his performance. I hoped that maybe at least some of that euphoria could also be attributed to the fact that he was there with me.

He leaned into me, gave me a nudge, smirked, and asked, "So... how are you liking your first *theatre* party?"

I laughed, knowing he was teasing me with one of the first things I'd ever said to him, back in September, waiting in line for the bathroom at Rymer's party.

I put my glass on a nearby table and mugged his same pose from that night; hands in my pockets and rocking back on my heels, and saying in a deep, midwesterner's accent, "It's cool. Ever-one's bein' reeeally cooool."

"Jesus, do I really sound like that?"

"Yes. That's what you sound like exactly."

That made him laugh, and in spite of my better judgment, it felt great to know that I still had the power to crack him up.

I was starting to feel the effects of the wine, but I probably would have been just as drunk off of my present company. After months of avoiding him, I'd almost forgotten what a drug Trip Wilmington could be. I'd almost forgotten how his grin made this great dimple appear in his left cheek, how his smile reached all the way up to his beautiful, blue eyes. I'd almost forgotten what it felt like to have him all to myself, the comfort of having him there to talk to, the way we didn't need to talk at all.

I was curious to ask him about a million things: I didn't know why he'd suddenly started talking to me again, I was interested to know when he'd decided to be in the play. I wanted to hear about the rehearsals, and what he possibly did in order to play his part so incredibly. But I didn't want to rock an already unsteady boat. We were hanging out for the first time in months. I didn't think hitting him with the Spanish Inquisition would go over too well.

So, I asked, "Hey! How'd hockey season go?"

He grinned that lazy, half-lidded-eyes smile at me, making my stomach do a little flip. "Pretty well, actually. We kicked ass all over the state and almost clinched a spot in the nationals, but blew it at the last minute."

"Aww, man."

"Yeah, tell me about it. It sucked." He tossed his empty beer bottle into the garbage pail and added, "But the coach was awesome. He actually asked me to be a part of his MVP team in the fall. If I join, I'll get to travel all over, meet pro players and stuff."

"Wow. Are you going to do it?"

Trip gave a shrug and shot a sham dirty look at me from the corner of his eye, which always managed to turn my insides to mush. "Still thinking about it."

I downed the last sip in my glass, and Trip offered to go get us another round.

I stood and looked out over the back yard, smelling the sweet, night air and feeling the tingly, numbing warmth of the wine taking effect in my legs. It was surreal, being there with Trip, picking up right where we had left off, wherever *that* was. I decided that whatever was happening, I wasn't going to rack my slightly alcohol-impaired brain trying to figure it out right at that minute.

It was hard to concentrate on anything other than watching Trip walk out of the house anyway- dressed sharply in a tan Henley and black slacks and grinning in my direction- because the sight was even more intoxicating than the drinks he was holding in his hands.

He placed them on the table, and gave a check over his shoulder before offering, "I just saw Vreeland trying to hit on Shelly Markham."

"No way!"

He came over to me, leaning his face close to mine. I shuddered at his nearness, feeling the delicious sensation of his breath at my ear as he added, "She turned him down flat."

"Lucky guy."

We both cracked up, then Trip grabbed my glass and handed it over to me. I took it, saying out the side of my mouth, "Whatrya trying to get me drunk tonight, Chester?"

I took a sip through a giggle and then realized he wasn't laughing, just standing there staring at me, holding his beer frozen in midair halfway to his lips. My brain did an automatic rewind, and when I hit play, I realized what I'd just said.

I looked at him wide-eyed, until the most obnoxious "PPPPHHHFFFFFTT!" escaped from my mouth and I doubled over laughing, Trip still looking at me thunderstruck.

He finally lowered the beer bottle and laughed out, "*Are you kidding me?* How the- How did you... Wha- Are you freaking *kidding* me?"

I didn't think I was going to be able to take my next breath; I was laughing so hard my stomach hurt. "Oh my God! Trip! I can't believe I just called you that. I-"

"How in *the hell* did you know that?"

I managed to get my breathing under control, fanned myself with my hand and then steadied myself against the table. "Okay, lemme just... Whoo! Okay. I'm okay now." I took a sip from my drink (as if I really needed one at that point) and confessed how I'd seen it on his driver's license way back on the day he filled out his application to work at Totally Videos.

"Are you serious?" He asked, looking at me like I'd just found the cure for cancer. "Do you know that I've managed to keep that under wraps in *every* school in *every* city I've ever lived in?"

"Yeah. I figured as much. Am I the only one who knows?"

He shook his head, still in disbelief that I had managed to sleuth him out. "Ho. Ly. God. Layla Effing Warren! Unbelievable. You know I have to kill you now to keep you silent, right? I mean, seriously. I have to end you now. So what will it be? Death by Manilow?"

I put the glass back on the table and found it took a little more concentration than necessary to stand back upright. I hoped Trip didn't notice, but I was definitely getting a tad tipsy off of the wine. "Firthst of all," *Shit. Was I slurring?* "my middle name is not 'Effing'."

Trip totally sniffed me out, realizing that I was definitely feeling the sauce. "Ya okay there, Lay-Lay?"

I dismissed his question with a wave of my hand. "And *B*..." I continued, "I kep that little tidbit of information to myself for..." I started counting on my fingers, Trip smirking at my impaired math skills. "...eight whole months! I didn't tell *anyone*. Not even *you*." At that, I poked a finger into his chest, adding, "So there, *Pal*."

Jesus. I was definitely drunk. How the hell did *that* happen? I guessed my immunity was only built up against cheap beer. Either that, or homemade wine packs more of a punch than storebought. I was only on my third glass!

But there was no stopping me now. "Thirdly... Oh, hey! Doritos!" I spotted the bowl of chips on the very table I'd been using to prop myself up and popped like three or four into my mouth before continuing. "I happen to *wike* Bawwy Maniwow-" (tortilla chips spraying from my mouth) "-and *Mandy* is the best song in the history of music! So there!"

Without thinking, I picked up my wine with a flourish, intending to punctuate my rebuttal with a dramatic final sip, when Trip intercepted my glass on the way to my lips with a, "Whoa there, pardner. I think it's time to cash in our chips."

"I'm fine."

"Layla. You're defending Barry Manilow with a vengeance. I wouldn't exactly say you're 'fine'."

I resisted the urge to belt into "*I Write the Songs*" and instead let Trip lead me out of the party.

On the way through the living room, I saw Shelly, still sitting on the sofa surrounded by her entourage. I broke from Trip's grasp and walked right over to her, pointedly interrupting whatever lame conversation she was in the middle of.

"Hey, Shelly," I said, loudly enough to cause her to flinch. She looked surprised to see me there and I could practically see her feathers ruffle. I put a genuine smile on my face and said, "It was good to see you again. Thanks for letting me crash your party."

Shelly looked genuinely flummoxed by my friendliness, and was only able to stammer out, "Oh. Okay. Goodnight."

Then I addressed the rest of the group. "Bye, girls! Have a good night."

I could see the shock on their faces and realized my niceties had sent them into a tailspin even moreso than had I knocked their leader down a peg. Trip didn't seem to notice as he put a hand under my arm and ushered me out the door.

Once in his truck, I started to get the spins. Jeez, what the heck did the Ferrantes put in that wine?

Trip barreled down the road and I thought I was going to toss my cookies. But we managed to make it back to my house without incident.

He escorted me out of the truck, but I broke free from his grasp in order to make my ritualistic lunge for a leaf off my tree. I guessed drunkenness wasn't even going to help cure my OCD. On the third try, I still hadn't managed to nab one and almost lost my footing upon my landing. Trip laughed as he balanced me back on my feet, then jumped up and grabbed one for me, handing it over and saying, "You have problems."

Tell me about it.

He walked me to the house, then asked, "You gonna be okay?"

I laughed and answered, "Yeah. I'm sure I'll be just fine." I leaned against my front door, looking up at his cobalt eyes, watching him watch me with amusement, and just launched in. "Hey- so, I gotta ask you... What *was* this tonight? Why the sudden urge to play nice?"

He dropped his head and answered, "Oh, I don't know, Lay."

He plucked the leaf from my hand, turning it over in his own, inspecting it with rapt attention. He massaged the back of his neck with his free hand, saying, "You know what? That's not true. I know exactly why."

He let out a deep breath, raised his head and said, "I was lying when I said my being on stage tonight was no big deal." His eyes got this faraway look in them, like he was talking to someone floating over my left shoulder. "Lay, I never felt anything like that before. I can't explain it. It was... *amazing.*" He ran a hand through his golden hair, then placed the leaf back in my hand, sandwiching it between his palms. "When I saw you backstage and realized you'd seen it, I was so... *grateful.* Grateful that you'd come there to share that with me. I knew I missed you, but I'd been so stubborn about it for so long... I don't know. It... I guess it felt more real having you be a part of it. You know?"

Actually, I did know. But Jesus, it felt awesome to hear him say something like that to me.

"I have a confession to make," I said, warily meeting his eyes, watching as he waited with baited breath for me to say something, *anything* that would validate him spilling his guts. "I didn't know you were in the play until the curtains opened."

Trip looked crestfallen, so I quickly added, "No, no. I'm *so glad* I was there, too! It was... It was just such a... such an *unexpected surprise.*"

I met his eyes just then, the months of anguish and separation just falling away. He put a hand at my neck, leaned in and whispered, "Surprises are good," before giving me a sweet, soft kiss on the corner of my mouth.

Needless to say, my insides turned to mush and my heart threatened to escape from my ribcage, even just from that small contact of his lips against my skin. But even still, I headed inside disappointed. I'd thought there was the slightest chance he was going to actually kiss me, but I guessed my drunken state and Dorito breath weren't really the biggest aphrodisiacs.

I leaned against the closed door and took a huge breath, trying to get some air back into my lungs. I grabbed a glass of water on my way up to my room, where there were five messages from Lisa on my machine.

Chapter 24
IMPROMPTU

I don't think the sun could have been shining any brighter that next morning. At least my throbbing head didn't think so. What a lightweight! Three stinking glasses of wine and I was actually suffering a bit of a hangover.

So, when my phone started ringing, I grabbed it off the hook quickly before my ears could explode.

"Hello?" My voice didn't even sound like my own.

"LAYLA! OH MY GOD!"

I held the receiver away from my ear, cursing first into my pillow, then next at Lisa. "Christ, Lis! Why are you *yelling*?"

Lisa didn't even acknowledge my blasting head and proceeded to launch into the details of her night with Pickford. "He said he loved me, Layla! On our way backstage last night, he just grabbed my hand and whispered 'I love you' into my ear! I couldn't believe it!"

I removed the pillow from my head, sat up and checked my face in the mirror above my dresser. Not good.

"Layla, are you listening? *Pickford told me he loved me!*"

I gave my skull a good shake and finally tuned in to what my friend was saying. I'd known that Pick had held off saying those three little words throughout the entirety of their relationship. He always explained that he'd never said it to any girl before and he wasn't planning on just throwing something like that around. I knew it infuriated Lisa, but she always made it seem like it was no big deal.

I guess, of course, until he actually said it.

"Lisa, that's amazing. I'm so happy for you guys." I fluffed up my pillows and sank back into them. "So, what, are you guys back together?"

Lisa gave a dreamy sigh on her end. "Yeah. I guess so."

I didn't want to rain on her parade, but it's not like their situation had suddenly changed. "But what about, you know, California?"

She was silent for a moment, then tried to sound chipper as she answered, "Well, we talked about it a lot last night and I mean, Pickford's right. Why wouldn't we at least make the most our time until he leaves for school? I mean, August is still three months away. Why wouldn't we just stay together until then?"

It was the first sensible thing she'd said in regards to her relationship with Pickford- a point of view I'd tried to convince her of myself during their seemingly premature breakup- but I wondered why she'd suddenly seen the light. "Why now, Lis? What's so different this time?"

She gave me an impatient, "Duh. I've been an idiot, okay? I admit it. I was an idiot. There. Are you happy?" She started laughing, and I couldn't help but laugh along with her.

I sure as hell wasn't looking forward to part two of The Big Breakup all over again in August, however.

Her tone changed, so I knew what was coming next. "So... On to more important business. WHAT HAPPENED WITH TRIP?"

I didn't even know where to start. We're friends again? I know I'm still in love with him? It's okay that he's not in love with me?

But I opted for the more evasive route. "We're okay. We had a really great time last night. He took me to the wrap party and I got drunk off the Ferrantes' homemade wine. I have the worst hangover!"

She laughed at that, saying, "Jeez. The theatre fags throw one hell of a party, huh?"

I reminded her that her boyfriend's sister was a "theatre fag", and could have just let the whole subject go at that. But something didn't feel quite right about it. I laughed and said, "Actually, a few of them were really nice. Heather's an absolute sweetheart."

Lisa surprised the hell out of me when she said, "Oh, yeah. Blonde girl, right? Kind of Mary Ingalls? Oh my God! We should set her up with Sargento! Wouldn't they look so cute together?"

Definitely not the reaction I was expecting. But her suggestion wasn't completely off the mark.

Before I could respond, she blurted out, "Oh, hey. I've gotta go. I told Pickford I'd go to church with him this morning. I'll call you back later, okay?"

Church? Who was this person and what had she done with my best friend?

I stuttered, "Uh, o-okay. I'll talk to you later. Bye."

I checked the clock on my nightstand and saw that it was past ten. I knew it was my God-given right as a teenager to sleep the day away, but I'd always been an early riser, and ten was actually a pretty late wakeup hour for me. I got out of bed, deciding that a shower would make me feel a little more like myself again.

I was lathering up my hair, belting out *"Weekend in New England"*, psychically willing Trip to call. It was like five months ago all over again, but this time... Well... this time, I wasn't planning on being a complete moron.

I was, however, only wearing a towel when I walked out of the bathroom and saw Trip at the bottom of the stairs talking to my father.

Our eyes met for only a second before I darted into my bedroom and slammed the door. I heard Dad say, "Well, I guess she was awake after all!" Then he laughed and yelled up to me, "Layla! Trip's here. Please put some clothes on before coming down."

Oh my God I could have just killed the man.

I stubbed my toe on my bed in my haste to get dressed, but managed to throw on a khaki miniskort and black tanktop through the pain. I toweled off my hair and finger-combed it, hoping I didn't look like a drowned rat on my way down the stairs to see Trip.

He was sitting at the kitchen table, making smalltalk with Dad when I walked in casually, as if I hadn't just been caught half-naked only five minutes before. "Hey, Trip. 'Morning, Dad."

I gave my father a kiss on the cheek and poured myself a cup of coffee as Dad excused himself to the garage.

Before I could even take a seat, Trip asked, "How's the hangover?"

I just about dropped the sugar onto the floor. "Oh, God, Trip. Was I a completely wasted mess last night?"

He sat back and smirked at me, this gorgeous boy sitting in my kitchen. "Nah. But you were definitely in rare form."

I brought my mug over to the table and sat down. But before the coffee had even hit my lips, he said, "Hey. Slam that thing down, we've got somewhere to be at twelve."

I lowered my mug just enough to give him a perplexed look over the top of it. "Where're we going?"

He grinned and said, "Just shut up and finish getting yourself ready. I'll meet you out front when you're done."

* * *

I sank back into my chair and crossed my feet at the ankles, fitting them between two of the seats in front of me. The Loews Theater had just undergone a major renovation, turning its three screen, rinkydink movie house into a massive, sprawling tenplex. Trip and I were in one of the newer theaters on the second floor, and I was enjoying the new, reclining seats they'd upgraded with plush leatherette and cupholders.

I grabbed the Diet Coke from mine and took a big sip from the straw. I was still feeling a tad dehydrated, and the soda was ice-cold and hitting just the right spot.

Trip had dragged me there to catch a matinee. Loews always reserved one theater to show classic movies on Saturday and Sunday afternoons; I'd seen *Sound of Music* on that same screen over the holidays, trying to get my mind off Trip at the time by losing myself in one of my all-time, favorite flicks. I thought it was fate or irony or whatever that I was sitting there at that moment not only with him, but while watching Franco Zeffirelli's *Romeo and Juliet*.

Mrs. Mason had originally intended to show it to us during class, but the nuns in the library had "lost" the video. Rumor had it that some scenes were pretty racy, and we figured the sisters had tossed it on a bonfire during a book-burning ceremony or something.

The movie turned out to be really interesting. I'd never seen it before. It was probably the first film that I didn't get to say smugly, "The book was better", as I'd started to share Trip's opinion of Shakespeare and realized that a lot of his writing was tedious, boring and hard to understand in its outdated speech.

But seeing his words play out onscreen was an entirely different animal. The visuals were beautiful, the costumes were gorgeous. The guy who played Romeo was pretty cute, too, so that was simply a bonus.

When it got to our scene, Trip gave me a nudge, saying, "Here we go," and I laughed while trying to concentrate on the screen.

Watching a movie with Trip wasn't like watching it with a normal person. He kept talking through the whole scene, pointing out how we should have done ours differently, gone with our original costume idea, changed the dialogue, filmed it in another location, etc. I was trying to tune him out. Up until that point, I'd just been content to watch a *professional director's* version of the film, without even thinking to compare it to ours. There was Trip, criticizing almost every decision we'd made. Finally, I couldn't take it anymore.

"Trip, I happen to *like* our film. I thought it was great and everyone else did, too." I lowered my voice and added, "*Obv*iously, it's not as good as this, but can you please just shut up and let me watch the movie?"

I gave a huff, crossed my arms and turned my attention back to the screen.

And that's when a handful of popcorn bounced off my face and scattered across my lap.

Chapter 25
CLASS ACTION

Trip and I didn't have much time to spend together over the following couple of weeks. After the prom- which Trip refused to attend for reasons unbeknownst to me- the partying had been put on hold as everyone readied for final exams. Everyone was hit with a case of senioritis, just riding out the minutes until graduation. The days seemed to be flying by so fast at a time I would have rather had everything come to a standstill.

It was scary to think that those were the official final days of my childhood, that I was going to be expected to grow up, go off to school and figure out what I was going to do with the rest of my life. I was pretty stressed out about the whole thing, but did my best to push all those thoughts to the back of my mind for the time being.

Graduation was the first week in June and the weather that Tuesday was looking pretty iffy. No one wanted it to rain, forcing the ceremony inside. Everyone kept their fingers crossed that the weather would hold out just long enough for us to get our diplomas and get to Rymer's afterparty without getting drenched.

Thankfully, aside from a few drizzly raindrops, our commencement ceremony went off without a hitch, and by the time it was over, the sun had actually peeked through for a brief instance before nightfall.

Kuman Royal was our salutatorian and he managed to bore everyone with an uninspiring speech. The boy had been a robot from the time that he was born, so I guessed all that studying didn't allow him to hone his people skills to the hilt.

But then Heather Ferrante took the podium as valedictorian and just rocked the place.

She spoke a lot about "who we were", ticking off our collective memories about talent shows and sporting events and favorite teachers, her mention of Mrs. Catannia bringing a few hoots and wolf whistles from the male members of the audience (as she was the original cougar/TILF/thing-we-had-no-official-name-for at the time), and her reference to the day when Rymer downed a record-setting fourteen frenchbread pizzas in the cafeteria brought about a collective laughing fit, while Rymer stood up and took a bow.

But when she started talking about "who we are" and "who we will be", the audience settled down in order to absorb every word. She talked about our hopes and our goals and about how scary it was going to be to start anew all over again. That we were, in fact, the future and that that responsibility shouldn't be taken lightly. But it was when she was wrapping up her big speech and said- and these words have stayed with me throughout my life- *"We know what we are, but know not what we may be"* - that I noticed a lump in my throat. For the slightest moment, you could hear a pin drop, but then everyone got over their sappy sentimentality as the place erupted in applause.

After the ceremony, we spent some time milling about, saying congratulations to one another and taking pictures. Lisa pointed out the shiny, black corvette in the parking lot sporting a big, red bow; a gift to some lucky, spoiled graduate being presented all showy like in some tacky movie.

I gave Mrs. Mason a high-five on my way out to the oval lawn, who took the opportunity to offer some parting words of wisdom as she smiled, winked and said, "Give 'em hell, Layla."

Trip was standing with his parents, so I went over to say hello. His face lit up when he saw me. "Layla! Hey, come meet my sister!"

I was introduced to Claudia Wilmington, in town from San Diego for the auspicious occasion. I knew that she was twenty-three and had been living out in California since she was eighteen, never having moved back in with her nomadic family after college.

I also knew that she was living with her girlfriend, and that her parents didn't have any clue about it.

I said hello to everyone, and Mrs. Wilmington was her usual chipper self, smoothing a hand over Trip's hair, trying to ready him for a photo. His father was friendly enough, but he seemed distracted as if he had somewhere else more important to be instead of at his only son's graduation. But they both said hello pleasantly, and Mr. Wilmington told me to get next to Trip for a picture, so I sidled up and threw my arm over his shoulder. Trip flashed me one of his evil grins and then scooped me up in his arms, the both of us cracking up as his father snapped the photo.

We said goodbye to his family and went to find my dad and Bruce. They were standing with Lisa, Pickford and the DeSantos, and we all said hello before the cameras came out. I managed to get a congratulations and a few snapshots out of my brother before he took off, but then my dad and Lisa's dad used up like twelve more rolls of film taking pictures of the rest of us.

On the way out to the parking lot, Trip and I spotted Heather and I ran over to give her a big hug. "Heather! What an amazing speech!"

For all her beautiful words that night, she stood there at that moment practically speechless. Finally, she stammered out, "Th-thank you."

I saw Trip give her a wink as I asked, "Are you going to Rymer's?"

She looked over my shoulder for a quick second before answering, "Oh, no, no. I don't think so."

"Oh, come on. It's going to be so much fun. He invited the whole class! You just have to be there, okay? Just grab a friend and go. I'm expecting to see you." I took a look at Trip and added, "*We're* expecting you. Please come."

Heather blew out the breath she'd been holding. "Yeah, okay. Maybe I'll show up for a little while."

"Thatta girl" Trip said, before we went our separate ways.

* * *

I pit-stopped home to freshen up, ditch my graduation gown and touch up my hair and makeup. It was tradition for the grads at St. Norman's to wear white on graduation day, and I loved the chiffon tank dress I'd found, the way the A-line skirt fanned out from hip to knee. Every step I took made me feel like a prima ballerina, the silky fabric floating around my legs.

I'd blown my hair out straight so that my graduation cap would fit on my head, but mostly, I was trying to look more classic and natural, like Michelle Pfeiffer at the end of *Grease 2*. I changed out my silver hoops for my diamond studs, put my St. Christopher medal on and did one last mirror check before running downstairs to say goodbye to Dad and Bruce. My brother and all the other underclassmen still had three days of exams to look forward to, and the public schools weren't due to let out for weeks. Seeing as it was a Tuesday, we knew that the town of Norman would belong exclusively to the senior Class of '91 that night.

I headed outside just as Trip was pulling in the driveway. On my way down to his truck, I could see him just sitting there behind the wheel smiling at me as I approached. By the time I opened the door, I realized the look I saw on his face could only be described as... proud.

"Hey, Chester," I offered by way of a greeting. I only called him that when we were alone; one, because I didn't want to sell him out, and two, because I liked having a secret kept just between the two of us.

"Hey there, Lay-Lay. Looking good, I see."

I smiled back in answer, caught off guard because I never knew what to say whenever he threw a compliment my way. He looked gorgeous in his dark blue jeans and white, button-down shirt with the sleeves rolled up. "You, too," I said, trying to keep everything in perspective. I mean, we were still taking these little babysteps, still working on getting our friendship back on track. I had to remind myself of that.

We got to Rymer's where the party was already in full swing. We made our way out to the back deck together, and I couldn't help but be reminded how it was Tess who'd been his date for the last deck party. And this time it was me. Well, sort of.

Rymer was in rare form- the full keg he'd picked up hours before was his treat- filling up cups and passing them out like candy on Halloween. I grabbed my beer and headed into the kitchen, looking for some bowls to put snacks into. I saw Margie Caputo, and before I could even say hello or wish her congratulations, she snipped out, "*You* came here with Trip?"

I was surprised by her tone and just answered, "Mmm hmm."

I went about my task, opening a bag of Ruffles and dumping them into one of the Tupperware bowls that was waiting on the table. Margie gave a snort and spat back, "So, what, are you guys like back together again or something?"

I folded the empty bag and threw it in the trash as I shot a confused look her way. When I saw the snotty look on her face, I decided to say, "Um, not that I owe you an explanation, but we're just friends."

She crossed her arms and added, "Well, no wonder. I heard you wouldn't give it up and that's why he broke up with you."

What?

I was stunned on about twenty different levels.

Firstly, I couldn't believe how Margie was talking to me. It's not like we were bestest buddies or anything, but we'd always been friendly with each other over the years. Yet there she was, talking at me as if our friendship suddenly didn't exist.

Mostly, I was surprised at what she'd said about Trip and me. People thought we were a couple at one point? And they thought we'd broken up because I was holding out on him?

I was fairly shocked to find I was the subject of a very misinformed grapevine. God. Didn't people have anything better to do with their time than talk shit about other people's lives?

I leaned against the counter across from Margie with my arms crossed, mirroring her same pose. I felt my anger rising like a heat wave up the back of my neck. Any minute, steam would start escaping from my ears.

"First of all, you have absolutely no idea what you're talking about." I leaned forward, trying to seem intimidating, and aimed two fingers in her direction to continue, "And secondly, it's none of your business!" I only half-registered that Lisa had entered the kitchen as I added, "What the hell is your problem tonight anyway? Are you serious?"

Margie snorted back, "Are *you*? What, you think a guy like Trip enjoys your company so much, he's willing to take cold showers every night?"

What was up with her? What a psychopath!

Before I could get over my astonishment and say a single word, Lisa piped up. "What do *you* care?"

Margie actually had the bad taste to look smug as she said, "Well, I got to second with him, which was further than *her*."

Lisa snapped back, "Yeah, in front of everyone, trampoid. Too bad you skipped first, probably because he couldn't risk taking the bag off your head."

Margie's jaw dropped open, but she didn't dare say anything back. She knew she'd been outmatched. She just gave a huff and stormed out of the room, leaving Lisa and me to look at each other in disbelief.

I would have laughed, but I was still too taken aback to find any humor in the situation. I mean, Margie and I didn't hang out every other minute, but we were sociable enough in school, and even if that weren't the case, I thought she had acted entirely out of line. I didn't know where the nasty streak was coming from.

Two hours later, we saw her making out with Rymer in the hallway, so Lisa and I figured she must have just been completely drunk. Or on drugs. Or had survived a massive blow with a blunt object to her head.

How else to explain not only the bad attitude toward me, but the fact that she was hooking up with *Rymer*?

Speaking of hooking up... Sargento and Heather seemed to be hitting it off, without any intervention from me or Lisa, so it was like they were meant to be. But even more unexpected was watching Cooper lavish attention on Heather's friend Becca all night. I knew she'd had a crush on him forever and I couldn't help thinking that if Coop hadn't spent the better part of the past six months nursing my broken heart, those two could have gotten something going a lot sooner. Now, with only a summer left before we all went our separate ways, I felt like I'd robbed both of them the chance to actually give the relationship a real go.

Standing there watching them gave me the smallest attack of jealousy. Not so much that Coop had finally gotten over me, but more because I'd spent my entire senior year basically single, in love with someone who would never see me as more than a friend. It was agony, but I was learning to deal with it, because I knew it was even more tortuous when Trip was totally cut out of my life. After half a year in that state, I'd already decided that having him as a friend was better than not having him at all.

I felt an arm slip around my waist and turned my head to see Trip smiling behind me. How did I live the past months, not seeing him smile at me like that? I gave his arm a quick squeeze as he asked, "Having fun yet?"

I could feel the length of his body pressed right up against mine from my shoulder to my calves. Yeah. I'd say I was having fun.

"Yep. Another Rymer party. Fun, fun, fun."

He laughed and released me from our hug. "Jeez, Lay. That dress is something else. I almost feel like I should take you out of here to ah, you know..." then he leaned in to whisper, "go *dancing*."

Such a tease.

I was thinking of calling him out for being a big flirt, but instead, the words that came out of my mouth were, "Actually, you think we could find somewhere to go talk?"

He raised an eyebrow, almost mocking me for suggesting we "go talk", which in high school world, was a euphemism for "make out". But he saw the serious look on my face and must have decided not to bust my chops. "Yeah, sure. I kinda figured you'd want to eventually. Let's start saying goodbye while we polish of our drinks."

"Sounds like a plan."

141

Chapter 26
GUILTY BY SUSPICION

We'd decided to head back to his house, knowing that we'd have the place to ourselves. His sister and parents had gone into the city to have a late dinner in Mr. Wilmington's new *TRU* hotel, which was slated for the grand opening in a few weeks.

Since we only had about a three-minute ride, I decided not to get into any in-depth conversation until we hit the house. I was looking forward to getting rid of the awkwardness between us, hash out any lingering kinks about our standoff and get up to date on what we'd both been up to in our lives since then. As great as it was to have him back in my life, there was still this implicit unease that hung like a cloud over our friendship.

When we pulled into the driveway, I couldn't believe the house I was looking at. It was a huge, stone mansion with oversized windows and a steeply pitched roof, the sheer size of the massive structure dwarfing the surrounding pine trees.

Trip's voice broke my gawking. "Oh, shit. They're home."

I noticed the Mercedes parked in front of the garage doors and wondered what the big deal was. I didn't really see too much of a problem. The Wilmingtons lived in a mansion. I was sure we'd be able to find some privacy somewhere in the humongous house.

I got out of the truck, saying, "Yeah, so?" and started to walk up to the front door, Trip asking, "Hey, you want to go to the diner or something instead?"

I tossed over my shoulder, "What's the matter, Chester? You don't have anything to eat here?"

He opened the door, saying, "You really gotta stop calling me that."

I laughed, then was immediately silenced by the sight of the foyer I was standing in. Easily the size of half my entire house, the room was three stories of white-painted federal paneling with an elaborate, curving staircase that reminded me of Twelve Oaks.

I'd never seen anything so extravagant in real life, but I tried to sound unaffected when I remarked, "This place is a real shithole, huh."

He just rolled his eyes.

I was going to ask which direction I should head in, when a light flicked on from the hallway upstairs and Mr. Wilmington's voice yelled down. "Terrence, is that you?" It was easily two in the morning and I hoped that Trip's parents were up because they'd just gotten home themselves, not because we'd woken them.

Trip started to shuffle me into the next room, saying, "Yeah, Dad. It's just me and Layla."

I shot Trip a guilty look, hoping he wasn't going to get in trouble for bringing friends home in the middle of the night when his father chortled out, "Layla? The Warren whore's girl? What's *she* doing in our house?"

I don't know how long I stood in that foyer, my jaw dropped wide open and my eyes bugging out of my head, but it was probably no more than a second. It felt a lot longer. It felt like I'd been slapped.

Trip looked as though he'd been punched in the stomach. His posture deflated instantaneously at the burden of his father's words. He turned toward me, all broken empathy, but I was only able to catch his eye for an instant before making a break for the front door.

I flew down the front steps and bolted down the walkway, my only goal to get as far away from the scene as possible, when I suddenly realized I had nowhere to go. Trip drove me there and I was miles from home. I didn't even have the comfort and sanctuary of my own car to assist in the escape.

I ran the length of the long driveway, my heart beating wildly even though it felt as though my blood had frozen in my veins.

When I hit the iron gate near the street, I stopped running. I sank to the ground at the curb, the full force of Mr. Wilmington's words sinking in and finding purchase.

Whore.

I guess I always knew that there had to be whisperings around town about my mother. Norman's a small town, after all. But the fact was, up until that point, no one had ever been so blunt as to actually say anything to me about it. I'd been suffering under the delusion that maybe, just maybe, everyone *didn't* know the whole story.

People always describe small towns as *quaint* or *cozy* or *familiar*. "You know who your neighbors are," they always seemed to say. But what you won't find depicted in a Norman Rockwell painting is how cruel those same neighbors can be. I suppose living in a small town isn't for those that have something to hide. I guess that realization is what made my mother finally leave.

At the time, I remember being so grateful that at least my father chose to keep the family right where we were instead of uprooting us and moving away. But I can't imagine what he must have endured in order to do so. Aside from the ghost of his wife that lurked in every familiar corner of town, he had to deal with the sewing circles, the store owners and the PTO. All those wagging tongues and "tsk, tsk, tsks" behind his back had to drive him batty. Oh, sure, there was sympathy. But I guess sympathy takes a backseat to a juicy bit of gossip any day of the week around here.

Where did those people get off? Wasn't it enough that my poor father was left to raise my brother and me all by himself? That Bruce and me were suddenly motherless? That the three of us had to endure the guilt, the unanswered questions, the *hole* that my mother left behind when she went away?

Whore.

Of *course* that's all anyone thought about my mother. Why wouldn't they?

No one knew her as I did, for too brief a time, dancing in the kitchen or frosting a lopsided birthday cake or singing showtunes at the top of her lungs to wake me up in the morning. The way she'd stand at the window and open the shades, the morning sun backlighting her honey hair and making her look like an angel.

144

No. To Mr. Wilmington and most likely the entire town, Kate Warren's entire existence can be summed up in one word: *whore*.

I swiped my arm across my dampened face and looked down at what I was wearing; unexpectedly assessing my clothes with new, albeit blurred eyes. Suddenly, my dress seemed too short, the sleeveless top showed too much shoulder. I loved that dress only a few short hours ago, but Mr. Wilmington's outburst had me feeling overly self-conscious. Exposed.

Whore.

I heard Trip's sneakers pounding against the blacktop and coming to a stop at my back. He blew out a heavy breath and silently sank onto the grass behind me.

I didn't lift my face from my hands.

"It's true," I said.

"What?"

"It's true," I reiterated before explaining. "About my mother. What your father said. That she's... she's a..."

"Layla, stop it."

I lifted my head, but I still couldn't find it in me to turn and look him in the face. "No. I told you my mother wasn't around, but you don't know the whole story. She *left* us, Trip! She was probably screwing half the town when finally, she just up and left us for one of her boyfriends. And everyone knows it. Including your father."

"My *father* is an *asshole*."

"Yeah, well, he may be an asshole, but at least he's still around. At least he's still *here*."

"Oh, you think that's *better*?"

"Better than being left behind? Better than watching your father overcompensate every single day because he's trying to make up for whatever part he *thinks* he played in her leaving? Better than being left to deal with the fallout of my mother's *stellar* reputation? Yeah. I think that's better."

Trip didn't know what to say, I guess, but it's not as though I was giving him a whole lot of air to respond, launching into a hysterical rant. "You don't know what it's like, to be a girl

145

without a mother! Having to do things like go on your first date, or start high school or get ready for the prom, knowing she's not going to be there. You don't know what it's like to stare down a random woman on the street, wondering if maybe this time, it could really be her. You don't know how impossible- how *completely freaking impossible* it is- to try and make sense of any of it, every single solitary day of your life, just wanting to know... *WHY?*"

I took a huge shaky breath into my lungs, trying to calm myself down. I'd gotten my crying under control, but I'm sure I was a puffy, red mess. "You just can't possibly know. I mean, your mom is so great!"

"Yeah, you're right, Lay. I *don't* know. And she is. But I look at it like she's the saving grace for the fact that my father's a total dick."

"But he seems so..."

"Nice?"

"Yeah. The way he smiles and jokes around and stuff."

"Well, he is. Nice, I mean. When he's not drinking."

Drinking... Wait- what?

I couldn't make sense of it at first. Trip was trying to tell me that his father was... an *alcoholic*? But it was just too weird that someone I knew was actually dealing with a thing like that, something you normally only see on TV. Yet there it was.

"He's like, multiple personalities or something. One minute, he's my dad, the guy that shows up to my hockey matches and is able to run a billion dollar company."

The word "billion" almost made me choke, and I hoped Trip was just throwing it around to exaggerate his point.

"The next, he's got a few scotches in him and he turns into the meanest, snarliest asshole you'd ever want to meet. I never know which guy is waiting for me when I get home."

I took the confession as something hard for Trip to tell me. It sucked that he seemed so embarrassed about something he had so little to do with. I finally glanced over my shoulder to see him sitting sullenly at the edge of the yard. His shoulders were slumped as he picked at the blades of grass between his feet. My personal concerns left me as I realized I wasn't the only one hurt and embarrassed back in the house.

I swung my legs around as modestly as possible, no easy feat while wearing a skirt and pivoting on my backside. Under normal circumstances, Trip would have reveled in the opportunity to catch a flash of girl panties, but he was a little preoccupied with his own thoughts at the time.

We sat in silence for a moment until Trip said, "I'm sorry about what my dad said in there. He had no right to talk to you like that."

I gave a shrug, touched by his words, but not knowing what to say. I mean, it wasn't *his* fault that his father said what he did. Why should Trip have to be the one to apologize?

I started picking grass along with him, arranging the occasional blade between my thumbs and blowing, trying to make it whistle. I always sucked at that. Trip decided to join me, with more success, showing off yet another of his innumerable skills. Always showing off. I rolled my eyes and flung my grass back from whence it came.

It was nice being there with him, sitting on the cool lawn in the dark; unspeaking and calm, sharing our secrets and trusting each other to keep them. Funny how our platonic status was bringing me comfort instead of anguish for once.

I leaned into Trip, nudging him off-balance in order to try and cheer us both up. I was thinking it was time to break the mood and get out of there, maybe grab some fries and gravy at The King Neptune.

"Hey Chester," I said. "Ya wanna make out?" I raised my eyebrows a couple of times for added effect. Very Groucho Marx.

I was expecting him to laugh. I was expecting him to take my hand, haul me to my feet and bring me with him to hit the diner.

I wasn't expecting him to turn his broken eyes to mine, skim a hand up my arm and whisper, "*Yes.*"

147

Before I knew what was happening, his palm was gliding up the side of my neck, slowly pulling my face to his. I was sure he could hear my heart beating out of my chest as he lowered his beautiful, full lips to mine and holy shit I was kissing Trip Wilmington.

My panic instantly gave way to the rush of pure heat his kiss instilled in me; all my wishful thinking, all my months of yearning, finally culminating in a moment I thought would never come. His lips were soft and insistent, his breath sugary and warm against my skin. I felt the pressure of his hand pulling my face tighter to his as he opened his mouth against mine, gently, allowing his tongue to make a brief exploration between my lips. He tasted so good, the heat of his sweet breath mingling with mine, my heart threatening to pound its way out of my chest.

I briefly considered the mortifying thought that it was only a pity kiss, but that idea was banished when Trip pulled back enough to whisper against my lips, "Do you have any idea how long I've wanted to do that?"

Not nearly as long as me, pal.

I slid my hands into the hair at his nape and his mouth opened fully over mine and the next thing I became aware of was his arms wrapping tightly around me as he lowered me onto the grass.

* * *

Lisa just about had a flipping heart attack on the phone when I told her about hooking up with Trip. I couldn't bear to get into the events leading up to said hookup, however, and just relayed the highlights. "Oh my God, Layla! So, you guys are like, dating now, right?"

"Lis- The truth is, I don't know and I don't care."

"Yeah, right."

"No, seriously. Whatever this is, I'm totally fine with it. I swear."

"Don't you think you're selling yourself a little short?"

"Actually, no. I'm happy enough just to have him back in my life. The hooking up is just a bonus. Seriously."

"Well, if you're happy, I'm happy for you."

"Thanks. Hey- How's Pick?"

"He's great. I'm just trying to savor every day right now. I don't know what I'm going to do when it's time for him to leave!"

"He's dead set on going, huh."

"Yeah. I mean, it's a really great opportunity for him. How can he turn down a full scholarship? Plus, he'll get to play basketball."

I felt like Lisa was trying to convince herself more than she was trying to convince me. But I simply said, "That's great!"

When she didn't elaborate, I knew her head had gone off in a daze just thinking about it. So, I tried to keep things cheery. "Hey, look on the bright side. We could maybe fly out there and visit him next winter! I've always wanted to go to L.A. and it would be nice to escape the freezing cold for a little while, don't you think? Maybe he can hook me up with Johnny Depp or something. I'm sure they'll be like best friends by then!"

Not like that was my best material or anything, but Lisa barely gave a chuckle. I figured she wasn't in a cheering-up mood.

"Hey, so I'll pick you up at nine-thirty tomorrow, right?"

She still had that far-off tone in her voice when she answered, "Yeah... Sure. See you then."

I hung up and started packing some stuff into my duffel bag. The whole crew had rented a house down in Seaside for a post-grad celebration. It sucked that we had to pay for a whole week even though we were only going to be there for half of it, but the houses down the shore don't rent by the day. Even the seediest places rented on a Saturday to Saturday basis. Since the rental arrangements had been made by Rymer and Sargento, I was pretty sure that our place was going to be the seediest of all.

Chapter 27
ANOTHER 48 HOURS

Lisa and I pulled up to the front curb of the rental house and almost died laughing. The place was a perfect, two-storied rectangle of *brown*. The roof and the siding were both covered in dark cedar shingles; the front door, the window frames and even the shutters were painted to match. The only bright spots on the entire façade were a ten foot, light blue smiling plastic whale over the front door and the row of pinwheels across the railing of the small brown balcony on the second floor.

Lisa got out of the car and stood on the sidewalk, nearly doubled over with laughter. "Holy Jesus, I can't even imagine what's waiting for us inside!"

But I had already decided I didn't care about that, because I had just seen what was waiting for me *outside*.

Sprinting up the driveway, wearing nothing but his swim trunks and looking as delicious as ever, was Trip.

He waved me into the driveway, miming where I should park. Before I could even put the car in gear, Lisa gave me the raised eyebrows and laughed, "I think I'll just meet you in the house."

The drive ran straight through to a garage in the rear, where the blacktop fanned out and took over half of the small backyard. I squeezed my car between Coop's Audi and Rymer's truck and got out. I was feeling a tad cautious, not knowing how I should greet Trip. I mean, was grad night just a fluke? A one-time thing?

I watched as he bounded toward me with the most elated grin, not even trying to hide how excited he was to see me. One look at Trip's face and I found myself vaulting the few steps that separated us and leaping into his arms. I wrapped my legs around his waist and landed a huge smooch against his smiling lips.

And then suddenly, the hello kiss took an entirely different turn.

He gave a brief look over his shoulder, before maneuvering us between the cars and backing me against Rymer's truck. I started to put my feet on the ground, but he buried his head in my neck and whispered heavily, "No, don't."

He caught me under a knee with his hand and hitched my left leg back over his hip. His other hand was tangled in my hair and his mouth opened over mine as he pressed his body against me.

His breathing sounded ragged and I could hear a low hum stirring in his throat, the sound making me catch my breath as well.

I could feel his rising need through the thin bathing suit, hard and insistent, driving into the bikini bottoms under my skirt. Wow. I guessed he really *was* excited to see me. Had I known *this* was waiting for me, I'd have violated every traffic law known to man just to get down in record-breaking time.

I almost melted into him, my body turning as gooey as the steaming driveway blacktop as I returned his kiss, running my hands along his neck, his shoulders, his bare chest.

It felt so amazing, his lips open over mine, his exposed skin under my palms, his demanding body pressed so intimately against me. I was half in a trance by the time he pulled his face back slightly and whispered, "Hi."

"Hi," I said right back, breathless and smiling into those gorgeous, ocean eyes.

"Took you long enough to get here."

Tell me about it. After an eternity of waiting, there I was, finally in the arms of Trip Effing Wilmington.

I laughed and said, "Yeah, it feels like it took forever."

* * *

Once Trip adjusted himself in his shorts and grabbed my bag from the trunk, we headed for the house. Turned out, the inside wasn't much better than the outside. Pickford was the first to greet us from his post in the kitchen, working an assembly line of sandwiches, apparently preparing lunch for the lot of us. Wow, that was pretty nice of him. Who knew he had a Betty Crocker streak?

"Hey, Pick," I said in greeting, while my eyes scanned the horrors of the room. Earth-toned, flowered wallpaper served as a backdrop for the dark walnut cabinets; a yellow formica countertop and avocado refrigerator rounded out the décor quite fittingly. I noticed that Trip was watching me appraise the room, so I pursed my lips and looked at him wide-eyed. He shrugged his shoulders and said, "You haven't seen the living room yet." Pick's head dropped and his shoulders shook as he laughed silently to himself.

I was ushered into a- yep, you guessed it- *brown,* paneled room, decorated in early Americana.

Make that *very* early Americana.

A thirteen-starred flag was strung up behind the brown leather recliner Lisa was sitting in. We exchanged a silent look of *whatthehell?* as I took notice of the bookshelves just crammed with every patriotic knickknack and memento ever created in the good ol' U.S. of A. Tacky eagle statues, framed pictures of civil war soldiers, commemorative plates, shadowboxes of medals... Did the owners of this dive forget that it was a beach house?

I said hello to Rymer and Sargento, who were sitting on the brown and orange plaid tweed couch playing Sega, the only modern thing in the room. It was as though the place had been sealed up during a bicentennial celebration and we were the first brave souls to have walked back through the door.

Lisa must have waited for me before slamming on our friends. "Hey, nice digs, guys. What, you couldn't find an older house? This place is much too fancy for us."

Rymer didn't bother looking up from the game he was playing. "Can it, DeSanto! What the hell do you expect for four hundred bucks a week?"

Lisa just rolled her eyes at me. I walked to the other side of the large living room and peeked my head down a small hallway. I scanned my eyes over the two bedrooms there, but decided I wasn't brave enough to check out the bathroom just yet. I turned toward the east side of the living room and took note of the screened-in side porch. At least the place was pretty big. Plus, we were on a corner lot only a block from the boardwalk, so that was pretty cool. I did, however, pray that that wasn't the only bathroom in the house.

Trip led the tour upstairs where there were three, slightly newer, slightly brighter bedrooms and, thank God, another full bath that looked somewhat clean.

He gestured toward the larger room, the one that faced the beach. I could see the pinwheeled balcony through the double sliders and figured it must be the master bedroom. Before I could even think of calling dibs, Trip said, "Forget it. Pick already won the coin toss."

He dropped my bag in the middle room, and said, "*This* is you. And that-" he added, pointing to the room directly next to it, "-is me."

I could see him fighting a smile, probably envisioning all the many ways he was planning on corrupting me throughout the weekend.

He gave a small bow and said, "I hope you'll enjoy your stay with us, Miss Warren. Please feel free to utilize my services at any time, at any hour. I am available to attend to your, ah, *every need* twenty-four-seven. Even in the middle of the night." He stepped closer and ran his hands down my arms, looking right through me with half-lidded eyes and smirked out, "*Especially* in the middle of the night..."

I just shook my head and kissed him lightly on the lips. I was mentally going over the room assignments when I realized our group was short by one. "Hey, where's Cooper?"

Trip's face took on a scowl. "Layla, seriously?"

"What?" I asked, even though I had suddenly realized how bad my question must have sounded to Trip's ears. I guessed it was probably kind of weird and uncomfortable for him, having to spend the following days under the same roof as my ex. My sympathy was followed- I'm ashamed to admit- by the thrill of realizing that he was actually a little jealous about the whole thing.

It was almost comical, the way his shoulders drooped, making him look wholly deflated, and, I might add, completely adorable.

"I just offer you an invitation to basically steal my virtue, and while you're kissing me, *that's* when you decide it's the best time to ask me about another guy? Jeez, Lay, talk about dejection."

It was the "steal my virtue" line that let me know he wasn't really upset. Otherwise, everything else from the look on his face to the tone in his voice would have made me think he was one-hundred-percent serious. Pulling a DeNiro on me.

I started to try and match his serious delivery, but I started laughing before I even got out one single word. Trip finally cracked, too, before I threw my arms around his shoulders and said, "Maybe you'd better try harder to keep me focused on you." *As if that was ever a problem.*

He was still laughing as he said, "Oh, yeah?" and dropped his face to mine for a kiss.

I could tell it was gonna be one hell of a weekend.

Chapter 28
PRISONERS OF THE SUN

Cooper, as it turned out, had been on the beach with Becca Bradley all morning. As Trip, Lisa, Pick and I made our way down to them, Heather Ferrante was walking up from the water. Huh. I didn't even know they were coming.

"Hey, everyone," Coop yelled in greeting. "We saved you a spot."

We laughed as we set up our chairs and blankets on the nearly vacant beach. There were only a few other people along our stretch of sand, and barely more than that walking the boards. Even though it was a sweltering hot, sun-shiny day, the official season didn't really kick off until the first week of July. Most kids didn't get out of school for another two weeks, so we practically had the whole town to ourselves. One of the very few perks of a Catholic education.

"Oh, hey, Coop!" I yelled three people down. "Pick made you guys some lunch." I twisted around to grab the small cooler behind my chair and passed it over Trip to Heather. Trip, of course, used the opportunity to try and steal a peek down my coverup. When he finally raised his eyes, I gave him a look that let him know he'd been busted. He grinned shamelessly, but before he could offer commentary, I stood up, facing his chair.

Coop and the girls were busy rifling through the cooler while Lisa and Pick looked as though they were in the middle of some sort of heated argument. I unzipped my white, terrycloth coverup and let it fall into the sand.

Ha! Trip stopped grinning.

I was wearing a lethal turquoise bikini that was scarcely more than four triangles held together with string. It was barely swimming season, but I'd managed to get in the occasional lap over the past few weeks. I was pretty pleased with the way my toned bod remembered to come back after a winter of neglect. Plus, I was rockin' some serious boobage in that bikini top.

Trip noticed.

I pretended to be oblivious as I sat back down on my chair, adjusted the armrests to recline and tipped my head toward the sun.

I heard Trip's chair creak a mere second before I felt his breath near my face, but still I kept my eyes closed.

His low whisper against my ear caused a tingle along my skin as he spat out through clenched teeth, "Jesus *Christ*, Lay."

I cracked one eye in his direction and saw a muscle twitching in his jaw and the wolfish look in his greedy eyes. I started to chuckle.

I was sitting there, stifling a giggle, so thrilled to have his full attentions as he whispered, "It's not funny, Layla. Look at me! I'm not going to be able to get out of this chair for an hour!"

I looked down at his lap and took notice of the huge... *towel* folded across his legs. And then I cracked up.

Just then, Pick stood and hauled Lisa to her feet. "Hey. Anyone want to take a walk down to the water?"

Before I knew what I was doing, I yelled, "Trip does!"

And then I just lost it.

* * *

We'd all grabbed some dinner at Midway and polished off our cheesesteaks and sausage and pepper sandwiches on the walk back to the house. No easy accomplishment while lugging all our beach stuff at the same time.

By the time we got back, Rymer and Sargento had wrapped up their Sega marathon and were already hitting the beer. They were ecstatic when Cooper handed them the greasy brown paper bag from Midway and dove right in.

I watched as Heather grabbed a roll of paper towels and brought them to the table for Sargento. I thought she must have had the patience of a saint. The girl hardly knew any of us, yet came all the way down to the beach on Sargento's invite. He then proceeded to spend the entirety of Day One holed up in the disgusting house playing video games, completely ignoring his guest.

But then, I saw the way he looked over at her mid-chew and gave her a wink. Heather just lit up like a firefly, smiling back at him.

Maybe the guy just needed to fine-tune his boyfriend skills. It'd been quite a while since he had a woman in his life. And damn. Lisa was right. They really looked so cute together.

I, on the other hand, must have looked a fright. I was sticky and sweaty from the day on the beach, my hair was twisted into a windblown knot on the top of my head, and after a sausage and pepper sandwich, all I could think about was brushing my teeth. "Yeesh. I think I'm gonna hit the showers. Anyone else need to get in there first?"

I flinched when I felt the can of ice cold beer Trip was holding to my neck. I turned as he cracked it open and handed it over. He tapped his can against mine and said, "Knock this back first."

Lisa cranked the radio and everyone grabbed a drink, and before long, the guys decided to get a game of Quarters going. I downed the last of my beer and finally excused myself upstairs for a much-anticipated shower.

I grabbed my bag from one of the bottom bunks of my assigned bedroom and headed into the bath. Stripping down in front of the mirror, I took note of my new tan lines, acknowledging my overly red nose and shoulders. I hoped a good scrubbing and some aloe would even out my skintone.

By the time I put on clean clothes and blew out my hair, I was feeling like a new woman.

Normally, we all would have headed up to the boardwalk for at least a little while, played some wheels and hit some rides. But even though it was summer for us, the official season didn't start until the shore towns said so. Most of the attractions on the pier were shut down during weekdays, until the influx of tourists started trickling in sometime near the end of June. A few booths got a jump on the season, but it was kind of depressing wandering around a veritable ghost town just to search out the random, open stand. Come Friday, though, the place would be hopping.

I headed downstairs and resigned myself to a night in the house. Not that I was complaining, however. Trip was at the kitchen table, laughing with the guys and looking like a bronze god. He must have braved the downstairs shower, because he was sitting there all clean and shiny, his gorgeous straw mane sporting new golden highlights from an afternoon in the sun.

He was busy bouncing quarters into a cup, so I grabbed myself a beer and took a seat on the counter next to Becca to watch. I didn't really know her too well, but I figured I'd better change that. If Cooper was as smitten as I suspected he was, this girl might be around for a while.

I put my beer can on the counter next to me, crossed my legs Indian-style and plunked a nearby bowl of chips in my lap. "Want some?" I offered to Becca.

"Yeah, sure, thanks." She reached over and plucked a single chip out of the bowl, nibbling daintily while we watched the boys' game. As hard as I tried, I could never pull off such a girly-girl move so naturally. Sad fact was that my inner tomboy was alive and well, especially around food.

I'd been mulling that over when Becca's words broke my train of thought. "Um. I uh, wanted to thank you for what you said to Cooper about me."

Wait, what? What had I said?

I guess the question played out on my face, because she clarified, "When you told him that you thought I was..." she lowered her voice and flushed a sweet shade of pink to continue, "so *pretty*."

A faint recollection of a long ago conversation with Coop played out in my mind. The previous spring, during Junior year while we were "dating", he and I were at his locker together. I'd noticed Becca sneaking looks at Cooper from across the hall, and mentioned it to him. What she didn't know is that my words were something more along the lines of, "Wow. Becca Bradley is actually *so pretty*. It's a shame that people don't notice that more." But I was hoping that Cooper had left that second part off.

I smiled at her and answered, "Well, you are!"

Her blush deepened as she smiled out, "Thank you." I held the bowl of chips in her direction, but she waved it away. See what I mean about how girly she was? I mean, who the heck only eats *one chip*?

I crammed a few in my mouth and was chomping away as she added, "Coop said that was the first time he'd ever really noticed me, because of what you said. He said that he never had the nerve to ask me out until Heather and I showed up to Rymer's grad party the other night."

My first thought was that Coop was so tied up in my BS and *that's* why he hadn't asked her out until then. But then I realized she wasn't trying to thank me for the compliment, but for the fact that she and Coop had finally gotten together, however indirectly, because of me. Wasn't I the one who insisted Heather and she go to Rymer's? Would they have ever shown up on their own to one of our parties otherwise? The honest answer was no. Only because, in the four years we'd gone to school together, that was the first appearance those two girls had *ever* made within our social stratosphere. I didn't want to throw my arm out patting myself on the back or anything, because truth be told, I wasn't the only one who deserved credit. When I connected the dots from Becca and Heather to me, there was still one degree of separation between us.

"You know," I started, nodding my head in the direction of the table, "the person you should really be thanking is Trip. I wouldn't have even met you girls if it weren't for him."

We both watched as Trip got to his feet, aimed an elbow at Cooper and yelled "Consume! Consume!" at the top of his lungs.

I shot a look at my new friend. "As you can see, clearly this is a man entirely capable of masterminding your fate."

That made us both crack up. I grabbed my beer can and held it out to hers, she tapped her drink against mine and we both took a swig.

Chapter 29
AFTER DARK, MY SWEET

I spent the bulk of my night hanging with Becca and Heather, seeing as "our men" were preoccupied with their drinking games all night. After Quarters came Beer Pong, and then Coop broke out a deck of cards to play Asshole. I talked the girls into joining in, and after explaining the game rules, Heather proceeded to kick each and every one of our butts.

Lisa and Pick had been anti-social all night, spending most of their evening out on the porch arguing, which wasn't normally their style. I wondered what was going on. By midnight, they were totally MIA anyway, and I figured they must have decided to turn in. I couldn't very well blame them for sneaking off to bed so early. We were all still trying to catch up on our shuteye since the allnighter after graduation.

By the time Rymer slurringly suggested that we play Strip Poker, I decided it was time to turn in, too. We'd been drinking since dinnertime, and even at my nursing pace, I was definitely feeling a little buzzed. Whatever snacks we had in the house had long since been demolished, our dinner sandwiches a distant memory, leaving no absorption in my stomach for all that beer.

The guys were flat-out drunk, singing along to *"Comfortably Numb"* when I stood up to take my leave. I gave a stretching yawn, apologized for being the turd in the punch bowl and went upstairs. I brushed my teeth and started to head into my room, but my feet had other ideas, succumbing to the tractor beam of Trip's room instead.

All the bedrooms had window fans, but they didn't serve as much defense against the day's blazing heat. The only areas that had air-conditioning were the kitchen and the living room, and after spending the past few hours downstairs, the warmth on the second floor was almost unbearable. I slipped under the sheets anyway, seeing as I was wearing only my bra and panties. Even though I was executing a pretty bold plan for Trip to find me undressed in his bed, I still wanted to maintain *some* semblance of mystery.

Whether the party broke up within minutes of my departure or Trip realized there might be a chance for an even better party upstairs, I have no idea. But I had just barely settled myself into his bed when I heard his footsteps coming up the stairwell.

The cocky bastard didn't even bother peeking his head into my room before strolling into his own, a sly grin playing at his lips as if he wasn't even the least bit surprised to find me there.

"Hi," he drawled, before swaying the few steps over and placing his hands at the foot of the mattress. He clutched the sheet over my toes with one hand and leisurely pulled it toward him, revealing my waiting form one excruciating inch at a time. The painstaking slide of the sheet skimmed across my skin, teasing me with the promise of what was to come. It was torture, having to wait, wanting only to get my hands on him, feel his lips crushing me. But he continued his unhurried motion, his eyes never leaving mine.

Once the sheet had cleared my lacy white bra, his lip curled up into a sneer. By the time he'd slid it down past my hips, he was practically licking his chops. By that time, I was feeling pretty worked up, but still a bit self-conscious.

I laid there, trying to look perfectly at home sprawled out half-naked on his bed as he snickered, "Well, look what we have here." His words were slightly garbled around the edges and he staggered a bit during his climb onto the mattress.

He crawled so incredibly slowly over me, kissing my ankles, shins, knees, thighs, along the way. It was taking him forever to make his way to my lips, but somehow, the waiting was turning me on almost more than the actual doing. He pushed my knees apart and filled the space with his kneeling form, running his hands along the outside of my legs, sending electric charges up my entire length. I let out a small moan which earned me a throaty chuckle from Trip. He moved further up, grabbing my hips, holding them pinned to the bed as his lips and tongue hit my navel, and I was finally able to put my hands on him. I combed my fingers through his golden hair and arched my back toward him, dragging a low growl from his throat as he laughed out, "Oh, no you don't."

He slid his body on top of mine, the weight of him pushing me back down into the mattress. He grabbed my wrists in one hand, forcing them up, imprisoning my arms above my head. His other hand was skimming across my collarbone, his mouth hovering an inch over mine. I tried to close the gap and kiss him, but he pulled back, denying me, a wicked smile on his devilish face, deliberately teasing me.

I could feel him harden against me; not quite the steel rod from that afternoon, but surely promising an appearance nonetheless. He buried his face in my neck, running his lips along the side, down to the hollow of my throat, between the lacy cups of my bra, back to my throat. My heart was threatening to burst its way out of my chest, Trip driving me insane without even having kissed me yet.

He was so hot, so completely male in everything he did, from the way he looked to the way he was looking *at* me. The sensory overload was almost unbearable. Trapped immobile, my arms pinned to the pillows above my head, my body imprisoned beneath his, those sweet, full lips just an inch away from my own, the delectable sensation of his hardened body pressing in just the right spot... Oh God, what could be better?

He released my hands and wrapped his arms around me, finally allowing me to touch him. I tried to tease him back, dusting my lips along his hairline slowly, cradling his mussed head against my neck. I could feel his lips brushing against my skin so softly, the full weight of him practically threatening to crush me, almost not even moving at all...

I registered his steady breathing which quickly turned to snoring and realized he had passed out.

Was he kidding?

He must have been drunker than I thought. Now *this* was dejection. No acting going on here.

I laid there, feeling all worked up and completely let down, when suddenly, I just started laughing. If this was how I was feeling about it now, I couldn't imagine what Trip was going to be feeling in the morning. I looked down at the sleeping beauty in my arms, wondering how hard he was going to be kicking himself the next day. After he'd seen the goods on the beach, I knew he'd been waiting out the minutes to get his hands on the merchandise. It's not like I had any designs on going too far with him that night, but I'm sure we could have had a helluva time working on some variables.

And now just look at him.

"Sorry, pal. You snooze, you lose."

I slithered out from under the dead weight of him, scooped up my clothes and headed into my room. I almost jumped out of my skin when I saw Lisa lying on one of the bottom bunks.

"Oh my God!" I whisper-shouted. "You scared the hell out me!"

Lisa swiped a hand across her face and apologized. "I'm sorry. Hey, is it alright if I sleep in here tonight?"

"Yeah, of course. But Lis-" My eyes had better adjusted to the light and I could see that she'd been crying. "I just assumed you'd be sleeping in Pick's room. What's going on?"

"Oh my God, I don't even know if I can talk about it." She sat up in the bed just then, intending to, in fact, tell me *all* about it, but she took one look at me and asked, "Um, Layla, why are you naked?"

I'd been standing there holding my shirt and shorts in front of me, not bothering to put them on for the short walk between Trip's room and mine. The rest of the guys wouldn't have had any reason to come upstairs and I'd assumed Lisa and Pickford were already long asleep, so I'd made a break for it. Thankfully, it was only Lisa who busted me.

"Don't ask," I replied, and threw the clothes onto the nightstand between our two bunkbeds. I scrounged around in my bag for a ginny-tee and cotton shorts, flashdanced the bra from under my top and climbed into the bed opposite Lisa. "Okay, so I'm not naked anymore, so spill it. What's going on between you and Pick?"

"What do you think?" She flopped back down on her bed and sighed dramatically, posing a question to the heavens, "God, why are you taking him away from me?" her words filtered on their way to Him through the bed above her.

I propped my head on an elbow so I could face her. "Come on, Lis. Not this again. You gotta cut it out. Why are you doing this to yourself?"

Lisa mirrored my pose. "I know, I know. I just can't stop thinking about it, you know? I just can't stop thinking about the fact that he'll be gone soon." She pulled the sheet up under her neck, warding off a chill even though the room was an oven. "What am I going to do without him?"

I knew that Lisa and Pick were pretty serious, but I'd always registered it as high-school-serious, not like life-or-death-serious. They were eighteen, for godsakes. I thought my friend was being overly dramatic. Like, okay, you're assigned a locker next to someone, but what are the odds that that person is actually your soulmate?

Then again, high school sweethearts got married all the time, didn't they? The DeSantos were a good example. My parents... not so much. But happy or not, married people had to meet *somewhere*. Why not high school?

Just then I thought about Trip, snoring away in the next room and my heart lurched. What a total hypocrite I could be. I made myself remember that my poor friend's world was coming apart.

"I don't know, Lis," I said, trying to come up with something positive to contribute. "I guess you guys will figure it out if it's meant to be."

I felt my eyelids getting heavy and added through a yawn, "But you gotta stop spending what little time you two have left together being miserable. There'll be plenty of time for that after he leaves, okay?" I snuggled down into the mattress and added, "And hey, when that happens, you'll still have *me*, right?"

Lisa yawned too. "Yeah. Some consolation *that*'ll be." I let out a tired snicker. If I wasn't half-asleep, I would have busted out laughing at her next line, because the last thing I remember her saying was, "Ya gonna grow a dick for me, too?"

Chapter 30
DELIRIOUS

That night, I had a dream that Trip was hovering over me. I could feel his hands braced on either side of my head, his sandy hair brushing my cheek as he nuzzled into my neck, running heated kisses along my collarbone. My arms went around him and pulled his body on top of mine, my legs wrapping around his waist, his hand sliding up my shirt, my fingers raking down his bare back, down to his thighs, pulling him tighter against me...

When I heard his laugh against my throat, I woke up and realized it was dawn. There he was, actually tangled in my arms, better than any dream could ever be. I looked over at the other bed and saw that Lisa was already long gone. I made a mental note to check in on her the first chance I got. Well, the *second* chance I got.

"Good morning," he whispered into my neck, the full weight of him pressing me into the pillows.

"Mmm. Good morning," I answered back, smelling the sleepy warmth of his skin. We twisted to our sides, facing each other, my one leg still draped across his hip.

The wakeup call would have been perfect if not for the word "DICKNOSE" written across Trip's forehead in black marker. I guessed Cooper at long last had found an opportunity to seek out his revenge.

I started laughing. "I'm gonna go out on a limb here and assume that you haven't seen a mirror yet this morning."

Trip looked at me like I was nuts before vaulting out of bed and heading for the bathroom. One second later, I heard him spit, "Sonofabitch!" which made me just crack up.

I heard the sink running and figured that Trip would come back to bed smelling not only soapy, but minty, too, and followed him into the bathroom. I thought it'd be best to brush the morning breath out of my mouth before we got too chummy.

He'd spent a considerable amount of time at the sink, but after he'd toweled off, there was still a grey shadow- along with a big, splotchy red spot- across his forehead. He threw the towel on the counter and leaned against the door frame, watching me as I finished brushing my teeth. "You're burned up pretty bad, huh?"

I twisted a shoulder toward the mirror. "Yeah. Think I'll skip the beach today and just stay inside."

A wicked smile decorated his face. "Want some company?"

I stepped back across the hall and slumped down on his bed in answer. He flopped back down half on top of me and groaned, "Remind me to kill Cooper."

I readjusted myself more comfortably underneath him before snuggling into his arms. The skin on my face and shoulders was feeling tight and raw, sunburned the day before and settled into its full damage while I was sleeping, and I was finding it somewhat hard to spoon with Trip. Which goes to show you how badly I was hurting!

After some breakfast in bed (Froot Loops), we declined the invitation to join everyone on the beach. Instead, we spent the entire day on that mattress; talking about godonlyknows and laughing our asses off.

The fact that he could barely touch me without me wincing kept our fooling around to a minimum. But neither of us minded too much. It was just awesome enough to be there with him, have him all to myself for a little while, just the two of us, no clock to watch, no time or space beyond that queen-sized bed. We only left to grab something to eat or use the bathroom, to change the radio station on his boombox or throw on a CD.

By the time everyone came back for dinner, we were surprised that it had gotten so late. We reluctantly came downstairs and helped to demolish the pizzas waiting on the kitchen table.

The weather had been cooling off considerably all day, so we decided to join everyone for a sunset game of wiffleball back at the beach, and Trip was astounded at how well I could play. He seemed more impressed than put off when I struck him out- *twice*- which made me laugh to myself at my own, private joke;

168

my athletic abilities had at long last become an advantage to me in the boy department.

We got back to the house and cracked a few beers before picking numbers out of a hat for the shower schedule.

When it was my turn, I grabbed a change of clothes and a towel and headed in. I had to shampoo twice to get all the sand out of my hair and was just rinsing off when I heard the door open. Guess who.

I poked my head out from behind the curtain to see Trip leaning against the counter, eyebrows raised.

I gave him a warning look. "Don't even think about it."

He started laughing. "Aww, c'mon, Lay-Lay. You're no fun."

I disappeared behind the curtain and said, "I mean it, Chester. Please don't."

It must have been the "please" that registered, because he acquiesced without further argument. "Fine, I'll just wait out here until you're done."

"Promise?"

"Yeah, sure. I promise. But at least give me the play-by-play of what I'm missing out on."

He was so bad.

I laughed out, "Well, right now, I'm rinsing the shampoo from my hair!"

If he really needed a rundown of what I was doing in there, I could have just continued with a basic explanation of my shower ritual. I could have chosen to say nothing at all. But I quickly came to the realization he had proposed an offer that was just too good to pass up. After how he'd teased me into oblivion the night before, I couldn't resist a little payback. Some wicked force overtook my body and turned me into a madwoman.

I dropped the joking tone and tried on a sultry voice. I wasn't quite the actor he was, but was able to suggest slowly, breathily, deliberately, "Actually, the water is so *hot* and it's sooo steamy in here. Mmm... I'm so wet, and God, it feels *so good*."

I thought I heard Trip choke.

I grabbed the bar of Ivory from the ledge, continued my commentary at a snail's pace, "Now, I'm soaping myself down, running my hands all. Over. My body. My neck, my shoulders... If only there was someone who could help me wash my back... or my *front*... Hmmm..."

When I didn't hear anything from Trip, I poked my head back out. He was standing there white as a ghost, his bottom lip slack and his eyes wide. "Layla, what the *fuck*?"

I giggled more to myself than at him. Oh, the power! It was thrilling, to say the least, being completely naked only one thin shower curtain away from Trip, knowing I was driving him crazy. How could I stop now?

"It's *so* slippery!" I continued. I took a deep breath and exhaled, adding, "And it smells like *heaven*... I'm rinsing off now, the hot water spraying me *everywhere*."

"That's it. I'm coming in."

Ha! At that point, I kind of wanted him to! But fun and games were one thing. Thinking about him actually getting undressed, the two of us naked in such an enclosed space... A small panic gripped me and I blurted out, "No! You promised, remember?"

"Oh, you little tease."

I laughed wickedly and peeked back out at him. He was unabashedly adjusting himself in his shorts, trying to get his body under control. I put a hand over my mouth and laughed even harder.

"It's not funny, Layla! Jesus, look what you've done to me."

I only had the nerve to glance down quickly at the bulge in the front of his shorts. It was enough to make me dizzy, thinking about that same piece of machinery driving against me the day before, first outside by the cars and then later half-naked in his bed. I wondered what the night would bring. Where else could this be heading?

I turned off the water and a moment later, his arm thrust beyond the curtain, offering a towel hanging from his hand.

I grabbed the towel, asking, "You sure you don't want to help dry me off?"

Okay, I admit it. That was just being mean.

His hand jerked back, disappearing to the other side of the curtain. "Jesus! Okay, just hurry up and get out of here. If you're not gonna let me in there, then you seriously need to get out of this room so I can take care of this."

I knew the "this" he was referring to was his raging hard-on, threatening to destroy him unless something was done to take the pressure off. I didn't know where the newfound boldness was coming from, but I decided that that something was going to be me.

I took a deep breath, wrapped the towel around my body and stepped out into the steamy bathroom. Trip looked pained, barely meeting my eyes when he said, "Out. Now."

I grinned, loving that I was the one responsible for getting him so worked up. But I didn't leave.

I stepped closer, backing him against the vanity, sliding one hand up his bare chest, the other across the front of his cargo shorts. He didn't hesitate to grab my wet hair in his hands and open his mouth over mine. The kiss was electric, jolting me down to my core, the feel of his mouth open over mine and his erection under my hands wildly exciting, out-of-control, the steamy room spinning.

My lips didn't leave his as I slid my hands to the button at his waist, lowering his zipper, letting his shorts and undies fall to the floor. I took him in my hand, the size of him startling me. I threw open my eyes, looking into his in disbelief. He grinned that shit-eating grin before kissing me again, obviously enjoying my moment of shock. Well, now it was my turn.

I gripped him firmly, the soft/hard feel of him straining into my palm, moving against the motion of my fist. When I pushed downward, he thrust forward, driving himself into my hand. I heard him moan into my mouth and the knowledge that I was the one to put him in such a state was empowering, exciting beyond anything I'd ever known.

I returned the favor, moaning back against his lips, which made him break our kiss and brace his hands against the counter in a

171

white-knuckle grip, his head thrown back to face the ceiling, eyes closed. His teeth clenched as he gritted out, "Mother of *God.*"

I would have laughed, but I was feeling a bit awed at that moment myself. I leaned over him and sucked at his collarbone, dipping the tip of my tongue into the hollow of his throat, running my teeth along the cord of his neck, biting his earlobe lightly, all the while continuing the rhythm of my hand.

I'd never been that uninhibited before, wanting only to please him with what little sexual knowledge I possessed. My brain long since liquefied, I could only follow the lead of my raging nerve endings, not even bothering to think and just doing whatever felt good. Because what I quickly learned was that if it felt good for Trip, it felt almost as good for me. He wasn't even touching me and yet I was so completely turned on, my heart racing wildly, every molecule within me threatening to implode. Every touch that wrung a moan from his throat, I intensified, every movement of my hand working on pure instinct and the hope that I was doing something right.

"*Layla,*" he said, and the mere mention of my name coming from his lips at a moment like that almost drove me mad. Desire pooled through me, all my pink parts tingly and alert, the sudden epiphany that I not only *could* go all the way with this guy, but *wanted* to. Wanted to be stripped down with him, wanted every part of his skin pressed against mine, feel him lying on top of me, hot and demanding, taking me right there on the bathroom floor... All I'd have to do is drop the towel...

But Trip was too far gone. "Layla, holy Jesus. I'm gonna... just keep... I... *ohhh!*" His body lurched forward as his cock went off like a bazooka, which fortunately, was aimed toward my midsection and into the towel I was wearing. His hand wrapped around mine, continuing the movement along his softening member slowly, the aftershocks dribbling out against my belly. It was the coolest thing I'd ever seen!

He slumped into me, his face against my neck, breathing hard, unable to complete a full sentence. "Holy sh... I can't... wow. *Wow.* Oh my God!"

I held him to me, loving that new side to him; vulnerable, spent... *mine*.

I didn't know what the hell we were doing, and, at that moment, probably shouldn't have cared less. I didn't know if we were legitimately a couple or what. Were we just screwing around? Was it just a friends with benefits thing? Throughout high school, I'd never even so much as gone to second with a guy who wasn't formally my boyfriend, and yet there I was, wrapped in the arms of a clothesless Trip Wilmington, the evidence of what we'd just done together glistening right there on my hand.

I mean, that was the first real live penis I'd ever seen, much less touched, much less prompted to explode, and Trip and I weren't even really going out! I don't know what it was about him that managed to turn me into such a sex-crazed lunatic, but I didn't spend too much time beating myself up about it. After four years of catholic school, I figured I *ought* to have felt guilty for what we'd just done. But the only thing I regretted at that moment was that we missed out on the chance to go even further.

Feeling him slumped against me, out of breath, naked and elated and holding me as tight as his wasted arms would allow, was nothing short of awe-inspiring. How could I ever feel guilty about something that felt so good?

"I'm in love with you," I whispered, the words leaving my lips before my coagulating brain was able to stop them. *Oh dear God, did I just say that out loud?*

My body froze instantly, stunned that I had actually let that thought slip out of my head and escape from my mouth. I could have just died right then and there.

Trip just gave a quick chuckle and pecked me on the lips, then bent down to retrieve his shorts.

Ohmygod ohmygod ohmygod. What did I just *do*?!!?

Trip bypassed any commentary on my proclamation, buttoning up and washing his hands at the sink, where I joined him, completely mortified, before I slipped out of the bathroom silently in order to let him take his damned shower.

173

I holed up in my room, locked the door and ditched the tainted towel in the dirty clothes bag. I got as far as dressing into a bra and panties before sinking onto the bed and completely losing my mind.

What the hell was I thinking? How could I have actually told Trip that I loved him? And oh God! He didn't even *try* to say anything about it! He didn't say, "I love you, too", which, let's face it, would have been awesome, but completely ludicrous and way too much to hope for. But he could have at least tossed me that time-honored, unrequited response of, "Thank you". He could have said *something* to let me off the hook for being a completely ridiculous freak with a broken brain filter. After just servicing him with a mind-blowing handjob, the least he could have done was that!

I threw the pillow over my face, hoping for an accidental suffocation. Then I wouldn't have to go downstairs and spend an entire evening in the same room with Trip, who, if he had any doubts about it before, had now been made entirely aware of the fact that I was in love with him.

Are you there, God? It's me, Layla. I know I just jerked off some guy who is not even my boyfriend in the bathroom of this crappy, brown house. But if you could find a way to kill me quickly and painlessly within the next ten seconds, I promise never to touch another penis again. Well, I'll be dead, so, I guess I promise not to whore it up in heaven. Which, of course is where you'll be sending me, right? I mean, I'd hate to think you'd deny me an eternity behind your pearly gates just because of one impetuous handjob. Thank you. Sincerely, Layla Warren. Amen.

Chapter 31
THE PRINCE OF TIDES

I must have passed out shortly after my unanswered prayer the night before, maybe even as early as ten o'clock, so when I woke up, it was still completely dark outside. I figured it had to be the middle of the night, so I tried to close my eyes and get back to sleep. But the extra shuteye, combined with my humiliation over what I'd said, kept me wide awake, tossing and turning for the next hour. When I saw a hint of grey seeping through the window blinds, I figured morning wasn't too far off, and decided to get out of bed.

My hair was an absolute rat's nest because I'd never gotten around to blow-drying it the night before, so I gathered the whole mass into a ponytail. I threw on a pair of black biker shorts and a chartreuse green tank top before tip-toeing out of my room.

I had to pass by Trip's door, so I did so as quietly as possible. But at the first creak on the top step, I heard him whisper, "Layla?"

I stopped dead in my tracks, hoping that he'd go back to sleep and leave me to go on my merry, mortified way, but of course I was having no such luck.

"Layla. What are you doing?"

I spat out a silent *dammit*, and took the two steps back to stand in his doorway. He was lying in his bed, the sheet tangled around his hips, his bare chest exposed, an arm propped behind his head. God. Even at five-something in the morning, the boy managed to look irresistible.

I could barely look him in the eye. "I can't sleep. I thought I'd go for a run on the beach."

There. Good enough. I managed to speak to Trip without blurting out any further avowals of my undying love.

I started to turn when he whipped the sheet off and said, "Hey, give me a minute. I'll go with you."

Shit. "Oh, okay. I'll meet you downstairs."

Since I didn't have to worry about waking him up anymore, I allowed myself to pee and brush my teeth before heading down into the kitchen. I grabbed a glass of water and was just finishing it when Trip showed up, dressed in grey nylon basketball shorts and a white T-shirt. I didn't allow myself to speak and just headed out the back door, Trip following on my heels. We walked across the street and up to the boardwalk, the hum from the streetlamps offering the only sound between us. But once we started down the walkway to the beach, I looked toward the ocean and couldn't help the, "Oh!" that escaped from my lips.

The sun was just starting to rise, offering a hazy orange glow along the horizon, shooting off purple and pink streaks into the rest of the ashy sky. In the minutes it took us to reach the water's edge, the sky had lightened considerably, the first edge of sun making its way out of the sea.

It was happening so quickly, this dawning of a new day, and my only instinct was to plant myself down to watch every second of it.

Trip sat down with me, and I wished things were different between us at that moment. All I could think was that I had possibly ruined everything that could have happened between us because I just couldn't keep my big mouth shut.

I tried to push those thoughts aside and just enjoy the view. But having Trip sitting right there with me was proving to stress me out, in spite of the peaceful sight in front of my eyes. Finally, I knew I wouldn't be able to pretend there wasn't an elephant between us.

"So, what, is everything gonna be all weird between us now?"

Trip gave me a confused look and asked, "Why? Because we..."

"No. Because I... Because of what I said after."

His head dropped down and his shoulders started shaking.

Glad to see he finds this so funny. Not.

"Jesus, Layla. You think too much. You were in a moment. You think I never blurted out something stupid in the middle of having sex?"

176

I didn't know whether to be grateful that Trip thought my confession was no big deal, curious because he'd mentioned having sex like it was an everyday thing, or angry because he thought what I'd said was "something stupid". I decided to just run with the out he had given me.

I started laughing, even though I was sort of dying a little inside. "Really? Like what? Tell me something you've said."

"Uh-uh. No way."

The majestic sunrise was only a blip in my peripheral vision, my main focus trained on Trip's reddening face. Holy crap, was he blushing? That made me start laughing for real. "Trip, tell me!"

"A gentleman never kisses and tells."

"Oh, shut up. You're no gentleman."

"True, but few people know that."

"Tell me, Chester!"

I nudged into him and he nudged back harder, knocking me off balance and forcing my elbow into the sand to stop my fall. He promptly pounced on top of me, laying me out flat on my back anyway, despite the efforts to save myself. He grabbed my wrists, pinning them into the sand next to my head and straddled my chest, his face hovering over mine. "Drop it, Warren."

"*Warren*? What are you, Rymer now?"

"That may be the worst thing anyone's ever said to me ever."

I started laughing, in spite of the weight of him practically sitting on my chest. "Ow. I can't breathe. Trip, you gotta get off."

He took mercy and rolled off of me, landing his butt on the beach. I got up on my knees, pretending to catch my breath and dust myself off before yelling, "Sucker!" and dive-bombing into him, throwing him backwards into the sand. He used the momentum of my tackle and rolled us both over, pinning me flat on my back again. Without the use of my arms, I was sputtering my hair out of my face and trying to spit the sand out of my mouth.

"Bleh! You jerk! No fair, you're bigger than I am."

"Yep. Stronger, too. Don't ever forget it."

"Trip! I think I have sand in my eye. Let me up."

"Oh, right, you big faker. Think I'm falling for that again?"

"No, Trip, seriously. I think I have sand in my eye."

He got up and I stood, brushing out my hair and clothes, making a big, phony show of trying to blink some non-existent particles out of my eyes. While he was busy dusting himself off, I went for a surprise tackle, diving right for him... just as he rolled out of the way, landing me face-down on the beach.

I cracked up, fully breaded now from head to toe, as Trip stood over me laughing. "You are the worst actress ever. Like I was really going to-"

His words were cut off as I grabbed his ankle and tugged, sending him ass-over-teakettle next to me. He looked stunned for a second, before he bared his teeth in a snarl, and I knew I was in deep shit. I got on my feet and made a run for it, Trip following right behind. I only got a few yards from him before he caught up, hip-checking me down to the ground once more. I tried to grab his ankle again, but he jumped back, then flopped down on his side next to me anyway.

"You just don't give up, do you, Warren?"

"Never, Rymer."

We were both cracking up, the beautiful sunrise barely registering on my radar. Nothing on God's green Earth was more beautiful than making Trip Wilmington laugh like that. How could any stupid sunrise possibly compare? After we'd caught our breath, dusted ourselves off and salvaged the last remnants of the brilliant dawn before us, I realized Trip and me were going to be just fine.

All I had to do was keep my trap shut from then on.

* * *

By the time we got back to the house, everyone else had gotten out of bed and was busy packing up to go. We had to check out by eleven and not only were we tasked with gathering all our personal belongings, but the place was an absolute mess to boot.

Lisa and I were cleaning out the fridge when Rymer staggered in, some random trollop at his side. He walked her to the back door, told her he'd call and kissed her goodbye. I shot Lisa a "*whatsgoingon*" look, but she was too busy trying to contain the giggle that threatened to escape her throat. I must have missed quite a show the night before.

Rymer closed the door and gave an exaggerated stretch. "Ahh. Good morning, ladies!"

Lisa raised her eyebrows at him. "Um, good morning, Rymer."

He saw the look on her face and asked, "What? You're the only one allowed to get laid around here?"

Lisa gave a huff. "Date rape isn't 'getting laid'. In fact, it's a crime."

We started laughing while Rymer floundered for a comeback. We were both surprised when he came up with, "Hey, fuck you, DeSanto."

"Whoa! Hey, hang on there, pal," she started back. "I was only busting your chops. Since when do you get so pissy about it?"

"You've been riding me all weekend, Lisa. Enough is enough already, okay?"

He stormed out of the room, leaving Lisa and me completely wordless and flummoxed.

"What was that?" I asked.

Lisa bit her bottom lip. "I don't know. You think I actually hurt his feelings?"

"I didn't know he had any."

That made us both laugh, but I knew she had a case of the guilts going on. "I have been kind of rough on him lately. Maybe I'd better go talk to him." She got up humbly to leave, but not before offering, "Jeez. Next time Rymer picks up some random skank from the boardwalk, remind me not to comment on it."

I just shook my head.

I don't know what Lisa said to Rymer during their conversation, but by the time we were loading up our cars, those two must have found a way to make nice. He actually helped us carry our bags out to my Mustang and loaded everything into the trunk for us. Wow. Maybe Rymer needed to get laid more often. Having sex seemed to turn him into an almost normal person.

Huh. Wonder what it could do for me.

As if Trip could read my thoughts, he emerged from the house at that very moment. He dropped his bag behind Cooper's car and came over to say goodbye. Everyone was coming and going through the house, but that didn't stop him from putting his hands at my waist and kissing me right there in the driveway. I tried not to think about the looks we were surely receiving from our friends and kissed him back, my arms looped over his shoulders right there out in the open, in front of God and everyone. I couldn't believe it! It was the first time Trip and I had ever freely let on that something was going on between us, and the public display floored me almost more than the things we did in private. Trip Wilmington was actually kissing me, without shame, in front of *everyone*.

Oh, the summer was going to be spectacular.

Chapter 32
CLOSE MY EYES

We hit The Barrens later that night, Trip and I arriving together. That wasn't so out of the ordinary- we used to show up at places together all the time- but that night, we showed up holding hands. We were almost giddy all evening, the two of us giggling like a couple of idiots into each other's eyes all night. I can only imagine it was fairly sickening to watch.

The next day, I invited everyone over for a pool party, and Trip didn't miss too many opportunities to show a little PDA. We spent the day swimming, making out, getting tan, making out, barbequing some lunch and making out. I kept waiting for one of them to bust our chops about it- certainly at any moment, Rymer would yell at us to "get a room"- but no one said a word. I may have been overly optimistic and self-centered about the situation, but I sensed that my friends were actually happy for us. As far as I was concerned, we were just long overdue to finally be together, so maybe everyone else thought so too. Not that they didn't have their own lives going on or anything, but I definitely caught the vibe that everyone seemed to be silently rooting for us, the unspoken approval uplifting yet humbling at the same time.

Trip and I spent almost every waking moment of that summer together, most of the time wrapped up in each other's arms. I can't remember a more consistently blissful time of my life than during that season after graduation, all of us soaking up the last days of childhood together, trying to make time go by more slowly. No one spoke much about the fact that we were going to be off in different parts of the country in just a few short weeks.

Heather and Becca had both set their sights on south Jersey schools, Princeton and Rutgers respectively, and even Rymer had gotten into Bergen Community College, a two-year school just a twenty minute drive away.

But that was pretty much it for the Jersey co-eds.

Cooper was slated to leave us first, spending the month of August doing intern work at some law firm down near his university in Maryland, trying to get a jump on some credits before the school year even started. Sargento was headed for Susquehanna all the way out in the boonies of Pennsylvania and Pickford was readying for his cross-country trek to L.A.

Lisa and I were prepping for our move to the city, doing the entirety of our dorm shopping together. We figured it would be best to nail down a coordinating design scheme, knowing all our stuff would be reunited in our apartment the following year. She was practically manic with her spending, obsessing worse than me over buying anything and everything she thought she'd possibly ever need for New York. I kept reminding her that there was probably a store or two in the city where she could buy such vital items like wooden spoons. Or lightbulbs. Or soap.

Trip, however, in spite of his excellent GPA and stellar SAT scores, hadn't even applied to a single school. He was planning to take a full year off; indulging in a few lost weekends before concentrating on his MVP hockey team in the fall, then doing some intensive travelling in Europe and Africa. Then and only then would he think about looking into college, hoping to play hockey at some university upstate, or even out somewhere in Canada, or some other place very, very far away.

A part of me was pretty jealous that he was going to be bouncing around the globe all year while I was stuck inside some classroom. The other part of me was terrified for him at the thought of not having a plan in place. I couldn't believe that he was not only unfazed about not knowing where he'd be a year from then, but that he was actually excited about it. I knew that even if he had asked me to go with him- which he never would anyway- I'd be too much of a wimp to say yes.

But we didn't spend much time discussing the future anyway. We both knew we were on borrowed time, the ticking clock always hanging over us, knowing we were going to have to say goodbye. For the first time, I truly realized how Lisa and

Pickford must have been feeling and understood why my friends were falling apart at the seams a little bit more each day.

Trip and I were great at playing the denial game, always living in the now, never discussing what our lives without each other would hold. It was impossible to think about our time together coming to an end, so I guess we always made a point to sidestep any questions about what was going to happen in the fall.

Two nights before Cooper was scheduled to skip town, however, Trip and I were sitting on my couch, snuggled up and watching *Animal House*. Out of nowhere, I started thinking about it, thinking about everyone leaving, about having to start a new life in New York, how I'd have to say goodbye to my friends, my family, my childhood, *Trip*... and my heart felt like it was being ripped apart. How was I ever going to let them go?

I blurted out, "Everything's changing."

Trip squeezed me a little tighter, knowing full well what I was talking about, the boogeyman in our midst finally being acknowledged. But he didn't respond right away, so I continued. "Everyone's going away soon. It's like we're not going to be *us* after that, you know? We'll run into each other at homecoming games or reunions or bump into each other randomly in town, but we'll never be *us* ever again, will we?"

Trip's voice was calm, soothing beyond his eighteen years when he answered, "It's called growing up, Lay."

"I know, but God. It really sucks."

I looked at him and saw the line drawn between his brows and the dimple working in his cheek- the look he wore when he was really thinking hard about something. "Yeah, it does. Is it harder for you?"

"What do you mean?"

"Well, you've known all these people your whole life. I've only known them a year and it's-" He swiped a hand through his hair before continuing. "-it's so much harder this time, even for me, to think about leaving. It's like, for all the cities I've lived in before, this is the first place that's ever felt like *home* to me. And I didn't even grow up here, with them, the way you have."

183

I put a hand to his face and said, "I've only known *you* for a year... Do you really think it's going to be any easier for me to say goodbye because I haven't known you as long?"

He held me tighter and kissed the top of my head. "Okay, point taken. C'mere." He slid down to lay on the couch, maneuvering me half on top of him.

We were silent for a moment, his hand moving in a caressing gesture along my back, trying to smooth our hurt away when he said, "You're right. This sucks."

I could feel him getting gloomy and realized this was why we never talked about it. I felt bad for bringing up our one, big, taboo subject and wished I could have stuffed the whole conversation back in my mouth.

"I'm sorry," I offered. "I'm sorry for even bringing it up. We still have a few weeks left and I don't want to spend them being sad, okay? Agreed?"

I turned to look up at him, just one split second before he was able to swipe the tear from his eye. Holy Jesus, I made him cry. My heart just about splintered in two when he tried to offer a wan smile to cover.

I felt helpless, guilty beyond belief for dragging him into my sorrow. I did the only thing I could think of, which was to grab him behind his neck and plant a kiss on him. Hard.

When I broke away, I realized I'd achieved my desired result, because Trip snapped out of his misery and looked at me like I was crazy. Well, at least he wasn't sad anymore. I'd managed to replace despair with confusion. At least confusion wasn't such a foreign emotion.

He sputtered out, "What the hell was that?"

I started laughing, trying to jolly us out of our sadness. "I don't know. Want me to do it again so you can figure it out?"

The old Trip was back, sounding like he was ordering another Coke when he replied, "Yes, please!"

So I kissed him again. I slid myself fully on top of him, pressing my mouth to his, licking him along the part in his lips until they opened for me. I wasn't normally the aggressor during

184

our makeout sessions, but I could tell by the growing knot against my hip that Trip didn't seem to mind.

Chapter 33
NECESSARY ROUGHNESS

On Cooper's last night, Rymer had us all over at his house for a going away party, but we knew it was pretty much a final gathering for the rest of us, too.

Rymer's was wholly the best location for the best possible sendoff for our friend. Walking out onto the deck made everything horribly real for the very first time, however. I realized we were actually going to have to start saying goodbye.

I spent a lot of time exchanging addresses with everyone, with promises to write whenever we could and call whenever we were going to be back in town. We knew it was the last official get-together, the last chance we'd all have to be assembled in the same room, the same *town*, at the same time. Such a previously casual occurrence, one which we'd taken for granted for the past four years. A pall hung over our evening, even though we all pretended to be having a great time. At least I knew *I* was pretending, anyway.

After a while, Coop announced he had an early morning and had to cut the evening short. Becca seemed sad, but I knew she wasn't devastated. After all, her campus at Rutgers-Camden was only about a two hours' drive from Coop's university in Baltimore. She'd only have to wait a few weeks, once they were both settled in, to see him again.

Unlike the rest of us.

After he'd said his goodbyes to everyone, I walked with him out the front door, trying to carve out a private moment. I'd pretty much said my peace with everyone else, but Cooper actually walking out the door kind of made things official. I wasn't ready to do it, to start the process of watching my friends leave me, one by one. And even worse, the chain of departures had to start with Cooper!

He'd been my rock for the better part of our school year, but that was nothing new.

I had a string of flashbacks from over the years starring Coop, realizing he'd been there in some way or another for practically my entire life. Cooper, who shared his Fruit Roll-Ups with me the day in first grade I fell off the slide at recess. Who talked his parents into buying me a new paintable ceramic Smurf kit when I was eight, because he'd overheard me crying to Lisa that I had just broken the one my father had given me for my birthday. Who came running out with Bactine the time when I was ten, and had wiped out on my bike in front of his house. Who suffered detention for an entire week when we were thirteen, after he'd punched Kevin Sullivan out right there in the gym for making a snide comment about my mother leaving.

And now it was his turn to leave me. Who was going to be the one to heal my heart once he was gone?

It seemed he was always my Superman, rushing in to patch me up whenever I'd gotten hurt. Now, he was the one causing my pain, and I knew there wasn't a Band-Aid in the entire world big enough to treat *that* wound.

"Jesus, Coop. I guess this is really it."

He met my eyes, the years of shared memories passing between us. "Shit," he said, "I'm really going to miss you."

I didn't have anything big enough to say to him. Nothing to sum up how important he was to me, how my life wouldn't have been the same without him.

"Keep in touch, okay? Don't just say yes and then not do it."

He wrapped his arms around me for a hug. "I will, I will. I promise." He pulled back, smiled and added, "You are totally gonna *own* New York."

It was so completely like him to recognize that while I was devastated about him leaving, the feeling was all wrapped up with fears about my own future as well.

I spent the ride home in complete silence, and to Trip's credit, he didn't try to get me to talk about it. By the time we'd pulled up in front of my house, I was drained.

I went to lean over and kiss him goodnight, but my body became possessed, moving on its own as my leg slid over his lap and straddled him in the driver's seat. I caught Trip's startled expression for a quick second before closing my eyes and opening my mouth on his.

I promptly rammed my tongue in his mouth, grinding my hips against his, feeling him harden in spite of his shock. I pressed against him with abandon, trying to make my mind go blank.

I unbuttoned my blouse but left it to hang off my shoulders as I knotted my hands in the back of his hair and pushed his head into my bra. He immediately slid his palms up to my breasts, grasping at the cups of pale blue lace as he lowered his mouth to the space in between. I slid my hands underneath his shirt, running my fingers along his bare chest as I felt his tongue tasting away at my cleavage, his erection pounding between my thighs.

I gripped his shirt in my hands and pulled it over his head before pressing myself to his bare chest and kissing him again.

We went to war with one another: I pulled his hair, he bit my lip. I raked my nails across his shoulder, he groped my breast. His hands slid up under my skirt, cupping a cheek in each palm and pulling me tighter against his rigid body. I rocked myself against him, causing him to growl and plunge his tongue deep into my mouth.

Things had heated up quickly, and I was all but lost in the incredible sensations taking over my body. I snapped out of the daze, however, when Trip suddenly stopped us.

"Hey, hey, whoa. Layla, wait, wait, wait."

He dropped his head and shook it, trying to rid himself of the spell that had consumed us. I tried to pull his face to mine again, but he put his hands at my wrists and held them still. "Layla, stop! What the hell's going on?"

I knew I'd been overly aggressive with him lately, and I guess I never stopped to consider the effect it was having on him. The poor guy was constantly put in the position of having to get his body under control whenever I assaulted him.

In any case, the moment was gone. I climbed off of him and back to the passenger seat, buttoning up my blouse and smoothing my hair back into place.

I looked at him then, watched as he put his shirt back on hurriedly. "Jesus, Layla. We're out in the street for godsakes!"

It was actually pretty funny, watching him try to regain control, chastising me for making him lose it. What he didn't realize, however, is that I never asked him to. I never asked him to be the overseer of our fate, ensuring that we didn't go too far whenever there was a chance of getting caught. When you're a teenager, there aren't too many opportunities for real alone time. We hadn't really been left on our own since grad week at the beach house, and since then, it had been tough to find a private moment. I guessed it was good that at least *one* of us was able to keep their head about it once we did.

I almost started to laugh. "Sorry. I don't know what got into me."

His eyes kept darting toward my house, probably expecting my father to come storming out at any minute wielding a baseball bat. Once he finally realized the coast was clear, he gave me a quick kiss and then said goodnight.

* * *

The next day, I went for a long swim before calling Lisa to see if she wanted to go microwave shopping. It was the last thing I needed to buy for my dorm room, and I didn't feel like being alone. After the toll on my emotions the night before- mopey to heartbroken to sexual deviant- I could have used a good dose of my best friend right about then.

She answered, sounding cheerier than I'd heard her in a long time. She'd been such a mess the past weeks, Pick's impending cross-country move never far from her mind, and it was nice to hear a bit of the old Lisa in her voice.

"What's with you today, Snow White? You sound like you're ready to shit rainbows over there."

189

She actually laughed, and I didn't realize how long it had been since I heard her do that. "Just having a good day, I guess."

"Well, that's good. Glad to hear it!" If she'd found something that day to finally be happy about, I wasn't about to start asking a million questions why. So, I just launched into one of our favorite topics. "Hey listen, I don't know if I should get the white or the stainless microwave. Did we decide on our kitchen design yet? Because I know I'm pushing on this, but I'd still really love to do a fifties look. Black and white floor tiles, teal walls. Ooh, hey. Maybe we can find one of those awesome formica tables, you know, with the steel chairs and vinyl seats? Wouldn't that look so cool?"

Lisa didn't respond right away and I thought the phone had disconnected during my ramble.

"Hellooo. You still there?"

She took a deep breath and then dropped the bomb. "I'm going with him to California, Layla."

Before the words could even form some sense in my brain, she launched into a sprawling diatribe. "I know it seems crazy, Layla. Believe me, I know it's like, ridiculous, right? I just... I just think that it can be like an adventure, you know? Like I can go start over in some brand new place and be whoever I want to be. And I'll be there with Pick! We won't have to say goodbye."

I blurted out without thinking, "But *we* will!"

I couldn't believe what I was hearing. She was moving to California with Pickford Redy? Did she just actually say that? She was leaving me? Lisa, the one person I could always count on to be by my side. The one person who needed me just as much as I needed her. I guessed she decided she needed Pick more.

The reality of what she was trying to tell me started to sink in, liquid fire boiling through my veins.

My voice got infinitely louder at that point as I dove right in, trying to find some sense in what was happening. "What about New York, Lisa? What about *our* plans?"

"Layla, I know and I'm sorry. I knew this was going to be hard for you."

190

Hard for me? Try impossible. Was she serious?

"You're barely eighteen! You're going to be one of those trashy girls that shacks up with her pimply boyfriend in some trailer somewhere and has twelve kids before the age of twenty! What are you *thinking*?"

Lisa tried making a joke. "Pick doesn't have pimples."

I ignored her attempt at levity and just continued my tirade. "What about *your* life, Lis? You're gonna follow him all the way out to the west coast and just completely give up your dreams for his? How can you just blow off F.I.T.? You've only been talking about going there forever. How can he ask that of you?"

"He didn't ask. He wants me to enroll in the fashion program at the Hollywood Arts Institute."

"But it's not New York! It's not the same thing!"

"Layla, I don't know how to make you understand. I *want* to go. I know that seems hurtful right now and I know all you can see is how I'm screwing up our plans, but someday I hope you'll be able to forgive me. I'm hoping you'll understand. One day, when you find that one person you know you're supposed to be with, you'll do whatever you have to do in order to be with him."

"So that's what you're doing? Being with your one and only true love, Pickford Redy? *Really, Lisa?*"

I knew I was putting some extra snotty into my voice, and at that moment, I didn't really care. She deserved it. How could she do this to me?

I heard her sigh on the other end of the phone, which pissed me off even further. I'd been yelling like a banshee during our entire conversation, only to hear her calmly respond to my remarks from her end. Where did she get off, expelling some wise-beyond-her-years sigh, talking at me like I was some petulant child and she was so damned mature all of a sudden? Not one month before, I was holding her freaking hair out of the toilet while she puked her guts out after too many shots of Jaeger. Four weeks later, she's trying out her June Cleaver impersonation?

"You know what, Lis? FUCK YOU. I hope you and *Pickford* live happily ever after. Have a nice life."

I slammed down the phone, so furious that I was actually shaking. It was the worst betrayal ever. I couldn't believe my best friend in the entire world was content to just throw me into the lion's den without even looking back. How the hell was I going to survive New York on my own? How could she expect me to?

I went downstairs and just shrieked the whole sordid story out to my father. The poor man didn't know what to do with me, stunned that I was slumped at his feet, laying all this information on him.

"Oh, Layla. I'm so sorry."

"Well, at least someone is! Lisa could care less!"

He finally realized he was holding a book, and placed it on the side table before offering, "I highly doubt that. She loves you, honey."

"Well, she obviously loves Pick more!"

"Be fair. I'm sure this was a hard decision for her."

"I doubt it."

I was being extraordinarily stubborn, and my father could tell he wasn't going to get through to me any time soon. He finally capitulated, throwing his hands in the air and attempted to distract me. "Well, it's too much to figure out tonight, right?" He got up from his recliner and held out his hand to me. "Come on. I'll buy you an ice cream cone."

I let him haul me up from the floor before he threw an arm around my shoulders and led me to the kitchen. "Everything's going to work out just fine, Layla-Loo. You'll see."

Yeah, right.

Not twenty-four hours after having to say goodbye to Cooper, Lisa decided to abandon me. I was so sick of how quickly everything was changing and I couldn't seem to keep up with it all. I had enough anxiety about having to leave my friends and family behind, say sayonara to Trip, my dad, my brother... and leave the only place I'd ever lived in my entire life. On top of which Lisa goes and lays all this new information on me. It was just too much to handle for one seventeen-year-old girl.

192

If that's what it took to grow up, then no thank you, I could do without it, thank you very much. It only meant letting go of everything and everyone I ever loved.

Chapter 34
DEFENDING YOUR LIFE

I found myself back at my old locker at St. Norman's.

There was a padlock on the handle, which was weird, because those things had been banned the year before. The school was trying out a new honor system, under the misguided fantasy that good little Catholic students like us didn't have any need to lock up our belongings from all the other good little Catholic students. I'd had a leather jacket, numerous writing implements and my senior yearbook stolen over the course of the year, so... I guess it was a pretty good system. Not. Thankfully, I was able to replace the yearbook, but I never did see that jacket again.

When I saw that the lock had my initials carved into it, I realized it was mine, the one I'd had ever since junior high. I'd left it in my locker all year, hoping for a reversal in the new rule. I must have unconsciously slapped the thing on there on the last day of school. I tried out my old combination: 0-6-16, and it popped right open.

I was expecting to find an empty space, but instead, there was a single, white rose. My heart starting beating faster, wondering if Trip had left it for me. The more I looked at it, the more I saw that it wasn't in the best of shape, wilting and browning around the edges, obviously due to inattention. The thing had probably been in there since grad night. I'd never had the greenest thumb, but I'm sure I could have managed to keep a single flower alive, at least for a little while, had I only known it was in there. I figured the best I could do at that point was to try and dry it out and keep it as a memento.

I went to grab it, intending to press it into my yearbook, when I noticed it was making some sort of noise.

Like a ticking.

And then I saw some strange wires protruding from it.

I looked at the floor of my locker and saw a brick of explosive material- what was that stuff called again?- and wondered who would have left a boobytrap for me. Why is it called a boobytrap?

But then I realized I shouldn't care about such details when all I really needed to concentrate on was getting out of there. Quick.

I tried to run, but it was like I couldn't get my legs to move properly, practically in cartoon mode, my arms pumping and my legs in a Roadrunner blur, but it wasn't getting me anywhere. I knew I only had seconds- for some reason, I was able to see the digital readout on the bomb, counting down in boxy, red numerals, even though I'd slammed the locker door shut before trying to run away.

I somehow made it down the hallway and could see the light from the front doors just steps away. But every step I took toward the exit, the further it moved away from me, until finally- tick, tick, tick, three, two, one- there was a huge *BOOM!* behind me!

The walls shook, the windows shattered, the floor rippled. I could feel the heat from the blast, lifting me off my feet, hurtling me airborne, my body flying across the foyer and out the door, the concrete stairs coming to meet me at a rapid pace. Falling, falling...

Falling out of my bed and landing on the floor.

I shook my head awake and untangled my sweaty self from the sheets, realizing I was safe and sound in my very own room. God. What a weirdo. That's the last time I fall asleep watching *Die Hard*.

I peeked out the window and saw that it was another sunny, summer day outside, so I grabbed the one-piece off my doorknob and got dressed to go swimming. The pool was almost too warm that time of year, having been steadily heated from the sun all summer long. But in the cool early morning, I knew it would feel just perfect. I didn't bother testing the temperature with my toes before diving right in, the oasis enveloping me with a watery calm.

It had been almost two whole weeks since my fight with Lisa, and we hadn't spoken to each other the entire time. It was the longest we'd ever gone without talking to one another- even when she went to Italy for a whole month one summer, we managed to get in a weekly phone call- and it felt really strange not having her there.

There was so much to talk about! I wanted to tell her about the blowjob article in the latest issue of *Cosmo,* and page one-seventeen had directions for making an awesome, fabric-covered bulletin board. I wanted to tell her how great things had been going with Trip and me, and I knew she must have been dying to fill me in about her plans with Pickford. I wanted to show her the pictures from graduation that my father had finally gotten developed- there was a really great one of she and I, and Dad had ordered two five-by-sevens so we could each take one to school.

To our separate schools, on completely opposite coasts.

Weeks before, when our New York plan was still in effect, Lisa and I had received our housing assignments within days of each other, both of us scheduled to move in to our respective dorms on the same date in August. Just one short day away.

I wondered when she'd be expected to report to Hollywood Arts. I wondered if she was even able to enroll at all. Didn't they have deadlines out in California? Didn't Pick need to be there early, too?

I did an Olympic turn at the pool's edge and pushed off with my feet, loving the feel of strength in my legs and the constant testing of my body's abilities.

Just one more day.

I came up for air, pausing at the deep end, throwing my arms over the side to hold my head above water.

I thought that Lisa and Pickford must have already left, probably days ago. Surely, they wouldn't still be slumming around Jersey when a glamorous and exciting city like Los Angeles was awaiting their arrival, right?

Then again... maybe I *wasn't* too late.

I hauled my sopping wet body out of the pool and toweled off.

* * *

I rang the DeSantos' bell for the first time in years. It had been forever since I actually did that instead of just giving a quick knock and waltzing right on in.

Lisa's mom answered the door. "Hey, Mrs. D."

Her eyes lit up, and my heart panged with guilt.

"Layla! How are you, sweetheart? I feel like I haven't seen you in so long!" She put a hand on my shoulder, ushering me into the house. "I'm glad I get to see you before you take off for the big city. Tomorrow, right?"

"Yes. It's really weird, I can't believe it."

She gave my shoulder a quick rub and yelled up the stairs. "Lis! Layla's here!" before turning back to me and saying, "Go on up. She'll be happy to see you."

Obviously, Lisa hadn't told her mom about our blowout.

Then she gave me a big hug and added, "Oh, my little girls are both leaving! Where does the time go?"

I hugged her back, but didn't know what to say. There were too many things running through my mind. So, I just said, "I'm glad I got to see you before I left, too."

I went upstairs and gave a knock on Lisa's door- again, another first- and she told me to come in. She was sitting in the middle of the floor, surrounded by boxes and clothes and books and stuff.

"Hi," I said, a bit sheepishly.

"Hi," she said back. There was an awkward pause while I was thinking of the right way to launch an apology, but Lisa broke the silence before I could. "Whadja come over to tell me to fuck off in person this time?"

The shocking words hurt, even knowing that I probably deserved them and a whole lot more. I looked at her, ready to face head-on whatever else was coming.

But then I saw the smile eeking its way out from her lips.

Vintage Lisa, so ready and willing to forgive. I hadn't even apologized yet, but all she ever needed was for me to just show up. She was always the bigger person, dammit, always so much more grown-up and thought-out and *cool*. It made me wonder what her payoff was for staying friends with me all these years.

"Okay, I deserved that." I decided to just lay myself out on the altar of humility. "But Lisa, Oh, God. I'm just so, so sorry for everything I said. I was selfish and rude and I don't know what got into me."

I sank down on the floor across from her as she said, "A little of the ol' bitch, that's what."

"Yeah. I guess so."

"Maybe a pinch of jealousy?"

I hadn't realized it until she said it, but there it was. No way could I even dream of taking off on such a huge adventure. "Yeah. That too."

"And maybe a big old dose of Trip Wilmington's man-goo?"

That one threw me, made us both start laughing. "Are you insane? What is wrong with you, perv?" Then, in answer to her ridiculously phrased probing, "And no, unfortunately. Virginity still very much intact, you freak."

She picked up a green piece of fabric and threw it at me, but I managed to dodge to the side and catch it in my hand.

"Look at you with the catlike reflexes!"

I was busy inspecting the Girl Scout sash in my hand, checking out all her badges. I had a similar one somewhere at home, with most of the same achievements. Except that Lisa's were lovingly sewn on in perfectly aligned rows, whereas mine where stuck on haphazardly with Krazy Glue. Needless to say, I didn't earn my sewing patch that year. "Where'd you dig this thing out from? You're not packing it, are you?"

Lisa reached out and I handed it over, watching as she ran her fingers over the embroidered disks. "No. I already packed my stuff for..." the word *California* had become a four-letter obscenity between us, and I sensed her hesitation to say it aloud. "...for the car. I also have a stack of boxes downstairs in the dining room which need to be shipped, but *those,*" she pointed to a pile of clothes in the corner, "need to go to Goodwill, and *this,*" she swept her arms around the scattered remnants all over the floor, "needs to get packed away for the attic."

"My God, Lis. Looks like you've categorized every single thing you own!"

"Pretty much, yeah."

I hopped up and grabbed one of the black garbage bags from a roll on the bed and started stuffing the Goodwill clothes in it. Lisa tried to protest, but it was easier to talk while we were both preoccupied with busy hands.

"So, when are you leaving?" I asked.

Lisa stopped sorting and answered, "Tonight. Midnight." She sounded resolute, doing that convincing-herself thing again.

"That's a weird time to start a trip."

"It was my idea, actually. It was the last possible minute that we could leave and still get there in time for class registration."

"But why? What were you wai-"

Oh.

I saw the look on her face and realized she'd been waiting for *me.* There was no way she was skipping town without us saying a proper goodbye.

"You knew I was coming today, didn't you?"

She laughed out, "I knew you couldn't leave without doing so first."

"Oh, you manipulative witch!"

I picked up her Cabbage Patch doll and went to hurl it at her big, poofy head when she stopped my act with, "No, not Cassidy! Don't do it!"

I was cracking up, even before looking into the dirty face of Cassidy Cleopatra Pink Poopypants Bourgeois. Obviously, we'd taken full advantage of the Rename-Your-Kid option on her birth certificate. I remembered that we'd also given her my mother's birthdate. That was back when Kate was still around and I liked her enough to bestow such an honor.

"You're right. That would just be taking things too far. Sorry, Cass." I laid her in a box near where Lisa was sitting, thinking that poor Cassidy had better be prepared for a very long hibernation.

"You know," she started in, suddenly intent on ripping off the Band-Aid. "Deciding to do this wasn't easy."

I acquiesced. "I know. I know that now."

She gave me a small, grateful smile, then continued with her explanation. "When Pick first suggested the idea- down at the beach, by the way, after grad- When he first asked me to go with him, I was ecstatic, thinking that he must really and truly love me." She absentmindedly tossed a few things into the box, adding, "But then, on the other hand, I almost immediately became... *resentful*. And angry. And scared. I mean, there was no way I could actually tell him yes, right? I just put my blinders on and focused solely on The Plan, you know? You and me. New York. End of story. It took me weeks of fighting Pick before I finally realized I didn't know why I was even fighting him in the first place."

She stopped tearing through the pile of stuff surrounding her legs and looked up at me. "Once I got over the idea of rearranging my entire future, rearranging *yours*-" at that, she tossed me a smirk, "I knew it was what I had to do. I knew it was what I *wanted* to do. Making the decision to actually go, however, was probably the hardest thing I've ever had to do in my whole life."

I knotted up the garbage bag and started on another one. "I know it was. I do. It's just that I wish-"

"It's just that you wish everything would never change. You wish someone could tie up your life with a neat little bow and have it presented to you all tidy and prepared so you'd never have to think about getting your hands dirty trying to figure anything out on your own."

Does this chick know me or what?

I couldn't even debunk her claims. As bad as it sucked, she'd hit the nail right on the head.

Then she said something that surprised me. "You're tougher than you think, you know. As awful as I felt about having to tell you I was bailing on New York, I knew- even if you didn't- that you were going to be okay. I wouldn't have been able to do this if it weren't for your... *strength*."

I'd never thought of myself as a strong person; it seemed I constantly let myself get knocked down at every turn. But maybe it was true that strength just came from getting back up again, each and every time.

I said, "Yeah, well, knowing that doesn't make any of this any easier."

"Tell me about it. I mean, first you flipped out and then my parents weren't too thrilled, but they eventually got over it. The Redys, however, are just completely freaking out."

She stopped just then and looked at me, realizing that's not at all what I meant. She opened her mouth- probably intending to give me a big lecture on why change was a good thing, how life is what happens while you're busy making other plans, blah, blah, blah- but nothing came out.

Finally, she just simply offered, "He really loves me, Layla. No guy has ever really... loved *me* before."

I knew what she was getting at. She'd had numerous boyfriends over the years, some great, some not so great. But most of the guys she'd dated always treated her like some kind of trophy. Like she was some beautiful, brainless party girl, their prize to show off to the world. No one had ever bothered to scratch beyond the surface. Until Pickford.

"What's not to love?" I asked, unable to stop the sheer corniness dripping from my brain. "Oh! You just reminded me of something!"

I went out into the hall and retrieved the picture of the two of us from graduation. I'd gone to K-Mart and bought a swirly, pewter frame to put it in, and had stuck a mini, silver bow on the corner. I handed it over, almost shyly suggesting, "I know it's stupid, but I thought it was a really good picture of both of us. You know

201

how we can never get one where we both look human... either I'm making some weird face or you've got your eyes closed or-"

"Layla, shut up. It's perfect."

I saw her smile as she looked at the two girls smiling back at her. "I'll find a spot of honor in our new home for it."

Her mention of her new home was enough to remind us of our impending reality. She was actually going to do it. She was going to move three thousand miles away with some boy who'd stolen her heart. Some boy who was going to take it, along with the rest of her, far, far away from me.

"He'd better be good to you," I warned, not having any clue what I could possibly be expected to do if he wasn't.

"He will be. He is," she said back.

The waterworks started then, the two of us crying like a couple of idiots, bawling like there was no tomorrow. We hugged and sobbed into each other for a solid minute, neither one of us wanting to be the first to let go.

"I'm going to miss you so much."

"Not as much as me."

"Will you come out to see us? Maybe over the winter like you said?"

I wanted to say yes, I really did. But I was too afraid of making any empty promises. After all, I didn't know what the next few months were going to bring. We broke our embrace, dried our eyes and I said, "I'll try. I swear. But come home every chance you get, okay? I can be back here within an hour of your call."

"Okay."

"Promise?"

"Pinky swear."

"Well, jeez. Now I know you really mean it."

That made us laugh a little, and I figured I'd better let her get back to her packing. By that point, our crying jag had almost become more of a celebration of the next chapter of our lives, rather than pure grief over having to say goodbye.

It was a weird set of mixed emotions I was feeling- happy and scared and excited and sad- as I actually walked out of her room and back down the street. Sure, she wouldn't be three houses down or even living in the same city where I could go see her any time I wanted, but I knew we'd still talk. A lot. Like every spare moment we got.

There was no doubt in my mind that Lisa and I would always be a part of each other's lives forever, so at least I took that small comfort away with me. It's not as though we had really said goodbye. It was more like see-you-later.

With the rest of my friends, I wished I could be as sure.

My father and Bruce were both planning to drive me into New York the following morning, giving us the whole day to spend together in the city while getting me settled in my dorm. So, Dad didn't mind when I told him I'd made plans with my friends for my last official night in town.

Which was good, because I still hadn't said goodbye to Trip.

Chapter 35
RHAPSODY IN AUGUST

I started the car but kept it in park while I gunned the engine, trying to kick-start the air-conditioning. I had it set to full blast, but the day had been a scorcher and it was taking a few extra minutes to get the freon flowing. Even nearing dusk, the heat was barely showing any sign of letting up. The physical labor of the past hour had left me overheated, my face damp with sweat, causing moist little tendrils to appear around the edges of my hairline.

I lifted the hair off my nape and turned at an awkward angle, trying to cool the back of my neck, then pressed my forehead right up against the vents in an attempt to dry my face. I fanned the top of my dress and checked to make sure I didn't have any hideous pit marks under my arms. Thankfully, the moisture had been confined mostly to my head area. I pulled down the visor mirror for a quick makeup check, and noticed that my waterproof (ha!) mascara had become smudged. I was grateful when a quick swipe with a tissue brought my face back to its pre-hike condition.

I pulled off my Converse high-tops and socks and slipped into my black, strappy thongs. If I thought the hike was bad wearing my sneakers, I couldn't even begin to imagine how I was going to make the trek in sandals. I figured determination alone would get me to my destination.

After only a few minutes, I was cooled off and presentable enough to put the car in drive and head up the hill to get Trip.

I pulled into the driveway and crossed myself that his father wouldn't answer the door. Trip assured me hours before that he was away on business- he knew that after my last encounter with the man, I wasn't planning on ever being in his presence again- but one can never be too sure. I was wearing a fairly snug, stretchy-cotton black dress which had spaghetti straps that tied into a lazy bow over each shoulder. It also had a plunging neckline, which was a little out of my comfort zone to begin with, so I supposed that any judgmental commentary from Mr. Wilmington would have hit a little closer to the mark that night. For insurance, I threw on a lightweight, button-down sleeveless top to cover any cleavage, tying the tails around my waist. I was yoinking at the bottom of the elastic skirt in a futile attempt to lengthen it as I made my way up the front walk.

I checked my reflection in the glass of the Wilmingtons' front door and decided I could still pass as good ol' Layla Warren: Catholic-girl, honor-student and all-around moral citizen.

I rang the bell, and mercifully, Mrs. Wilmington answered.

"Hello, Layla, come on in."

"Hi, Mrs. Wilmington!"

The Wilmingtons' house had central air, so any residual heat from my ordeal vanished within one minute inside their blessedly refrigerated marble foyer.

Trip's mom closed the door behind me, asking, "Are you all set for New York?"

I'd been trying all day not to think about it, but there it was. I gave her my standard reply. "Yes. I'm excited, but kind of scared too."

She started to tell me that the greatest adventures in life were like that, when suddenly, she did a double-take. "Oh, my, don't you look pretty tonight!"

I could feel my face flush. "Thank you."

She gave me the once-over and added, "Where are you two headed tonight all dressed up?"

"Oh, uh," I hadn't thought about the fact that my dress could provoke suspicion (which was stupid, since I'd spent practically every other summer day in T-shirts and shorts) and hadn't devised a proper ruse for my semi-formal attire ahead of time. So, I improvised. Chances were good that we'd swing by Rymer's at some point, and I figured Trip's mom would buy that as reason enough to get all decked out. The truth was, I wasn't wearing some dress to impress anyone at some stupid party. I was wearing the thing to affect one person and one person only. So, I played dumb. "Oh... There's a birthday party tonight. You think I'm overdressed?"

I could hear Trip's clunky feet thudding down the stairs as Mrs. Wilmington said, "Oh, no. You look terrific. Whose birthday is it?"

Yes, it was Rymer's birthday and yes, he was having some sort of family party. But I was feeling pretty guilty about pretending that we were on our way right at that moment to actually *attend* said party and I didn't want to continue lying into that sweet woman's face any longer. Mercifully, Trip rounded the corner just then and answered for me. "We're just going to Rymer's, Ma."

I watched as he walked across the foyer, registered what he was wearing. He had on a pair of jeans and a grey T-shirt, which on anyone else would have looked ordinary, but on Trip looked like a magazine ad for some expensive cologne. His hair was still wet from a shower and he looked great, devastatingly gorgeous as usual.

He offered a "Hey" in my direction as he grabbed the small, insulated cooler bag from next to the door and swung it over his shoulder, the muscles in his arm stretching the shirt taut around his bicep, making my stomach flip.

There was an unmistakable sound of cans clanking with ice coming from the bag, but his mother didn't make any attempt to confiscate it. She even bypassed the lecture and only raised a knowing brow. "Please be safe tonight, Terrence. And Layla-" I could feel her wanting to say something about being a responsible designated driver, but then she must have realized who she was talking to. To her, I was Saint Layla, after all. It's not as though she had any reason to suspect that I was actually planning on fucking her son's brains out that night. She smiled and said, "Have a good time."

Chapter 36
MY BLUE HEAVEN

I followed Trip down the front walk toward the driveway, asking, "You're bringing your own beer?"

He laughed and answered, "Yeah. Who the hell can afford Rymer's prices?"

I giggled at that as I slid behind the wheel and ditched the shirt. Trip was fiddling with the radio, but I knew the exact second he must have finally looked over at me.

"Jesus, Layla! What the hell are you wearing?"

His mouth was parted, assessing me with a thrilled look on his face, which made me feel ecstatic and nervous and proud all at the same time. I bit my lip to try and keep myself from smiling, which was answer enough for him.

At the bottom of his driveway, I made a right turn, causing Trip to stop ogling me and spout, "Yo! Where you going, dummy? Rymer's is *that* way."

I kept my eyes on the road, knowing there was no way I'd be able to look him in the eye when I said, "We're not going to Rymer's. We've got some unfinished business to attend to. Just shut up and let me drive."

Without even looking at his face, I could tell that he was figuring things out, registering what was up with the tight, black dress and my evasion of any specific details. A little too confidently, he asked, "Where we going then?"

"Forget it, Chester. You'll just have to wait and find out."

He didn't have to wait very long.

I pulled down a dead-end street only a few blocks from his house and parked the car where the road met the woods. The sun had begun to set and already, the surrounding trees were blocking out any trace of light, hiding us away in a pool of shadow. I cut the engine and Trip grinned that killer smile, surely under the assumption that I'd chosen the secluded place to "park" and said, "Okay, then... I like where this is going..." He leaned over toward me, sliding a hand up my leg and going in for a kiss. I let him do it, but only for a second or two. I knew how easy it was to get swept away once we got going, and letting him nail me in my car was not part of the plan. It was all I could do to tear away.

"Trip, stop."

He looked at me, puzzled, those sapphire eyes searching my face for an answer. "Then why did you-"

"Not here." I was holding back a smile, but he saw my lips twitch. He smiled himself, relieved that I wasn't cutting him off, coming to the realization that I had some sort of better idea.

I bounded out of the car and popped the trunk. Trip came around the back as I was unpacking a few things. "Here," I said, loading his arms with a citronella bucket, pillows and two blankets.

I grabbed the small boombox, the bottle of white wine and stuffed the glasses I'd snuck out of the house in my purse before closing up the car and stepping into the woods.

Trip was a few steps behind me when I heard him tease, "I don't know what you have planned, Lay-Lay, but I wish you would have told me to wear my hiking boots."

I ducked under a branch and responded, "At least you're wearing sneakers. Try traipsing through the woods with these things on."

Trip teased, "Didn't *you* know where we were going tonight?"

"Ha ha. Yeah, of course. I just didn't think that a pair of clunky old boots would really complement my outfit," I teased. "It's not that far anyway. Right up ahead is this great spot I want to show you... There's an amazing view."

I heard him give a huff. "Well, the view in front of me is pretty amazing already. What, did you pour yourself into that thing?"

I gave a modest smirk over my shoulder, but the truth was, I was loving the fact that I had Trip practically drooling. I knew he found me likeable enough to be my friend and cute enough for us to hook up on occasion, but all that was nothing compared to when he found me *desirable*. I was overcome with a perverted sense of power, feeling the scales shift ever so slightly, allowing me the upper hand for the first time in our relationship. Not that Trip went out of his way to wield control over me, it wasn't his fault that I'd fallen in love with him. He never led me on or made me believe that we were anything more than what we were, which, in itself, had always been pretty great. But after spending almost an entire year panting after him, it was nice to finally see some sort of balance of power between us, some sort of point scored in my column.

The feeling was dismissed almost immediately, however, when I realized that I didn't *want* to have power over Trip. The only thing I ever wanted was *him*.

I stepped over a log and around a huge boulder, emerging from the treeline into a small clearing. Lisa and I had found the place years before and while I'm sure we weren't the first nor the last explorers to venture there, it never became a popular destination. There were dozens of hiking trails throughout those woods, and twice as many lookout points along the ridge giving beautiful views of the valley. This spot was more off the beaten path and very secluded, which is why I picked it.

Trip stepped out onto the grass and almost dropped the blankets he'd been holding. There, in the little clearing surrounded by pines and scrub brush, was the turquoise tent I'd set up an hour before. It was the tent I'd used for sleepovers with Lisa in the backyard and "camping trips" with Bruce in the living room. In all the years I'd owned it, it never found its way into actual nature. Until now.

Trip was stunned. "You did this? You came all the way out here lugging that huge thing and set it up yourself?"

I couldn't have been more proud. "Mm-hmm. Impressed?"

Trip ditched the blankets and candle on a nearby rock, came over and wrapped his arms around me. "Yes. You're unbelievable." He kissed me then, made my knees go weak. "It's gonna be a hell of a night, huh?"

I'll say.

"I hope so. Hey- crack open that bottle. Let's have a glass of wine while we watch the sunset."

I gave Trip the opener from my purse and he went to work on the cork. "Damn. This is a great idea and all, Layla. But I've never done this before." I came over to help, but I had no idea what I was doing either, so between the two of us, we'd managed to get the broken cork *into* the bottle. No matter, as long as we'd be able to get the wine out, who cared? Trip poured us each a glass, then he followed me through the pines a few feet to the rock ledge. He bounded the few steps up a boulder then held out his hand to help hoist me up. Miraculously, I was able to climb up without spilling my drink all over the front of my dress. We sat down side by side, our elbows and hips touching as I wrapped my legs under me. Trip had his knees up, his arms stretched straight out over them, the glass dangling from between his fingers.

"This is beautiful," he said, looking out over Norman Valley from his perch at the top of the world.

We were probably about ten minutes too late for a perfect sunset, as we were only able to catch the last hints of pink and purple before the sky went navy. But he was right. It was beautiful. And so much nicer to watch without a sand fight distracting from the show.

The memory panged at my heart, thinking that there'd never be another shared sunrise or sunset for us ever again. I considered the fact that I'd be gone in just fourteen short hours from then, but I buried the thought almost as instantly as it had appeared. I refused to let our last night together be turned into a glum occasion.

We sat there sipping our drinks for a few minutes, unspeaking in the early dark. When our glasses were empty, we hopped off the rock and headed back to our tent. My stomach was in knots, nervous and anticipating what was going to happen next.

Trip lit the citronella bucket I'd packed- brilliant planning on my part, if I do say so myself- offering a soft glow throughout the small clearing and staving off any mosquitos we might encounter out there in the woods. I grabbed the bottle of wine off the ground and Trip grabbed the radio and blankets. We headed into the tent, kicked off our shoes and set up camp. I laid the blankets out over the floor while Trip found us a good station on the radio. The quarters were pretty cramped as we moved around inside the tent, but after we'd set everything up, there was plenty of space for us to both sit across from one another. Trip poured us another round and tucked the bottle into the corner so it wouldn't spill.

His cerulean eyes looked right into mine as he raised his glass in a toast.

"To Layla. A girl who never stops surprising me."

My heart just about broke out of my ribcage, but I managed to clink his glass and smile.

"So, what now? We gonna roast marshmallows?" he asked, trying to keep the mood light.

I had no idea if he truly knew what I was up to. Thinking about it made my heart race and turned my palms sweaty. I tried to maintain the conversation along with the grip on my glass. "It's nice here, right? Lisa and I found this place years ago, but I haven't been up here in a while."

Trip took a sip before answering, "It's great. I've hiked the trails through here a bunch of times, but I never came down this way." He shook his head and laughed out, "I still can't believe you hauled all this stuff up here on your own."

"I'm a girl of many talents."

"Yeahyouare."

I gave him a shy smile and then promptly changed the subject. "Are you mad that we're missing Rymer's party?"

Trip stretched out on his side, propping his head up on his hand. "How could I possibly be mad? Layla, this is awesome."

"You think *Rymer's* gonna be mad?"

He smoothed a hand over my knee and then kissed it. A shudder ran through me at the intimacy of that. He raised his mischievous cobalt eyes and asked quietly, "Layla. Did you really bring me up here just so we could spend our whole night talking about Rymer, for chrissakes?"

211

Chapter 37
LET HIM HAVE IT

Trip rolled onto his stomach and continued to slide his hands up my legs, his fingertips grazing my thighs at the hem of my skirt while peppering my knees with soft kisses.

My heart did that slamming thing again, watching him kiss me so tenderly and feeling his hands running along the outside of my legs. I combed my fingers through the golden hair above his ear, my palm coming to rest on his nape.

That was all the invitation he needed.

He slid his arm around my waist and pulled me underneath his body, my skirt bunching up above my legs in the process. I could feel the weight of him on top of me and the iron-like vise of his strong arm wrapped around my middle as he lowered his mouth to mine.

There was a sweet taste of wine on his lips mingled with his hot breath and within seconds I was yielding to the perfection of it all. I wrapped my arms around him and I guessed the knee-kissing had gotten him all worked up ahead of time, because I could already feel him harden against me as his mouth opened over mine.

Making out with Trip was always like this. My love for him combined with his hunger for me, the force of which made for spontaneous combustion, this unstoppable *thing* between the two of us.

I felt myself spinning, wrapping my legs around him and pressing back, and when I heard the moan escape from his throat, I was lost. So lost, in fact, that I hadn't realized he'd pulled the top of my dress down and was working the clasp on my front-closure bra. I peeled off his shirt before his mouth made its way to my breasts, cupping them with his hands as he licked and played and tormented me with his tongue.

Out of nowhere, his movement stopped.

My eyes flung open in a panic, sure that he'd found my half-naked body revolting, and I looked down to see his chin resting against my chest as he stared up at me. "What?" I asked, anxiety-ridden.

He gave me an evil grin, which, thank God, managed to dispel my insecurities- my fear over his abrupt halt to our makeout session was replaced with instant relief. But then he shocked me all over again when he said, "Take off your clothes. I want to try something."

I suppressed my astonishment as I watched Trip army-crawl over to the corner of the tent before stripping off my dress and bra under the covers. For the time being, the panties were staying put.

Trip came back, kneeling over me with the half-emptied bottle of wine, and the sight of him hovering over me shirtless was positively dumbfounding. Before I had a chance to process that, he pulled the blanket down, exposing me to my waist.

"Trip!" I said in embarrassed surprise, reaching down to cover myself up.

His grip on the blanket tightened, denying me. "No. I want to look at you."

I was feeling incredibly exposed, but thankfully, it was pretty dark inside our tent. Besides, when Trip Wilmington tells you to take off your clothes, you don't think about it. You just do it. And if he tells you he wants to look at you? You thank your lucky stars that he must see something about you that he likes. You lie there, trying to act laid-back, as if getting naked with the eighth wonder of the world is an everyday occurrence for you. You send up prayers of gratitude to the gods of good fortune... and then you let him look.

His smile was wicked as his eyes ran the length of me. Without another word he bent over to kiss me again, as his hand trailed down the center length of my body from my lips down to my belly button, searing me in half. He raised himself up and before I knew it, he'd drizzled some wine into the hollow of my throat; the cool, gold liquid forming a rivulet down the same path his hand had just taken. He put the bottle down and lowered his lips and tongue to my neck, tasting the droplets away with his hungry mouth. He took his time, working his way from my throat, down the center of my chest, kissing and licking all the way down to my abdomen.

I giggled when his tongue tickled my belly button, which made him laugh, too. I took the opportunity to skootch down and kiss him on the lips, before announcing that it was my turn.

Trip stretched out on his stomach and I tipped the bottle, drizzling a stripe down his back. I started kissing him between his shoulder blades and followed the route of his spine with my tongue. The wine had pooled into a little well at the small of his back, which I licked away from his jeans as I ran my hands over the muscles at his shoulders. He gave a grunting laugh, obviously enjoying his torment.

I thought it was so incredibly exotic what we were doing to each other, leisurely sipping wine from one another's skin. Like we were some sophisticated married couple vacationing at a five-star hotel on the Riviera and not just two kids in a tent out in the woods of Jersey. It felt so wild and thrilling and so extremely grown-up, the two of us there alone, tasting each other like it was the most familiar thing in the world. I mean, it's not like I thought grown-ups spent all their free time drinking booze off of each other's naked bodies, but I definitely felt like Trip's and my makeout session was a little more intimate than just your average pair of teenagers, getting drunk off a bottle of Boonsfarm and necking out in the woods. I didn't think the effect would have been quite so drugging had we cracked open a few cans of Meister Braus before sticking our tongues down each other's throats.

Trip rolled over and threw an arm around me, taking my body underneath his before burying his head in my neck. His mouth was at my ear, his hands were everywhere else. I was starting to feel the slight effects of the alcohol, but not enough to deaden my encroaching nervousness about the situation. I kept thinking that at any moment, my panties were destined to join my dress in a pile in the corner and then there'd be no turning back from there.

I made myself remember that that was the reason I'd brought him there in the first place and the thought fortified my resolve. I put my hands at the side of his face and he took the cue, sliding his body up the span of mine and kissing my mouth again. But this time, he pressed his hardened length so intimately between my legs that I thought we'd both go up in flames.

I knew things were moving too fast, but I didn't stop him. The more he moved against me, the more I convinced myself I wanted him to. I didn't recognize my own hands as I watched them unbuttoning his jeans and sliding down his zipper. His hands were braced on either side of my head, his face trying to gauge just what in the hell I was doing. His eyes were dark, wild, questioning, searching.

"Layla?" he scratched out, one word asking if this was really happening. Asking for permission.

I ran my hands up his chest in answer and met his eyes with my own. Wordlessly, silently, he found confirmation there and quickly went about the task of stripping the rest of the way down. I slipped out of my panties as Trip maneuvered himself on top of me, under the blanket.

His mouth was at my breast and my hands were in his hair as he fumbled with the condom out of my sight. I thanked God that Trip had one in his wallet. It was the one thing I hadn't taken care of ahead of time, assuming that guys just always carried those things on them at all times. Thankfully, it turned out I was right in this case. I hadn't registered what a gamble that had been until after he'd put it on.

By then, my heart was beating like mad, my nerves were a tangled mess. Instead of allowing myself to appreciate how awesome it felt to have Trip kissing me, touching me, melting for me, my brain refused to turn off. Normally, making out with Trip was amazing. Feeling his lips and body pressed against me was the most insanely remarkable experience in the world. But this time, all I could think about was how every kiss, every touch was leading us toward a much bigger destination, and I was terrified.

As freaked out as I was, it would have completely sucked to have come all the way up there just to *not* have sex. So I had no illusions about what was going to happen.

Chapter 38
TREMORS

Once he got positioned, the reality of the situation hit me like a bag of bricks. Things had suddenly become very real, and instead of acting like the irresistible vixen I'd assumed I'd play, I was suddenly struck by the magnitude of what we were going to be doing.

I didn't get to think too much about it, because the next thing I knew, Trip was inside me.

Damn! It really hurt!

It felt so awkward and painful and my body flinched and I gritted out, "Ow!" but Trip must have thought I was moaning in ecstasy or something because he started making noises of his own against my ear. I tried telling myself to relax... I figured I was only in pain because I was so tensed up and panicky. But instead, my traitorous body started to rack with uncontrollable trembling and I could not, for the life of me, make it stop. Trip was kissing me, his tongue buried in my mouth, his erection buried between my legs, when he finally registered my frazzled nerves and asked, "Are you alright?"

How to explain? I dragged him up there, I planned the whole night, I *wanted* this to happen. There was no way to turn back now. Not that I wanted to, but it was just that I was so scared at that moment. "I'm fine."

He went back to kissing me, but the shivering wouldn't stop. He raised his torso above me on unsteady arms. "Layla, you're shaking. You sure you're alright?"

I thought about tossing out a line like, "Better than alright" or some such movie nonsense, but the truth was, I wasn't prepared for my first time to be *that* uncomfortable; after only one short minute into my life as a non-virgin, it felt like I was being ripped in two.

I decided to be honest. "Trip, I'm sorry. I want this to happen, I really do. I just... It's just that I'm *so nervous!*"

Trip slid out of me with a grunt and rolled over, but still he pressed close against my side. He pulled the blanket up around us, trying to get me to stop shaking. "Don't be sorry. It's our first time together." He let out a little laugh and continued, "I mean, truth be told, I'm a little nervous, too. Was I rushing it?"

I put an arm across my face to stop myself from crying at the sweetness of his words. "God, no, Trip, not at all. You're..."

Amazing. Incredible.

"...You're doing everything right, really. I guess I'm just freaked out because it's my first time, you know?"

Trip started to say that it was alright, but then abruptly, he sat up just then and looked at me.

"Wait. You mean *our* first time, right? As in you and I have never done this with each other, right?"

I looked at Trip like he was from another planet. What, did he think I'd been sleeping around? "What do you mean?"

"I mean Cooper Benedict, Layla. Don't try and tell me you guys never-"

His face changed just then as his jaw went slack and understanding dawned across the rest of his features. "Oh, Jesus. You're telling me that this is, that you and me, that you never-"

"Yeah," I said, embarrassed. "I thought you knew."

He let out with a heavy breath and then settled back in against my side. He threw an arm across my waist and pulled me close against him, whispering in my ear, "Layla, I'm so sorry. I would have- I wouldn't have just- Jesus! I didn't know. I'm *sorry.*"

My body had stopped shuddering by then, but the tenderness of his apology and the way he was holding me started the tears flowing. I swiped at my face, trying to disguise my emotional outburst. Jeez, I'd gone from sex kitten to bundle of nerves to weeping crybaby inside of five minutes. Trip was going to think I was psychotic. "Don't be sorry. You were great, really. I'm sorry I didn't say anything before. I just thought you knew."

"I *should* have known. Layla, I never- Babe, wait. Are you crying?"

I answered without thinking, "No," which was an obvious lie.

Trip rolled over, angling the top half of his body over mine, looking me in the eyes.

"Oh, God. Please don't cry. I'm so sorry. I'm so *sorry*." He dropped his face to mine, kissing my tears away, whispering his apologies over and over again. His lips found mine, kissing me so gently, so sweetly.

He peppered his kisses with softly spoken avowals of affection, everything from "I'm sorry" to "I'm an idiot" to "Did I hurt you?" But the one that really got me, the one that just about completely *killed* me, was when he brushed a strand of hair behind my ear and whispered, "You know I'm crazy about you, right?"

And then I knew.

I looked into his eyes- those searching, hopeful, beautiful blue eyes- and I knew that at least for that one night... he was *mine*. Even if he didn't admit it out loud, even if it wasn't forever, even if it was just for that one moment- that one glorious, blessed moment- Trip Wilmington had actually fallen in love with me.

The sweetness of his words, combined with the gentleness of his lips should have broken me, sent me into a full-on bawling fit. But instead, the endearments served to melt me in a way his hands and mouth had tried to just moments before. I felt myself heating up again, back on the Trip Wilmington roller coaster ride all over again.

I wrapped my arms around him and kissed him back, loving the feel of his bare skin against mine. He tangled his hands in my hair as I lightly raked my nails over his back and I could feel him harden again. It didn't freak me out this time. It felt empowering, the way I could turn him on so easily just by kissing him, touching him, drive him crazy. His tongue plunged into my mouth, his hands touching every part of me within reach and I met his hunger, grasping his shoulders and arching my back toward his body, writhing against him with that familiar, aching need.

He buried his head in my neck before I heard him whisper, "Ah. *There's* my girl," the sound of his throaty laugh sending shivers down my spine, this time in a good way. I kissed him then, hot and searching, my mind and body giving over to him completely, my fears crumbling against the assault of his sweet mouth against mine.

His palm cupped my breast before replacing his roving hand with his lips, his expert mouth drawing its tip between his teeth lightly, teasing me, slaying me with his gifted tongue. Just when I thought I was going to die, he moved on to the other one, giving it the same treatment. The feel of his mouth on my bare skin was phenomenal, turning every inch of my body into a quivering mass of pure sensation, my nerve endings on the verge of exploding.

I almost passed out when his fingers slid between my thighs, gently easing one into me, sending a hot current through my body, every molecule threatening to detonate. I pressed myself against his hand, which sent us both completely over the edge, Trip's body doubling over, his raspy voice breaking when he laughed and begged, "Jesus, stop *moving* or I'm not gonna make it! You're killing me."

Ha! *I* was killing *him*? How enthralling, knowing I was able to do that!

There I was, Layla Warren: Sex Goddess.

I'd managed the unthinkable task of turning Trip Wilmington into a defenseless, panting piece of mortal flesh. I guessed he was human after all and it made me love him all the more. And being wrapped up in the arms of someone you love is just about the greatest feeling in the whole wide world. I finally understood why sex was such a big deal. Because at that moment, all I could think about was how I wanted to be as close to him as possible, to feel him inside me- wanting me, making love with me.

There was no room for nervousness this time as he positioned his body over me again and aligned his hips over mine, his hardened length straining toward my body, waiting this time, excruciating, unyielding, holding out with a torture that consumed us both.

I wrapped my legs around his waist, crushing us closer together, surprising him with the effect my movement had on him. He lifted his face just long enough to shoot an impressed look my way, which had the intended effect of cracking me up.

"Oh, just *do it* already!" I laughed out, and Trip didn't wait for me to change my mind. He slid into me slowly, checking my reaction every centimeter along the way. Huh. It didn't hurt so much this time. It still felt weird, but once he was all the way in there and started to move inside me, it actually started to feel... pretty good.

Then, it started to feel *really* good.

And *then*, it started to feel *amazing*!

He started driving into me at a steady pace and I was able to match his movements with my own, raising my hips toward his demanding cadence. I could hear him breathing hard against my ear, aching, dying for me, causing me to lose my mind. I decided to return the favor, offering some noises of my own. When I did, Trip started trembling all over, wrapping his arms around me like a vise and ramming into me rhythmically; faster, *harder*. I probably should have been in some state of orgasmic euphoria or something, but what I was really consumed with at that moment was how fascinating it really was. Like, you hear about sex all the time, but there we were, actually doing it! We were *having sex*!

His voice brought me back to him, seductive and rough in my ear when he whispered, "God. You feel *so good*," which caught me by such surprise that I almost died.

I completely lost whatever hold I'd maintained over my own control as I groaned louder, arching my entire body up to his, smashing myself against his smooth, sweat-slicked chest, watching the muscles of his jaw clench as he dropped his head and cursed under his breath.

I knew I had driven him over the edge because he started slamming into me harder, his hand at the small of my back lifting me to him, rigid and insistent and deep inside of me, his string of half-words and animal noises rocking me to my very core. His hips crashing against mine, his body pounding away at me, his

221

breathing ragged, losing control, sinking, soaring, *dying*, his voice finally rasping out, *"Oh God... I can't..."* before letting out with a final, tortured groan, his shaft quaking fiercely inside of me again and again and again, his arms ultimately giving out from the effort of coming so violently. He collapsed on top of me, the full weight of his spent body on top of mine; panting, laughing, growling.

I could barely breathe, but I figured there were worse ways to go. Had my life been smothered out at that moment, I would have died a happy girl. I shifted to try and find some breathing room, and Trip must have taken the hint. He let out a heavy breath then rolled over onto his back, grinning ear to ear, dropping an arm over his face and exclaiming, "Holy shit!"

I was still flying high at that moment, registering the delicious afterglow of what had just transpired between us. I finally saw what all the fuss was about. I pulled the blanket up to my neck and said, "Nice, Chester. I always dreamed my first time would end with a sweaty guy yelling obscenities."

He laughed his ass off, snuggling into me, a heavy arm around my shoulders, pulling me to face him, both of us trying to get our breathing back to normal. "Sorry. But christ! I don't know what else to say."

I nestled in against his arm, unable to stop myself from smiling. "Hmm. Well, let's see. I let you get me drunk and deflower me out here in the wilderness... How 'bout thank you, you ingrate?"

He was still grinning that gorgeous, white, elated grin as he said appreciatively, "You're right. Thank you."

I started to say, "You're welcome", but Trip had reached down to remove a little something from under the blanket, a little something that currently, was sheathing my new favorite thing about him. Before he even pulled his hand out from under the covers, he said, "Uh, Babe? Don't know how to break this to you, but..."

My first thought was, *Ohmygod! The condom broke!* For one horrifying second I was sure that I was pregnant, that I'd never go to NYU and that I'd have to tell my father, who would immediately drop dead of a heart attack upon hearing the news.

So, it was almost an odd relief that all Trip was trying to tell me was that there was "a little bit of blood" down there.

Oh, God, how embarrassing! I was pretty mortified, but immediately grabbed my purse and dug out some Wet-Naps and tissues, thanking the good Lord up above that I at least had something we could use to clean ourselves up.

Trip grabbed a few of the towelette packets, slipped into his boxers and exited the tent, affording me some privacy.

I lifted the covers and peeked with one eye closed... and saw the small stain that was spotting the blanket under me, along with the mess of my inner thighs. Gross! Why does loss of virginity have to be so undignified?

I did a quick cleanup, found a pad in my purse and put my clothes back on, then rolled the stained blanket into a ball, which I shoved in the corner of the tent before going outside.

Trip was just inside the edge of the trees, naked except for his undies. Seeing him hanging out in the woods in just a pair of boxers was so out-of-place that it was comical. It broke the tension enough for me to laugh out, "Well, that was pretty horrifying," trying to make light of the disgusting situation. I mean, what was I supposed to say? I was humiliated. And Trip was probably completely grossed out.

"Oh, so sex with me is horrifying? Nice, Lay."

I took the opportunity he offered to dismiss the Texas Chainsaw Massacre back there in the tent and asked, "Did you just call me a nice lay, you perv?"

Trip did a double-take, realizing how I'd twisted his words around and started laughing. He leapt toward me and threw me over his shoulder, smacking my butt, telling me to cry uncle. I couldn't twist out of his iron grip and I was *not* letting him win, so I reached down and grabbed the waistband of his boxers and gave a good tug.

"Wedgie defense!" I yelled as he put me down post haste.

223

"A wedgie? Really?" which cracked us both up as he adjusted himself in his shorts.

It was a downright shame that Trip had to eventually put his clothes back on. I thought he should forget about travelling or hockey or college and just set up a booth on some beach somewhere, selling tickets to random girls who'd gladly pay good money to see him shirtless. His chest should rank right up alongside the Grand Canyon as one of the Lord's most miraculous creations.

We packed everything up and trekked back to my car. Neither one of us said much, and I knew we were both thinking the same thing. My impending departure loomed over us, that actuality suddenly very real and very imminent. In just a few hours, I'd be in New York; no more Norman, no more Trip. I knew he was waiting for me to skip town before getting on with his travels, and since we never discussed either of those things at length, I wondered where he'd be heading first.

We loaded up my car, and as I slammed the trunk, I saw that Trip was just standing there looking at me. I met his eyes, trying to commit every detail of his beautiful face to memory, not so easy to do considering my vision was starting to blur from unshed tears.

Without hesitation, he put his arms around me, holding me tight against his chest. "We're not doing this now, okay? I'll come over in the morning, but I. Can't. Do. This. Now." I could hear his teeth clenched together as he said that last part, which gave me the strength to clamp down on the waterworks as well. Tears had been threatening for weeks, never more so than in the past few minutes, but I was determined *not* to ruin our last night by bawling.

I pulled back to let him know it was okay, I understood, that we could postpone our big theatrical scene for a few more hours.

And then I saw the look on his face.

I almost fainted dead away. There was Trip, his expression telling me everything I ever needed to know. Back in the tent, I was fairly certain that he'd fallen in love with me. Looking into his eyes, that thought was confirmed, right there on his face. He was looking at me with such adoration; those broken, blue eyes offering a window into his heartache, dying inside as he watched me slipping through his grasp.

He may as well have been screaming "I love you".

I'd won our school science fair in the fourth grade, my "Phases of an Egg" presentation eclipsing the dozen or so baking-soda-and-vinegar volcanoes presented by the rest of our class. I'd taken gold in our town's Junior Olympics when I was ten, and got to stand up on the top of a three-tiered pedestal after placing first in the Fifty Yard Dash. One time, when I was fourteen, I'd received a Presidential Physical Fitness certificate from Ronald Reagan, when I logged a record-breaking eighty-two situps in the span of a minute.

But nothing compared to the sense of accomplishment I felt- no award, no ribbon, no trophy- no achievement lived up to the unfathomable triumph of having won the heart of Terrence C. Wilmington III.

Chapter 39
THE HARD WAY

I took a last look around my room, knowing it would never be the same again. Sure, my *Water Lilies* comforter would still be where I left it on my mattress, my furniture would remain in its rightful place. But the next time I would walk through that door, I'd just be a visitor.

I ran my fingers over the pictures around my mirror, taking in the images of my life from over the years. Yesterday, I was a little girl riding a bike; in a few short hours I'd be riding out the rest of my life.

Doesn't it just go by in a blink.

Dad had packed all my stuff into the car hours before: The movie posters I'd bought on my last day at Totally Videos, the bedding set I'd picked out with Lisa. The mini-fridge Bruce had gotten me at graduation, the computer from Dad, the bags upon bags of clothes, a box of my favorite books. I stood out in the driveway looking at all of it: My New Life, crammed into every spare inch of our family car.

Trip's truck pulled in just then, and he looked almost beaten as he got out and made his way toward me. No kiss hello, no hug. Just his hands jammed in his pockets as he offered a nod of his head and a formal "'Morning" at me.

In the old days, I would have freaked out by his lack of emotion, especially considering how we'd spent the previous night. But I knew that he was being standoffish purely out of self-preservation. What else could he be expected to do?

"Hey, uh," he started in, not quite sure what to say. "You, uh, you okay?" referring to my near-fatal hemorrhaging the night before.

Some of my embarrassment had left me by then. I mean, I'd come to the conclusion that if something like that was going to have to happen someday regardless, I'm glad it had happened with him instead of some random guy. "I'm fine. A little mortified, but I'll live."

"You know, that was a first for me, too."

I looked at him, ready to call him out for being a rotten liar when he clarified, "I've never been anyone's First before."

I forced a laugh and said, "Well, I can only imagine you never will be again after that horror show."

His eyes met mine then, the broken look on his face almost tearing my heart out, the sad, sad realization that our minutes together were numbered. After all the months of postponing the inevitable, there we were, left with mere seconds to spend with one another.

He came over to me, grabbed my hands in his and planted a sweet kiss on my lips. "No, probably not. But only because I can't imagine ever wanting to *be* with anyone else ever again."

My stomach wrenched, actually causing me physical pain. How could he say something like that to me? My heart was already shattering into a million pieces and I was already doing all I could not to break down in tears.

"Trip... *don't.*"

Oh God, please don't say it. Please, please-

"I'm in love with you, Layla."

I dropped my head as the tears came rolling down my cheeks; despite my resolve, I was completely incapable of stopping them. You'd think that I would have been bursting at the seams with joy, finally hearing him say the words I could only dream about for the better part of an entire year. But I was too crushed to feel any sort of elation at his admission. And the truth was, I already knew how he felt.

"Trip. Stop!"

"No, Layla. I won't stop." He moved closer, cradling my head to his chest before continuing. "I know you're leaving and I would never try to keep you from going, and I guess I have my own path to follow as well. But don't ever ask me to stop loving you, because I can't. Don't ever think I'll be able to forget you, because I won't."

I was actually sobbing against him then, my shoulders heaving, my tears dampening the front of his T-shirt, causing tiny, dark blue spots to appear across his chest.

I wanted to freeze us in time, like one of those museum displays that Holden Caulfield was so fixated on, or seal the two of us off from the world with plexiglass like Thomas Edison's desk.

I was about to tell him I loved him, too, that I didn't need to go, that we could both stay right there at home forever and ever, amen. It could be so easy for us to just decide to stay right where we were, loving each other for the rest of our lives.

We don't have to say goodbye.

But the words caught in my throat and I didn't say anything.

He kissed the top of my head and asked, "But I want you to promise me something, okay?"

My eyes were spilling over and I could barely breathe, but I managed to ask, "What's that?"

He put his hands on either side of my face, looked right into my eyes and said, "Be happy. Wherever you wind up. And know that I'll be thinking of you, wherever I am." At that, he bent his face to mine and I let him kiss me for the last time.

Oh, the drama! Is there anything so powerful as the love of two teenagers being ripped apart?

He tore his mouth from mine and shook his head, defeated. "I can't do this. It's too hard."

He reached into his truck through the open window and pulled out a pale blue envelope. He placed it in my hands before swiping his thumb across my dampened cheek, his knuckles grazing my neck. I was trying to think of something to say, some memorable, monumental, perfect parting words.

But for some reason, I found a smile cracking through my tears, and the words that left my lips were, "Stay gold, Ponyboy."

At first, Trip looked at me stunned, like he couldn't believe I was being so blasphemous as to make light of such a serious situation. But then, he started to smile too; a beautiful, final, charming grin, just for me.

After he'd gone, I watched, too depleted to be emotional as his truck drove down my street for the final time. I looked down at the envelope in my hand and decided to go have a seat in the backyard to open it.

When I did, the first thing I saw was a picture of Trip and me from graduation, the one his father had taken when Trip had scooped me into his arms. I looked at the smiling faces in the image, smirking to myself when I remembered how later in that evening, we'd shared our first kiss.

The photograph had been sandwiched by a piece of folded looseleaf notebook paper, and I recognized what I was holding immediately. I couldn't believe that I'd finally gotten my hands on Trip's Mind Ramble from our very first week in English class together.

I put the picture across my lap and unfolded his note.

Hey Dummy. What are you working on in art class? You missed Rymer blow Coke out his nose at lunch today. Although, something tells me that's not the first time that's ever happened.

Shit. Mason wants a mind ramble.
Romeo was a complete tool who had no balls. Which is it? Rosaline or Juliet? Make up your mind dude.

Okay forget this. I can't write about stupid Shakespeare when you're sitting two inches away from me and I can smell your hair. Coconut? Smells like summer. Okay so I just caught the look you shot me over your shoulder and you need to know that I can't even breathe right now. I haven't even known you that long but from the first time I saw you, I've been knocked out by how hot you are. No. You know what? Not just hot.

You're beautiful.

The kind of beautiful that doesn't go away. Do you even know how beautiful you are? Christ. Stop looking at me! Killing me.

Do you know what that does to me? Seeing you look at me like you're half in love with me? Are you? If I write it does it make it true? So let it be written, so let it be done. Haha.

Anyway, mind ramble mind ramble mind ramble.
The only thing rambling through my mind is how much I want to grab you out of that chair and kiss you right now. Kiss you the way you need to be kissed- and kiss you often.
Oh God I must sound like such a loser. By the way, if anyone's reading this, I should state right here that MY NAME IS SONNY AETINE. There. Nothing to hide.

Nothing to hide? Okay fine. Here it is.
I could be in love with you.
There it is. I wrote it.
I'll write it again.
I really think I could be in love with you.

Oh man, I'm going to have to burn this thing so no one gets their hands on it. Especially those wiseguy friends of yours. That Cooper guy seems like he's ready to murder me whenever you look my way. No way I'm going to get on THAT guy's bad side my first week in town.
Guess I'll wait it out.

The letter ended there along with the last grip on my life as I knew it.

Trip loved me.

I held the paper to my chest, expecting a sobbing fit to come again, waiting for an all-consuming blubbering outburst to overtake my wasted soul. I'd shed more tears in the past weeks than I had in my entire life, but there was nothing left to cry about.

I thought about the people that I had loved in my life and the never-ending list of people that had left it. Everyone both here and gone... from my mother, to my family, to my friends.

I thought about Cooper, who'd loved me unconditionally, practically from the day that we had met. Who cured my hurts and built me up and never asked for anything in return.

I thought about Lisa, probably somewhere in Ohio by then, striking out and starting over with Pickford in a place so very far away. Lisa, who I shared everything with, who'd been in my life for so long, I could hardly remember a time before her. Lisa; my partner in crime, my role model, my sister, my friend.

I thought about Trip; my beautiful, blue-eyed, golden-haired god, getting ready to hop a plane to who knows, living a life of adventure, and taking me with him wherever he went in the world.

I carved out little spaces within my heart; little, lovely mausoleums where I could lock each and every one of them away inside, keep the memories safe and close to me forever.

And then it was time to go.

About the Author:

T. Torrest is the author of many books, although she prays that only a handful of them will ever see the light of day. She was a child of the eighties, but has since traded in her Rubik's Cube for a laptop, and her catholic school uniform for a comfy pair of yoga pants. Ms. Torrest is a lifelong Jersey Girl... She currently resides there with her husband and two boys.

A Note from the Author:

I want to thank you for reading my story! I'm working very hard to finish "Remember When II: the Sequel", which should be completed by June 2013 (Flip the page for a preview). If you enjoyed this book, I ask that you tell your friends, loan it out, and please, please leave a review. Friend me on facebook or follow me on goodreads.com. I love hearing from readers and am curious about your book club discussions! Lastly, if you'd like to drop me a personal message, my email is: ttorrest@optonline.net. I always do my best to write back!

Thank you.

BOOK CLUB DISCUSSION QUESTIONS

1. Were you surprised by the ending? Do you think Layla and Trip should have ridden off into the sunset together?
2. How do you think Layla's mother's abandonment affected her? Did you notice how she never referred to her as "Mom"? Do you agree with Layla's opinion that her mother was manic-depressive?
3. We don't get to hear too much about Layla's dad. What's your take on him?
4. How do you think Mr. Wilmington's drinking affects Trip when it comes to his own alcohol use?
5. What did you think of Lisa and Pickford's decision to move to California together?
6. How do you view Layla's friendship with Lisa? Was their relationship realistic?
7. Every chapter in RW is the title of a movie from 1990 or 91 and there were a ton of other eighties/nineties references. Which ones stood out for you?
8. It's hard to ignore the running Shakespeare theme throughout the story. What did you think of Trip and Layla's "balcony scene"? Can you guess what Shakespeare work Trip's "Mind Ramble" was based on?
9. Popularity is also an issue that gets addressed repeatedly throughout RW. How did you feel about Layla's evolving thoughts on the matter? What group were you a part of in high school?
10. Let's discuss Cooper, shall we?

11. Who did you envison as Trip? Was it your high school crush or someone famous?
12. Casting call! Who would you like to see in the movie version of Remember When?

Preview Chapter
Excerpt from *Remember When II: The Sequel*
PART TWO
2000

I made myself eat breakfast that morning, but it was difficult to do with my stomach so tied up in knots.

It had been one week since I found out Trip was in New York, five days since I finagled a press pass to attend the junket and twenty-four hours since Lisa dropped off the Armani suit she'd lent me from her designer wardrobe.

Multiply that by the nine years it had been since I'd last seen Trip, and it all added up to the thirty-seven times I felt like throwing up that morning.

I checked my reflection in the mirror, again, adjusted the thin silver belt at my waist and smoothed away some non-existent wrinkles from my slacks. The suit was sleek, black and nicer than anything hanging in my own closet, and I was grateful to have it. I'd left the blazer open, revealing a white silk shell underneath, trying for a casual look even though I was feeling anything but. I cursed my frazzled nerves and tried to get myself under control.

It was strange enough to think about being in the same room with my old high school sweetheart, but it was positively surreal to have to reconcile that eighteen-year-old boy with the uberhot movie star that he'd become.

There isn't a girl alive that doesn't want to feel like she's left some sort of imprint on every single one of her exes, and I was no different in that regard. But how many girls have to deal with their ex becoming a famous movie star who has since been with no less than half a million other women, most of whom were beautiful Hollywood movie stars themselves? How would I even rank in such a grouping?

I grabbed my satchel, took a cab up to the *TRU Times Square* and made my way into the lobby. I'd been by the hotel numerous times, but never had any reason to go inside. One look at the place, and I was sorry I never bothered to check it out before. The décor was modern- not usually my style, but incredible nonetheless- white floors, white furniture, white everything except the walls, which were painted in a deep, dark navy. The lighting was done in tones of blue and green and purple, splashed across every surface and sofa in the expansive room.

My Steve Madden heels clacked against the white marble floor as I headed toward the front desk, trying very hard not to seem impressed by the expanse of my surroundings. My brain flashed back to graduation night, standing inside the Wilmingtons' foyer for the first time, overwhelmed by the size and beauty of the massive home.

The Wilmingtons' *hotel* was infinitely more imposing.

I resisted the urge to pivot my head around the space, take it all in like some wide-eyed tourist who didn't know how to play it cool. I *lived* in the city for godsakes. I didn't need to look like a sightseer in my own backyard.

I approached the front desk where a model-thin concierge stopped tapping away at her computer to look up apathetically at me. She had a severely cut black bob which dusted her impossibly high cheekbones, and large, almond-shaped green eyes that made her look almost feline.

She gave the briefest intimation of a smile before offering stoically, "Welcome to *TRU*. How may I help you."

New Yorkers always get a bad rap for being rude. The thing is, they're not normally mean, they just don't have time for anyone's bullshit. This is something I inherently knew my whole life, but had just recently learned to project myself.

I flashed my press pass, laminated and hanging from my neck by a long black nylon lanyard. "Layla Warren, *Now!* Magazine. I'm here to meet Mr. Kelly." It was the code name I'd been given to be granted access to The Great Trip Wiley, up-and-coming movie star, already in need of a pseudonym in order to protect his privacy.

238

The concierge suddenly took a genuine interest in me. Her eyes fully met mine and she gave me a quick once over before asking, "Mr. *Johnny* Kelly?"

I got the impression that she had not only just sized me up, but found me lacking. Either that, or she was immediately able to see right through me with my every hair in its perfect place, standing there in my borrowed suit and trying to disguise my sweaty palms.

I did a mental eyeroll. *Yeah, okay, sweetheart. You caught me. Yes, I'm freaking out about my meeting with Trip Wiley. No, I'm not looking to compete with you for his hand in marriage. Clearly, you've got it all over me and I don't need to be viewed as a threat, as Trip is only one "chance encounter" away from falling madly in love with YOU.*

But I just raised my eyebrows and gave her a, "Yep."

She was all business back at her keyboard, tapping away as she asked, "Junket or one-on-one?"

Now, I should mention here that my editor, Devin, was very clear on the fact that I was only scheduled to do the junket. If you're unfamiliar with what a junket is, let me enlighten you.

A press junket is basically a lion's den of desperation. Normally, anywhere from five to twenty writers are crammed around a table in some stuffy room eating complimentary doughnuts and drinking weak coffee for a gazillion hours. Finally, at some point, they are granted an audience with the celebrity in question for all of thirty minutes. In that short amount of time, questions are rapid-fired at said celebrity, each writer trying to get as many of theirs answered before an assistant comes in and excuses the haggard interviewee to their next appointment. Then the writer has to piece together the melee in order to come up with a cohesive story, all the while making their article look as though they've scored the exclusive of the century.

It was all rather uninspiring.

Seeing as I had absolutely zero experience with the competitive nature of a press junket, I wasn't much looking forward to fighting it out with the other seasoned writers in the room.

So, even though I knew there was a good chance I'd be found out by Trip's people anyhow and there was a *definite* chance I'd be reamed out by my editor, I took the shot.

"One-on-one," I managed to say.

I placed my company card on the desk, refusing to worry about the consequences of the unauthorized charge. If I managed to pull off the interview, Devin would gladly go to bat for me on the expense report.

Concierge Cat tapped away on her computer while I waited to be called out for my deception. But eventually, she simply slid a room key across the desk and told me to head on up to 4116 via the elevators located just off the main lobby.

I played aloof as I signed the receipt and grabbed the keycard, casually strolled over to the alcove, and made my way into a private elevator.

The second the doors closed, however, I started dancing; punching the air and cabbage-patching like a white girl. I hoped I wasn't being monitored.

But I had done it! I was going to turn my little sideline story assignment into a feature article! I was on my way to an exclusive, one-on-one sit-down with the fastest rising star in Hollywood. Chances were good that I'd be able to parlay the interview into a cover piece with photos and a full-length story. Maybe Devin would finally see that I could actually write more than just boring old advertising copy. Maybe this would be a big turning point for my career.

I was so busy daydreaming about my impending promotion to CEO of Howell House Publishing that I'd forgotten to flip out about the fact that I was going to find myself back in the same room as Trip in just a short while. He was probably only a few doors down from my suite at that very minute, getting ready to head into the conference room at the end of the hall.

I slid my keycard into the lock box, opened the door, and was greeted with the sight of an exquisite space.

The entrance opened into a large living room area, decorated in pale, neutral tones with dark wood furniture. There was a kitchenette to my right, with cabinets done in the same dark wood, but the counters were cobalt, offering just the right splash of color. There was a table and chairs to my left and a sitting area directly ahead, set up in front of a large window. The curtains were pulled back, allowing a flood of natural light into the room, and I couldn't resist its pull, drawing me to check out the view of Broadway far below.

I wandered into the adjoining bedroom and walked through the huge, marble bath. The décor was the same, soothing neutral, with just the right splashes of blue to make it interesting.

I settled myself into the beautiful, well-appointed living room and grabbed my bag. I dug out my cell phone and put in a quick call to Trip's publicist, letting her know my room number, and crossing my fingers while I heard her rustle through a sheaf of paper. I exhaled when she gave me the first appointment time following the junket for the half-hour between 12:30 and 1:00, only one short hour from then.

I set up my recently acquired digital tape recorder on the coffee table and took a seat in one of the blue plush chairs next to it. I reminded myself not to fidget as I became aware of my growling stomach. I didn't think I had enough time to order room service, and besides, I was already pushing the limits of my company card by being in a room in the first place. I thought that I sure could have gone for one of those complimentary doughnuts right about then. I rifled through my purse and managed to come up with a flattened and crumbled granola bar, which I scarfed down without any semblance of grace.

I had to check my teeth in the bathroom mirror, so I used the opportunity to pee and then readjusted my entire outfit and fixed my hair. Again.

I sat back down in the chair and checked the time.

Damn. Still had half an hour to wait.

I reviewed my notecards, found a decent music station on the TV, rigged the door to stay open a crack, peed *again* and went through my outfit adjustment/hair touchup for only the millionth time that morning. Then I started to wonder what was in the

241

minibar. I took a quick peek in the fridge, but decided against indulging in a drink, even though my nerves were pretty well shot.

I still had some time to kill, wondering if movie stars actually held true to their schedules, when the room phone rang loudly, startling me enough that I actually jumped.

It was Trip's publicist on the other end, letting me know that they were on their way over to my suite.

I hung up the phone and ignored the lurching in my stomach, trying to acquire my long lost sense of cool. *Get a hold of yourself, Warren.*

I took a deep, steadying breath and tried to remain calm. But my zen ritual was interrupted by a knock on the door, before it was whisked open by a pretty and efficient-looking Sandy Carron, holding a clipboard and wearing a bluetooth headset.

"Hellooo!" she called out as she scurried into the room. She came right over to me with an outstretched hand leading her way. I always found it strange when two women shook hands. It seemed like a necessary act in a roomful of men, but when it was just two ladies, a kiss on the cheek almost seemed more appropriate. I got up out of my chair to greet her as she stated, "Ms. Warren from *Now!* Magazine. Pleasure to meet you. I'm Sandy Carron."

I shook her hand and couldn't help but peek over her shoulder for Trip. Sandy definitely caught my wandering eyes, but was nice enough not to call me out for it. I guessed she was used to the many females coming and going through Trip's life who made complete cakes out of themselves on a regular basis.

"Mr. Wiley is just finishing up the junket. He'll be in momentarily. Can I get you anything? Would you care for some coffee or a cold drink? Something to eat, perhaps?"

Oh, right. Like after waiting a whole hour, I was going to risk getting food caught in my teeth or get busted scarfing down a bacon cheeseburger at the zero hour with Trip Wiley on his way into the room.

"No, thank you."

242

She gave a quick glance over her shoulder. "Well, I'm going to have some bottled water sent over, just in case Mr. Wiley decides he wants some, if that's all right." When I didn't protest, she spoke into her headset. "Hunter, could you bring some water to forty-one-sixteen? Great, thanks."

Sandy started to go over the protocol for the interview when a call interrupted her instructions. A hand went to her headset and she said, "Okay, wonderful. I'll be right there." She turned her attentions back to me and said, "Mr. Wiley is ready for you now. I'm just going to pop down the hall and escort him here."

Just then, Hunter (Trip's assistant's assistant, apparently) came in with an ice bucket filled with four bottles of some kind of water I'd never seen before, and Sandy offered on her way out the door, "Please feel free to help yourself. I'll be back in just a moment."

Sandy the whirling dervish was gone, taking Hunter the Assistant with her and leaving me alone in my room once again. I decided to bust open one of the bottles of *VOSS* water, which was ice cold and would undoubtedly have me racing for the bathroom all over again. But I was grateful to have something new in that room to occupy myself during my wait.

I didn't have to wait long.

Within minutes, I could hear voices coming down the hall and my stomach did an anxious somersault. Before I knew it, Sandy was back at my door, holding it open for her charge...

...and there was Trip, once again, walking back into my life.

* * *

There was a tangible shift in the air of the room, a gripping, electrical aura that stimulated the space surrounding his presence like a gravitational pull. I'd noticed this phenomenon when watching his movies, seeing the man that had emerged from the boy I once knew; but actually being in the same room with him was an entirely different animal. Trip *Wilmington* had been a gorgeous teenaged boy, no question. But Trip *Wiley* was a gorgeous young man just exuding raw, unabashed sex at every turn.

It was only slightly impossible to remember how to breathe.

I registered the jeans and black T-shirt Trip was wearing, along with the backwards jeffcap ineffectively attempting to contain his overgrown hair, which kicked out around his ears and behind his neck regardless. He was scratching the stubble at his chin and was five steps inside the room before he finally looked up, saw me... and froze.

He literally did a double take, shaking his head in a futile attempt to rid himself of the sight of his old friend standing before him. I guessed he remembered me after all.

I bit my lip to keep from grinning, and broke the silence with, "Hey Chester. How's it hangin'?"

His mouth went slack, but the corners of his lips were turned up into a smile. His eyes went wide as he said incredulously, "Layla. Effing. Warren."

I started to giggle. "Hi."

He came at me, arms outstretched, and wrapped me in a tight bear hug, as if not one single day had gone by.

Still smelled like soap and sugar, the bastard.

"Layla Warren! No way! How the hell are ya?" He swung me around and I almost caught a shin on the coffee table before he set me back down on my feet. He pulled back slightly, still keeping his hands on my arms. "Jesus! Look at you. Still as beautiful as ever."

I smirked a "yeah right" look at him, but didn't call him out on his bullshit. Instead, the smile remained plastered to my face, as I was completely unable to stop beaming at him like a lunatic. But he was looking down at me with absolute euphoria and grinning ecstatically himself, so I didn't bother trying to keep my enthusiasm in check either. That familiar electric current was passing between us like lightning, that indescribable, all-consuming *thing* that he and I have always shared.

244

"Sandy!" he called over his shoulder. "Sandy, come meet Layla. She was my... well, hell. She was my very first costar!"

I laughed as Sandy came into the room saying, "We've met already, Trip." I guessed since I was obviously a friend, Sandy allowed herself to drop the formal address. She shot me a conspiratorial look and added, "But she didn't tell me you two already knew each other." She shook my hand again, as if I were a brand new person for her to meet, which, I guess, under the circumstances, I was.

Trip still hadn't taken his eyes off me, grinning ear to ear like it was Christmas, blinding me with his perfect white teeth.

Sandy was the first of the three of us to remember that we were all gathered in that room for more than just a friendly reunion. She started her schpiel about sitting in during the interview, and about the ground rules regarding acceptable topics for questioning, and godonlyknows knows what else. I couldn't hear much of anything with Trip looking at me the way he was. It had been years since we'd seen one another. And Jesus. Suddenly, there he was, standing right there two feet away from me.

Trip cut her speech off with, "Hey Sandy. Can we bump the next interview back so I can *grab something to eat*?" His palm slid down my arm, then he took my hand in his and kissed my knuckles. He was looking into my eyes, but his words were directed toward his publicist. "This is the girl that got *away*, Sandy. I'm going to need more than just a few minutes with this one."

I deciphered that *"grab something to eat"* was obviously their code for when Trip required privacy. I knew he was only teasing, but the fact that he and his publicist/assistant had obviously worked out some long-standing arrangement in order to perpetuate his sexual appetite was mildly unsettling.

I shook my head laughing at him, but directed my commentary toward Sandy. "Actually, I happen to know from firsthand experience that he *won't* need more than a few minutes."

Sandy slapped a hand to her mouth, poorly concealing a choking smirk as Trip's jaw hit the floor and he laughed out, "Ouch! You're breaking my heart all over again, sweetheart."

Sandy had to fight her laughter as she excused herself from the room, assuring Trip that she'd take care of the scheduling conflict.

I smiled back at him, registered his teasing. I was still in awe that I was right there looking into those deadly blue eyes after so many years and thought, *Oh, my sweet, handsome, beautiful Trip. Your heart was never mine to break.*

And that's when he leaned down to kiss me.

Acknowledgements:

I'd like to take this opportunity to thank some very important people who, whether they know it or not, helped to turn the mere idea of this book into a reality.

To my parents, thanks for always encouraging me (and for not weirding out over the more graphic scenes in this story!). I am the person I am today because of you. I hope that's a compliment.

To my sister, who, after reading one of my short stories years ago, stunned me with her flattery by saying, "Wow. You need to find something to write about and *write*." Welp. I finally did it. Here ya go.

To my high school girls (special shout-out to Dana for help on the cover): I am amazed that we still tolerate each other after all these years. The teenaged characters in this story are compiled entirely from little bits of each and every one of you.

To my high school guys: Ditto.

Lastly, I of course want to thank my boys for their enduring patience. I love you bunches. Now that the computer has finally been surgically removed from my lap, let's go play.

To Michael, my super understanding, rock star husband: That goes double for you. ;)

Made in the USA
Middletown, DE
18 October 2015